The 911 ca
dispatcher, speaking calmly and clearly, ordered
bulance to the stated address, and then notified the closest officer to the scene, Jim Donnegan, who was on
patrol about eight miles away.

"There's a burglary in progress at that address," the
dispatcher told Donnegan. "There's an injured victim
and the perp may still be in the house."

Squealing to a stop in front of the Wilsons', Donnegan
quickly checked the building. Walking around the house
first, Donnegan noted that there was a light on in the
garage and the front door was ajar.

Right arm extended, pistol in hand, Donnegan ventured carefully into the house, mindful of the dispatcher's warning that a burglar might still be inside.
Glancing in the rooms on the ground level and finding
them empty, Donnegan proceeded cautiously up the
stairs. Before he could get all the way to the top, he
noticed a woman's purse and two pink plastic garment
bags lying on the steps, apparently where they had been
dropped.

Beyond the items, through the banister that bordered
the stairwell on the top level, Donnegan could see a
form. Moving closer, he determined that it was a man
sprawled on his back. Since he was expecting the worst
because of the dispatcher's warning, the officer was not
surprised to see that the man was surrounded by a pool
of blood . . . .

BLOOD SISTER

KEN ENGLADE

ST. MARTIN'S PAPERBACKS

BLOOD SISTER

Copyright © 1994 by Ken Englade.

Cover photograph courtesy Associated Press.

ISBN: 0-312-95203-1

Printed in the United States of America

St. Martin's Paperbacks edition/March 1994

10 9 8 7 6 5 4 3 2 1

For Mark and Marion

Acknowledgments

Many people provided valuable assistance in compiling the material for this book, some of them much more than they realize. To all of them I am grateful because without their help this story would never have been told. I am intensely aware that for more than a few of those who opened their hearts and their histories to me, the experience was excruciatingly painful. I will never be able to show my appreciation to them beyond saying that I will be eternally indebted to them, and that I pray I have not added to their distress.

Among those to whom I am particularly appreciative for background information are Jo Ann Chiri, Julia Wilson, Brenda Cerha, Sandra Mitchell, Nancy Nelson, Tommy Ford, Kay McDowell, Bobby Smith, Blake Hudson, Bobby Cummings, Steve Means, Barbara Smith, and Alex Weisskopf. In addition, I owe special thanks to Heidi Hizel, who helped keep me on track when I was prone to wander.

Express recognition also is due to the lawyers who helped make the legal aspects of the case intelligible— Roy Miller and Marc Sandlin—and especially Jimmy Fry, whose insight and willingness to help far exceeded what I could have hoped to expect. I wish him a bottomless basket of hush puppies.

Author's Note

Some of the dialogue represented in this book was constructed from available documents, some was drawn from courtroom testimony, and some was reconstituted from the memory of the participants. In order to protect their privacy, a few of the characters have been given fictitious names. Their names will be put in italics the first time they appear in the book.

K.E.

ONE

ACCELERATING UP GARTH ROAD, *MARION Hancock* experienced a momentary twinge of indecision. I don't even *know* Tim Morgan, she thought. Do I really want to go to his party?

Easing her foot off the pedal, she considered turning her dented Chevrolet around and heading back down the mountain, pointing it toward her apartment and forgetting she had ever heard about the candidate for district attorney of Madison County Alabama and his political fund-raiser. Then she remembered that she had promised Betty that she would be there.

Yes! Hancock commanded herself, stepping on the gas. I said I would go, and I will!

A minute later she swung onto Chandler Road and passed the turnoff to Boulder Circle, the quiet cul-de-sac where Betty lived with her husband, Dr. Jack Wilson, a popular ophthalmologist and one of the most colorful members of the Huntsville medical community. She could stop and talk to Betty, she thought, maybe get some last-minute encouragement. In the weeks she had known Betty, Hancock had come to regard both her and her husband as friends. But Betty was more than that; she was a confidante as well.

Hancock had met Betty some two and a half months

before, when she joined Alcoholics Anonymous, seeking help to combat her alcoholism. Betty, who was an established member of the group, took an immediate personal interest in her, assuming the role of older sister, mentor, and confessor to help her through the first ninety days of her membership in the organization, a period regarded as extremely crucial because during that time frame a new member either begins forming habits that lead to recovery or slides back into old practices of substance abuse. Hancock was determined to take the road to recovery, and at the time, any help she could get was more than welcome.

Since their first meeting, Hancock had seen Betty five or six times a week, often twice a day if she counted the recovery group meetings. They had lunch and dinner together. They went to an endless chain of movies together because Betty was a confirmed enthusiast of the big screen, an entrenched Richard Dreyfuss fan, and a sucker for cinematic melodrama. And together they regularly made the hour and a half drive into Birmingham, a city where Betty seemed to know every boutique, every specialty shop, and every upscale jewelry store. They would spend the day tromping from one shop to another while Betty, joking about "spending Jack's money," stocked up on pricey skirts and blouses; flashy rings, bracelets, and earrings; new purses and belts fashioned of leather as smooth as velvet. "I like nice things," Betty would usually say as she piled her purchases unceremoniously into the trunk of her Mercedes. "Like this car," she would add, pointing at the vehicle with pride. "I love it. What can I say? Somebody has to drive a Mercedes."

Betty sometimes acted strange, Hancock had to admit. While she could seem like an affectionate big sister one minute, expressing compassion, concern, and extraordinary generosity, the next she could be almost like a total stranger: cold, unfeeling, and hardhearted. In the blink of an eye, Betty's sweetness could turn to meanness, especially when she was talking to or about her husband, Jack. Once, Hancock remembered, she had stopped at the Wilsons' house to pick up Betty so they could go to an AA meeting. The two had been in Betty's bedroom and Hancock was freshening her makeup. Betty was sitting on the floor, laughingly recounting an anecdote, when Jack innocently stuck his head in the door. "What's for dinner?" he asked pleasantly. Betty had glared at him, all of her previous humor disappearing in an instant. "Don't you *dare* embarrass me in front of one of my AA babies!" she screamed at him.

But that was Betty, Hancock told herself. It was part of her complex and often puzzling personality; it was what made her what she was. On balance, Hancock felt, Betty had been a good friend. When she needed a shoulder to lean on, Betty's was invariably available. And when she felt low, Betty never failed to cheer her up with her quick wit, her graphic and clever scatological observations, and her obvious lack of inhibition.

Her first glimpse into Betty's ribald sense of humor, she recalled, came soon after she joined the program. She had been standing with Betty, waiting for a meeting to start, when Betty steered her to a group of men. Snuggling up to one of them, Betty nestled her petite five-foot-two frame into the tall man's arms. "This is Jim," she said, giggling, grabbing his posterior. "He's got the cutest little ass in the program."

At the same time, Betty could be surprisingly sensitive. She seemed to realize how confused Hancock felt in those initial weeks as a new member, and went out of her way, virtually adopted her, in an attempt to help make the transition from an alcoholic to a recovering alcoholic as smooth as possible. It was toward that end, Betty had said, that she suggested to Hancock that she attend the Tim Morgan fund-raiser.

She and her husband had known Morgan a long time, Betty explained. In fact, she had lived in the same apartment complex as Morgan back in the early seventies, after her divorce from her first husband and long before she met Jack. After their marriage, Betty and Jack kept the relationship with Morgan alive in little ways, mixing socially from time to time and always being friendly whenever they were thrown together by circumstance. Once, Jack called the assistant district attorney for some legal advice, and was so grateful for the help that he presented Morgan with an eel-skin briefcase that still was one of the lawyer's most treasured possessions. It had not been a particularly close friendship, Betty admitted, but it was an enduring one that both Betty and Jack were anxious to maintain. In that light, it seemed natural for Jack and Betty to be among the first to offer their support when Morgan announced that he was a candidate for a job that had been snatched away from him by what he considered to be political whimsy.

When Betty first suggested to Hancock that she should attend the Morgan party, Hancock had hesitated, insecure and lacking confidence, not quite certain that she was ready to venture into society. But Betty was not a woman to take no for an answer. "You should come to this party," she had urged. "It'll give you a chance to meet some new people."

Hancock had to admit that made sense. As her weeks in the twelve-step program went by, she found herself making steady progress and she could feel her self-assurance growing. Now it was late spring, and she perceived that it was time to begin working seriously toward building a new life, to start looking beyond the day-to-day struggle and begin devising a plan for the future. Even though recovery was a battle that had to be fought daily, sometimes even hourly, the contest did not preclude an abuser from considering what the rest of her life was going to be like.

The logic of Betty's argument as to why she should attend the party made it easier for Hancock to justify her decision as she drove past the sumptuously landscaped half-million-dollar homes that lined Chandler Road, each of them resplendent in the day's fading light. It was a long way from her neighborhood, Hancock thought, summoning forth a mental image of her own small apartment and comparing it to the exquisitely landscaped dwellings she was cruising by. Up here, she said to herself, things *are* different. The paint looks fresher, the lawns thicker, the shade cooler, the foliage more lush. Spring is truly here, she thought, reflecting on how the winter had passed in a blur, seemingly inconsequential compared to the mental and physical ordeal she was going through as she determined to kick her old self-destructive habits. Where had the time gone? she wondered. Too soon, it seemed, the dogwoods and azaleas, the vivid heralds of spring, had dropped their flowers. But they had been succeeded by dazzling beds of impatiens and begonias, she noted happily, whose eye-catching brightness was balanced by hanging baskets filled with sedate Boston ferns or emerald-leafed bougainvillea. Although it was too early in the season for them to bloom, the crepe myrtle and magnolia were budding, promising visual and olfactory delights to come.

On her right, between the trees that were decked out in their new summer greenery, over the residences in Greenwycke Village, Hancock could see into Jones Valley, and beyond that, the glint of the Tennessee River as it snaked on its southeasterly course toward Guntersville Lake. It was early evening, the period that Southerners call suppertime, and the sun was setting majestically behind the hills, blurring the outlines of the less ornate homes and strip centers that filled the dale. As she watched, lights began to twinkle on, making the city look like a table covered with an olive-colored cloth onto which a large handful of diamonds had been cast.

Forcing the last of the lingering indecision out of her mind, Hancock turned onto the side street, where the party was being held at the impressive new home of *Dr. and Mrs. Davis Johnson*. Originally, the fete was to be given at Jack and Betty's, but was switched to the Johnsons' because the physician and his wife felt it was a good opportunity for them to show off their dream house, which they had just finished decorating. Despite her resolution to quit worrying about what she was doing, Hancock felt a brief stab of self-consciousness as she parked her plain-looking Chevy on the street among the shiny new BMWs, Volvos, Acuras, and Saabs that already lined the curb.

Climbing out of her vehicle without bothering to lock it, Hancock paused to study the house where the party was being held. It was a sprawling, two-story, pink-stucco building beautifully landscaped and strategically placed within the shelter of the surrounding hardwoods. Gazing at the house glistening in the setting sun, Hancock thought it looked more like a home that belonged in Miami or Palm Beach than in the hill country of northeastern Alabama. She was further impressed when she was ushered inside, mumbling her greetings in a large foyer whose floor was covered in gleaming white and green marble. To her left was a large living room, decorated with a modern white sofa and matching side pieces. Against the far wall was a massive fireplace, also finished in marble. Since the outside temperature that evening was in the seventies, there was no fire glowing in the hearth, although Hancock could imagine how comfortable the room would seem if the logs had been lit. A few paces away, a makeshift bar was tended by a uniformed professional who had been hired for the evening, along with the piano player who was crafting soft music in the background. Beyond the living room was the dining room, which was dominated by a large oak table laden with platters of cheese, shrimp, thinly sliced roast beef and ham, plus a tempting selection of pastries. Before she could decide in which direction to move, she saw Betty rushing over to greet her.

As Betty approached, Hancock noticed, she pointedly brushed past a dark-haired woman that Hancock had met previously but did not know well.

"Hi, Betty," Hancock heard Brenda Cerha say. Instead of replying or even acknowledging the greeting, Betty stared straight ahead and kept walking. A look of disappointment and humiliation flickered across Cerha's face. She opened her mouth, and Hancock thought she was going to say something else, but she shrugged instead and turned to a man in a well-cut dark suit, forcing a smile.

Cerha, twice widowed, was somewhat of a legend in the Huntsville medical community. Her second husband, Vladimir, a physician who had defected from Czechoslovakia, had committed suicide by shooting himself in the head while they were in bed together several years before. Vlad had been Jack Wilson's best friend, and Brenda and Betty, both nurses at a local hospital, had become equally close. But soon after Vlad's suicide, the friendship between Betty and the new widow abruptly dissolved, for reasons that most members of the tightly knit community, much less Hancock, did not understand. Once best friends, they now appeared to be worst enemies, even though Cerha had mentioned to others that she would like to mend the rift.

Since Cerha, whose first husband also had committed suicide, had never remarried after Vlad's death, and since she maintained a certain distance from the group, she had come to be regarded among the members of the local medical clique as a woman of mystery. Cerha wore her raven hair straight, with the ends tucked under, and her skin was alabaster white. She bore a remarkable resemblance to a character familiar to late-night TV viewers, especially horror movie fans. Because of that resemblance, and Cerha's esoteric reputation, and possibly because of her rather macabre past, she was dubbed "Elvira."

Studying Betty as she maneuvered across the crowded room, Hancock's eyes widened in surprise. Although she invariably bought expensive and stylish clothes, Betty was notoriously inept at putting together a matching outfit, often mixing the wrong colors or wearing garish costume jewelry with chic dresses. Tonight, though, Hancock observed, she looked stunning in a black cocktail dress with a beautifully cut bolero jacket, a garment that did little to mask the low-cut bodice or hide Betty's surgically enhanced breasts. Around her neck was a remarkably effective necklace, a simple gold chain with a huge diamond centerpiece, which was complemented by a pair of simple diamond earrings. Betty almost never wore cosmetics, not since she had her eyebrows and lips tattooed and had undergone extensive facial surgery, including at least one face lift and two rhinoplasties. And, while there were times when her lack of makeup made her look deathly pale and somewhat surreal, not unlike the Joker character played by Jack Nicholson in the movie *Batman*, this was not one of those moments. In Hancock's opinion, Betty looked as pretty that night as she had ever seen her.

"I'm glad you made it," Betty squealed in delight, grabbing Hancock's hand and squeezing it affectionately. "Come on," she said with a tug, flipping her dark pageboy, "there are some men I want you to meet."

TWO

BOBBY CUMMINGS LOOKED ON WITH quiet amusement as Hancock was led away, smiling to himself and silently commenting on how radiant Betty looked.

A shy, unobtrusive stockbroker, Cummings, like Hancock, was a friend of the Wilsons, almost a member of the family. Like Hancock, Cummings also had met Betty through the twelve-step program, and, again like Hancock, he had not known at first what to make of her. Watching her as she introduced Hancock to a slim dermatologist, noting how she threw her head back and roared at something Hancock had said, Cummings recalled the first time he had seen Betty, how she had strolled almost casually into a meeting wearing a mink coat and diamond rings. Since most of the members had lost their fortunes as well as their self-respect because of their addictions, Betty's ostentatious dress was decidedly out of place. Cummings had taken one look at her that evening and rashly concluded that she would not last long in the program. Later, he admitted how wrong he had been. That was almost five years ago, Cummings recollected in surprise. Not only had Betty stuck it out, apparently remaining sober while others reverted to their previous self-destructive behavior, but she had become one of the group's more active members, being among the first to greet and offer assistance to newcomers, and struggling to perfect a public-speaking persona so she could extol the advantages of the program. Despite that misleading first impression, Cummings had become friends with Betty and then, through her, with her husband Jack. Cummings and Jack had hit it off immediately; Cummings had become not only his friend, but his broker as well.

As with Marion Hancock, it was because of Betty that Cummings was at the party. While he hobnobbed frequently with the city's wealthier residents, including many of those in that very room, he rarely attended events like Morgan's fund-raiser. As an entrepreneur whose livelihood depended on his relations with a cross-section of the population, Cummings felt it was better to maintain a policy of political neutrality. This line of reasoning, he believed, was especially valid in Huntsville, a city whose residents were sharply divided along political lines. Cummings had been born and reared in Huntsville. His family had resided there for generations and was well-known. Still, he admitted, his hometown was a rather strange place, an anomaly in the region, having little in common, other than the fact that they were all in Alabama, to sister cities like Montgomery and Mobile.

But that had not always been true. Until the late forties, Huntsville was a sleepy Southern hill town, not very different from other communities at the tail end of the Appalachian chain, cities like Chattanooga, Tennessee, which was a few miles to the northeast, or Rome, Georgia, which was about an equal distance to the southeast. Founded in 1819 as a village called Twickenham, it was the first community in the newly formed state of Alabama. The town developed as a market center on what was then the American frontier, and evolved into a cotton and textile center, a pattern it maintained through the Civil War and into the middle of the twentieth century. The impetus for Huntsville's divergence from the paths followed by similar Southern cities was World War Two.

After the war, Washington decided to headquarter the country's rocket and missile programs at the Redstone Arsenal, a military installation just west of the city. As a first step, a sizable contingent of Germany's brightest and most imaginative scientists, including the famous Werner von Braun, were sent to Alabama to get the program under way. Before long the rocket facility became a magnet for other high-tech industries. Once McDonnell-Douglas, Boeing, TRW, Rockwell, and others began moving in, a floodgate opened that forever changed Huntsville's character and mores. Almost overnight the city was transformed from a relatively small Southern community whose major export was cotton, to a full-fledged city whose workers supplied the world with boots, tires, telephones, and rocket parts, not to mention the technology of the space program. The George C. Marshall Space Flight Center, as the program came to be known, went on to become NASA's largest field operation.

In little more than the blink of an eye, Huntsville's once somnolent streets were bristling with people speaking in strange accents about topics and concepts that were totally foreign to natives. Coffee shop conversations, which once centered on boll weevils and the cotton market, mutated to principles of boost and lift; from Auburn and Alabama football, to throw-weight and solid fuels. Engineers moved in next door to farm equipment dealers, and children of physicists took schoolroom seats next to those whose fathers ran grocery stores or operated cranes. By 1990 Huntsville's reputation as a professional oasis was well-established. Alabama ranks forty-seventh in the country in the percentage of its residents who have high school diplomas, but the city of Huntsville, with 166,000 people, has seven hundred holders of doctoral degrees in nonmedical professions, as well as twelve thousand engineers.

During that period of transition, the city's political climate changed as well. By the mid sixties the so-called Solid South was falling apart as a direct result of a massive civil rights upheaval set in motion by liberal Democrats in Washington under the direction of a Texan, President Lyndon Johnson. Southerners whose families had been Democrats for more than a hundred years began registering and voting as Republicans because the GOP had evolved into the more conservative party. This switch, in turn, led to a peculiar politicosocial flip-flop. Many of Huntsville's new residents were liberal Democrats from other areas of the country. Once in Huntsville, they joined with the local Democrats, whose social beliefs were decidedly less liberal but who continued to exist as a sort of subculture within the population, remaining loyal to the party of their ancestors. The result was an odd mixture: liberals and conservatives found themselves tied together under the Democrat banner, while many original Democrats had become Republicans. At times it could be very confusing.

During this period, too, the South itself had changed in many ways. Blacks and whites were attending the same schools, unlike thirty years before. By the time of Morgan's fund-raiser, all official vestiges of segregation had long been abolished. While some social barriers remained, they were disappearing, too, some more quickly than others. Attitudes, even among native Southerners who had grown up with segregation, had metamorphosed. The crowd at the fund-raiser was a good example. The host and hostess for the evening were black, and blacks were scattered plentifully among the guests, laughing, eating, drinking, and talking politics with other guests, some of whom probably had gray Confederate uniforms packed in trunks in their attics and portraits of Rhett Butler–type figures hanging in their dens—a situation that could not have existed a bare quarter century earlier. Change, however, particularly social change, is not manifested equally among the residents of what sociologists like to call the New South. In many ways, the South has indeed mutated, but in some ways it remains the South.

Some modern Southerners remain unequivocally conservative, while others are just as unequivocally liberal, a difference that has come about almost capriciously, seemingly unrelated to an individual's background. Betty, for instance, was born in Gadsden, Alabama, a steel-mill town seventy miles south of Huntsville, on July 14, 1945, into a family whose socioeconomic status was unarguably middle class. Her father was a policeman and her mother worked in a textile factory. As Betty went through her formative years there, the elementary and junior high schools she attended were segregated, as were all the city's public facilities. Her arrival at Gadsden High School coincided roughly with the desegregation movement, but her class, when it went into the world in 1964, was the last all-white one to graduate from the school. Given her background, it would not have been surprising if Betty had been a staunch conservative, as were many who grew up in that era. Yet Betty's social and political beliefs were undeniably liberal. At every opportunity, she championed black causes and actively sought out black friends. And, as would be pointed out later, perhaps to her detriment, at least one member of her stable of lovers was a black.

Race, however, is not the only factor of importance in the South, not excluding Huntsville. Class and politics are considerations, too. While the Morgan fund-raiser could claim to be racially integrated, the other two criteria were noticeably in effect, creating a different kind of segregation. Almost everyone at the party, Cummings and Hancock being conspicuous exceptions, was connected in one way or another to the city's medical community, a society whose members stood subtly apart from the city's scientific community—which was composed chiefly of engineers and physicists—and from the professional group, which included administrators, lawyers, and computer experts.

The political orientation of those at the party was equally obvious: they were almost all liberal Democrats. It was, in fact, largely because of this continuing Southern obsession with politics that the party was even being held. The guest of honor, Tim Morgan, had recently taken on the role of political martyr.

Morgan was a slim, well-groomed man in his mid-forties, with a neatly trimmed salt-and-pepper beard and a slow, warm smile. A self-effacing lawyer with a quick legal mind, Morgan had been in the prosecutor's office since the early seventies, almost twenty years. When the district attorney—Morgan's boss, Bud Cramer—was appointed to fill a vacant seat in Congress, Morgan, a Democrat like Cramer, temporarily took over Cramer's job until someone could be formally named to the post pending an election. However, within weeks the state's Republican governor appointed another assistant district attorney, fellow GOP member Morris "Mo" Brooks, to fill Cramer's chair. One of Brooks's first acts, influenced, according to Morgan, by politics, was to fire Morgan. As a result, Morgan almost immediately announced that he would oppose Brooks in the election scheduled for the following autumn, some four months in the future. The party at the Johnsons' was an attempt to raise funds to help his campaign.

When Cummings had proclaimed his reluctance to attend the event, citing his long-standing public commitment to political neutrality, Betty was determined to change his mind.

"It will be good for you, Bobby," she had argued. "Besides," she added, "I really want you to come."

Once he was there, the soft-spoken Cummings wondered why he had been hesitant to attend. Moving comfortably among the well-heeled partygoers—the men clad in expensive and expertly tailored dark suits, the women in stylish cocktail dresses, literally dripping jewelry—Cummings made small talk about the delightful spring that northeastern Alabama was experiencing and the vagaries of the financial markets.

Pausing to survey the room, he spotted Jack Wilson standing against the living room wall, nursing a Coke and looking lost. A tiny, frail man, barely five-foot-four and weighing only 122 pounds, the ophthalmologist's physical appearance belied his sharp wit and native intelligence. Vision problems forced Jack to wear thick-lensed glasses that magnified his dark eyes, giving him an owlish appearance. He also had overlarge ears that seemed to float away from his balding head, and a sharp, jutting chin—all characteristics that Jack himself lampooned. Cummings recalled seeing one of Jack's prescription blanks, which depicted the doctor in caricature, magnifying glass in one hand, a carpenter's box labeled "Eyeball Repair Kit" in another, pursuing a huge, two-legged orb.

As usual, Cummings noted dryly as he watched his friend, Jack was dressed like a man who shopped for his clothes at the Salvation Army. In contrast to the fashionable suits that draped the other physicians at the party, Jack wore an old tweed sport coat and a twenty-year-old, eight-inch-wide tie snuggled up against his Adam's apple in a knot the size and shape of a tennis ball. Jack was known throughout the area as a lovable eccentric, and his manner of dress did nothing to contradict his reputation. Absolutely nothing the ophthalmologist did, Cummings thought as he greeted his friend, except for his medical procedures, could be considered conventional. For one thing, Jack hated to wear shoes. As often as not, he padded around his office in his stocking feet, slipping quickly and silently from examining room to lab, his progress marked only by his ever-ready laugh. Thinking about shoes prompted Cummings to look down. Since this was a party, Jack apparently had compromised his habits by donning a pair of scuffed brogans.

Who could look at this man, Cummings asked himself, and guess that he was worth more than six million dollars, and was adding to that cache at the rate of another million dollars a year? The answer, the stockbroker knew, resided in Jack's personality and his ophthalmologic skills. He was loved and admired throughout northeastern Alabama; patients flocked to him in droves. His files contained more than fifty thousand charts. Plus, Jack was a workaholic; his practice was not only his job, it was his life. He customarily opened his doors at seven in the morning and did not close them until five. Sometimes, on really busy days, by beginning early, staying late, and racing between treatment rooms, he saw as many as ninety patients a day. Often, Cummings had heard, Jack even slept in the office, grabbing a pillow from a waiting room settee and spreading a blanket on the floor.

"I just talked to Betty," Cummings commented, taking a position on Jack's left. "I asked her where you were."

Jack half turned and cocked an eyebrow. "What did she say?"

"She said she didn't know." Cummings smiled. "She said she wasn't talking to you."

Jack guffawed. The tribulations of his and Betty's marriage was a standing joke between the men. Cummings had been an ally a couple of years before, when Betty had told the stockbroker that she was going to divorce her husband. She didn't love Jack anymore, she explained, adding that she could no longer tolerate his peculiar habits. Furthermore, she added, she was disgusted by the fact that he had to wear an ostomy bag as a result of an operation he was forced to undergo soon after they were married. Most of his large intestine had been removed, necessitating the use of the pouch. She had been thoroughly revolted once when he tried to make love to her and the bag burst, soiling the sheets. As a result of that incident, she told friends, she had banished Jack from her bed. From then on she referred to him, even among people she hardly knew, as "the old shitbag."

Summing up her reasons for planning the divorce, Betty had told Cummings that she was "just tired of feeling humiliated in front of others."

Cummings kept working on the couple until he convinced them to see a marriage counselor; as any friend would do, he told himself. Soon afterward, Jack told him that on their first visit, the counselor had directed each of them to draw up a list of grievances so they could have a basis for working out a possible reconciliation. Betty's list, Jack had confided, was three pages long, beginning with things like, "He picks his nose" and "He scratches his butt."

"And what about your list?" Cummings wanted to know.

"There was only one thing on it," Jack had replied.

"What was that?" a curious Cummings had asked.

"I said I wanted her to start treating me as well as she did her friends in AA."

They must have worked out some sort of arrangement, Cummings decided, because Betty never filed the necessary legal papers for a divorce. Neither she nor Jack ever told him why, and he thought it none of his business, so he didn't inquire. The possibility of a divorce was never mentioned again, at least not to him.

When Jack stopped laughing about Betty's latest comment, Cummings asked him if they were still on for lunch the next day. In an uncharacteristic move, Jack had called the stockbroker a few days earlier, saying he wanted to meet with him because he had something to tell him. Although Jack had been very mysterious about the topic, Cummings deduced that it had something to do with the doctor's portfolio.

"We'd better postpone it," Jack said. "Betty and I are going on a vacation to Santa Fe the day after tomorrow, and I need to spend some time with her before we go."

Cummings readily agreed, although, given his relationship to the couple, he was surprised that he had not known about the vacation plans.

"Do you want to set a date now?" Cummings asked.

"No," Jack replied, "I'll just give you a call when I get back."

Without expanding upon his reasons for asking for the meeting, Jack drifted off. As his friend walked away, Cummings looked at his watch. He'd been here long enough to leave without seeming rude, he decided.

Cummings did not know it until later, but Marion Hancock had left just a few minutes before, in a somewhat agitated state.

After Betty steered her away to introduce her to a series of guests, mostly men, Hancock saw immediately that Betty was in one of her difficult moods.

"I want you to meet someone," Betty said to the first man they had come upon. "This is Marion Hancock. She's my *very best friend,*" Betty simpered. "I know you'll just love her. Isn't she beautiful?" she asked, adding with a wink: "And she's available, too."

After three or four similar encounters, Hancock began to feel acutely embarrassed. Claiming a prior engagement, she told Betty she was going to have to leave, but would see her the next evening at the twelve-step program's weekly speaker meeting. "Thanks for inviting me," she called behind her as she fled, her ears burning. "I'll see you tomorrow."

THREE

A FEW MILES AND HALF A WORLD AWAY, while the impeccably clad, politically conscious members of Huntsville's medical community sipped white wine or scotch and nibbled daintily from the Johnsons' smorgasbord, an unemployed handyman named James Dennison White, wearing worn and wrinkled jeans that bagged in the seat and a loose-fitting tee-shirt, lay stretched out on the queen-sized bed in a second-floor motel room, gulping lukewarm Budweiser from a can distractedly staring at a flickering TV. His faded blue-and-white-plaid flannel shirt was tossed haphazardly across a chair, and a pair of down-at-the-heel work boots lay in a small pile in the middle of the floor.

A short, skinny, balding man of forty-two who lived in an untidy trailer outside a tiny community southeast of Birmingham called Vincent, White would not have been invited to the Morgan fund-raiser under any conceivable circumstance. A man with a prison record and a history of substance abuse, an eighth-grade dropout whose most treasured occupational memories included his days as a short-order cook, White would have been as welcome at the Johnsons' as a member of the Ku Klux Klan in full regalia, with or without a cross and a can of gasoline. All of which was just fine by James White. On that Thursday night, May 21, 1992, he was far too tired to go partying anyway.

He stretched and yawned. It had been a long day, beginning shortly before three that morning when he locked his trailer behind him and climbed into his battered eight-year-old Ford pickup truck to begin the drive to Huntsville. The three-hour trip had not been unpleasant. Pumped up with Bud and a handful of the tiny over-the-counter caffeine tablets he called "fast ones" or "white crosses," the miles had clicked away.

Arriving in the city a little after dawn, White drove to a parking lot outside an office building at 333 Whitesport Drive, a blocky, two-story structure jammed between a shopping center and a hospital. Climbing out of his truck, he limped up to the building, trying to work out the kinks from his hours behind the wheel, but unable to do anything about a permanently stiff knee, the result of a fall at a construction site a couple of years before. Squinting in the early morning light, White studied the piece of paper taped to the door, an inexpertly typed notice that read:

> These premises protected in off
> duty hours by deadly snakes and
> mobile laser strike beams
> Have a good day
> Jack Wilson, M.D.

White grinned, exposing a row of badly neglected teeth. Yep, he told himself, this is the right place all right. Furtively looking around to see if he had been noticed, he scurried back to his truck and scooched down behind the wheel.

For more than an hour he sat there, staring at the building and cursing the comings and goings of a surprising number of early risers: joggers, insomniacs, and hospital workers changing shifts. About seven, when the parking lot began to fill up, he started his pickup and cruised across the street to a spot in the almost empty shopping center lot, leaving a puddle of cheap motor oil on the pavement behind him.

Settling down again, he reached across the seat and pulled a small plastic bag onto his lap. Nervously, he checked its meager contents: a length of heavy twine and a pair of thin plastic gloves of the type favored by health care workers. As he tensely fingered the cotton cord, a stray thought crossed his mind: Maybe I should have brought the pistol. No! he told himself instantly, remembering the strong distaste for firearms he had acquired more than twenty years ago, when he was humping through the boonies of Vietnam. It's better off where I hid it, he told himself. A gun is too noisy.

A little after eight, when cars began pulling into the shopping center lot, White got out of the truck and slammed the door in disgust. Hurrying across the blacktop as quickly as his limp would allow, he found a pay phone in front of the grocery store. Dropping a couple of coins into the slot, he punched a series of buttons for a long distance call.

"Call me back," he said without preamble when the party at the other end answered, and read the number off the phone in front of him. A minute later, precisely at 8:08 A.M., the phone rang and White snatched up the receiver.

"I can't do it," White would later claim he told the caller. "There are too many people around."

He listened for a few seconds. "I can't do that either. I don't have enough money for a motel."

He listened again. "Okay. I'll meet you at the Chick-Fil-A at Parkway City Mall at lunchtime. But you'd better have some money."

By eleven, according to White, his alcohol/caffeine buzz had disappeared. His stomach was growling and he couldn't decide which he wanted more, a beer or a

burger. By noon he was sitting at a table in the designated restaurant, hovering over a paper cup half full of
cold coffee and the remains of a sausage biscuit. He was
brooding over his bad luck and the poor timing of his
morning activity when a stylishly dressed brunette joined
the line at the counter. White rose and got in line as well,
separated from the woman by several other customers.
He watched as she paid for her order and walked briskly
to a table. He paid for his sandwich and was walking to a
nearby table when the woman crossed the room and
walked up to him. In her hand was a paper bag that
carried the restaurant's logo.

"Will you throw this in the trash for me?" the woman
asked politely, handing the bag to White.

Controlling an impulse to wink, White scurried away
and surreptitiously peeked inside. At the bottom of the
bag, under a neatly wrapped sandwich, was a crisp one-
hundred-dollar bill. Palming the cash, he threw both
sandwiches in the refuse can and exited the restaurant
without a backward glance.

With his spirits elevated considerably as a result of the
sudden monetary windfall, White drove to a nearby
K mart, where he dropped a packet of men's under-
shorts, a razor, a small bottle of aftershave lotion, a
toothbrush, and a small tube of toothpaste into a basket
and walked to the checkout counter. He paid for the
items with the one-hundred-dollar bill he had retrieved
from the bag, a transaction that would be readily identifi-
able later when investigators showed up at the store and
asked to see the sales tapes for the day.

White left the strip center and drove a few blocks to
the Ramada Inn, where he explained to the clerk that he
wanted a single room for one night and he wanted to pay
in cash. Like many establishments in the age of plastic,
the motel chain has a policy that anyone renting a room
and not using a credit card had to present some type of
identification with a picture on it. White dug in his

pocket and pulled out a worn wallet. Reaching inside, he extracted his Alabama driver's license and flipped it across the counter, along with two twenty-dollar bills he had received in his change at the discount store. The clerk photocopied the license, handed White $7.65 in change, and gave him the key to Room 222. A computer recorded the time of the transaction as 12:47 P.M.

Three hours later, after a short nap, a somewhat refreshed White got in his truck again and headed north on Memorial Parkway, toward downtown Huntsville. He took the exit that would lead him past Parkway City Mall and drove east on Drake Avenue. Some five minutes later he turned north again, this time heading up the mountain on Garth Road, following the same path that Marion Hancock would traverse some three hours later. When he got to Chandler Road, he turned right and drove to the intersection of the first street on his left, Boulder Circle. Leaving his truck at the intersection, White hobbled up the street until he got to the point where it dead-ended in a turnaround. For several minutes he stood staring at the brick home immediately in front of him.

Compared to the other houses on the block, number 2700 was a plain sister. While its neighbors were artfully landscaped, the Wilson residence had only a few scraggly shrubs under the front windows and a single, immature oak to offer scant shade over the brick path leading to the front door. Two faux gas lights bracketed the unadorned entrance. The dwelling, while obviously expensive to construct, had no character or personality, more closely resembling a campus sorority house or a unit in an office park than the home of one of the more prominent members of the city's medical community.

Walking a few paces to his left, White saw that a driveway had been carved out of the hill and plunged rather precipitously toward the back of the property. After about seventy-five feet the drive curved sharply to the right and ended in a double garage in the southwest quadrant of the house. The house's three occupants, Jack and Betty Wilson and Betty's youngest son by a previous marriage, twenty-three-year-old Trey Taylor, commonly entered and left the house through the garage and seldom used the front door.

Looking at the house head-on, it appeared to be a two-story structure. But there was a level below, which wasn't visible from the road, and it included the garage, Trey's bedroom, a laundry room, and a TV room. One door off the garage opened onto a short flight of stairs that led to the main level, which from the street appeared to be the first floor. There was a sitting room, a dining room, a kitchen, and a library on that level. At the back of the house, opening off that floor, was a large wooden deck that overlooked an Olympic-size pool and a rock garden, neither of which could be seen from the street. The staircase that came up from the ground level continued upward one more flight, opening onto a small hallway bracketed by bedrooms on either side. Coming up the stairs, Jack Wilson's room was on the right, Betty's on the left. In the other direction, toward the front of the house, was a guest bedroom and, opening off Betty's bedroom, a huge master bath that included a combination shower and steam room.

While he stood staring at the house, White realized that he himself was being watched. Spinning as quickly as he could on his game leg, he came face-to-face with one of the Wilsons' neighbors, who had decided to take advantage of the pleasant, cloudless late afternoon by mowing his lawn. Feeling that he needed to demonstrate some reason for being on the street, White did the first thing that popped into his mind: he pretended to be a health enthusiast out for a brisk walk. Extending his arms over his head, he simulated a series of stretching exercises, meanwhile watching the neighbor out of the corner of his eye. After a couple of minutes of that cha-

rade, acutely aware that he looked as out of place on
Boulder Circle as an apple in a crate of oranges, White
bustled as quickly as he could down the street, anxious to
get away before the neighbor could approach him and
ask what he was doing there. He reached his truck un-
challenged, slid as quickly as he could behind the wheel,
and sped away. The neighbor would remember the encounter and later describe in detail the strange-looking
man and his light blue truck with a fender that was a
different color from the rest of the vehicle.

Back at the motel, according to White, he made another long distance call, only to discover that the person
he wanted to speak to was not there. He dialed a local
number, talked for several minutes, and hung up. Then
he left the room and drove to a nearby fast-food restaurant.

After a meal of fried fish and weak iced tea, White
went back to the motel and reached for the telephone,
punching in the familiar long distance number, using the
middle finger of his right hand since the index finger was
a stub, the result of another work accident. It was 6:46
P.M. Again the person he wanted to talk to was not at
home, so White hung up abruptly. Finally, at 8:03, about
the time Tim Morgan's fund-raiser was reaching its peak,
he claimed he connected with the person he'd been trying to reach earlier.

"Don't worry," he said into the phone. "I'll try again
tomorrow."

He was silent for several seconds, listening. "Okay,"
he said at last, "I understand." They chatted for several
minutes before White ended the conversation. "I'll be
careful," he promised. "I love you," he added, and hung
up. That call lasted six minutes.

Placing the phone back on the night table, White rose,
put on his boots, and walked downstairs to the front
desk. Because he had paid cash for the room, he also had
to pay cash for any long distance telephone calls he

made, although local calls were free. He gave the clerk $10.75, went back to his room, stripped off his clothes, and slid under the sheets. He was asleep before the last of the Johnsons' guests said good night.

Whether these phone calls took place as White claimed would later become a hotly contested issue.

FOUR

JAMES WHITE MIGHT NOT HAVE RESTED SO
well if he had known that even as he slept he was being
sought by police. About four-thirty that afternoon, about
the time White was surveying the Wilson house, Detective Don King of the Shelby County Sheriff's Office in
Columbiana, another small community in the middle of
the state south of Birmingham, received a call from a
woman who identified herself as Janine Russell. The
woman said she was calling from Vincent, about thirty-
five miles from where King was.

"I'm not sure how to say this," Russell began, "but I
think there's a doctor in Huntsville that's fixing to be
murdered."

Taken slightly aback, King asked her to repeat what
she had said. "Who's going to be killed?"

"I don't know," Russell said. "All I know is he's a
doctor and his wife has a twin sister who lives near here."

King considered what the woman had said. Maybe the
alleged killer was her boyfriend and they had a fight and
she was trying to get even. Maybe she was high on alcohol or drugs, even though she didn't sound it and had not
been slurring her words. Maybe she was hysterical about
something. Maybe she was nuts. Or maybe, he thought,
she knew what she was talking about. Since she was talk-

ing about murder, King decided he could not afford to take a chance.

"I'd like some more details about what you're saying," the detective told her. "Will you meet with me? Will you come over here and talk to me?"

For what seemed like a long time there was only static on the line. Finally, Russell spoke. "Okay," she stammered. "I reckon I can do that."

It had begun about a month before, Russell said once she was seated across from the detective. Her friend, James White, would get boozed up and start blubbering about killing someone's husband. At first, Russell admitted, she figured it was just the alcohol talking and White was trying to make himself look like a big man. She had to chuckle when she thought about that: little ol' James being a killer! He liked to talk a lot when he was drinking, she told King, but she never thought of him as mean or dangerous. He was good with his kids, she added, and he was always good with her kids, too.

Anyway, she said, collecting her thoughts, it began with White telling her he was having an affair with a local school teacher named Peggy Lowe. At first she thought that was pretty fanciful, too, she told King, because Peggy was a proper lady, a first-grade teacher who was active in the First Baptist Church where her husband, Wayne, was music director and a deacon. They had three children, including one in college and one still at home, and they lived in a nice home on Logan Martin Lake just west of Vincent, toward Talladega. But according to White, Peggy and Wayne were having some serious problems.

"Not financially," she added, "but just that they had a marriage in name only and that Peggy was staying with her husband only because of the kids." She began to believe White was telling the truth about his relationship with Peggy when he asked her to babysit for him several times when he went to meet her. And she had been with White a few times when Peggy called, and watched the transformation in him when he knew who it was on the line. "He would just light up like a Christmas tree," Russell said.

What did that have to do with murder? King asked, growing impatient.

"I'm getting to that," Russell said.

At first, she told the detective, White told her that he was planning to kill Peggy's husband Wayne. "He said she was going to pay him a lot of money," Russell said nervously.

"I thought you said it was someone in Huntsville who was going to get killed," King said.

"That's what I'm getting to," Russell added, a little irritated at having her storytelling pace interrupted. The next thing she knew, White wasn't talking about killing *Peggy's* husband anymore, but about murdering the husband of Peggy's twin sister who lived in Huntsville.

"It was just all crazy," Russell said. "I didn't know what to think. I mean he just kept telling me all this stuff, and I didn't pay him a whole lot of attention. I didn't think it was true."

Well, King asked, what made her think it was true now?

White kept on about it, Russell said, talking about how he had a contract and about how he had to make a trip.

What kind of trip? King wanted to know.

Russell shook her head, indicating she was not sure. "I'm assuming that that's when he got the first part of the money," she added.

Well, did he have money? King asked.

Russell nodded. "I know he had a lot of money at one time. I thought it was from money that his sister had owed him, that he had told me she had finally paid him back. But then he told me that he had accepted half of the money for the job he was supposed to do."

What about this contract? the detective asked. Did he say any more about that?

"He referred to it twice," Russell said. "He said he had it in writing. That it was as good as gold, but that they hadn't signed it. He said they wouldn't sign it until it was done."

"Did you ever see it?"

"No," Russell said. "Who has it or what it says, I have no idea. I told him all they're going to do is get you to do all this stuff and get in all kinds of trouble, and then you're going to be the one bearing it. I told him it was the stupidest thing he could do."

Then why do you think he was serious? King asked. When did you think he wasn't just talking in his drink?

"Last Monday night—" Russell began.

"That would have been May eighteenth?" King interrupted.

"I guess so," Russell said, "whatever Monday was."

"Okay," King nodded. "What happened then?"

"That's when he told me he had to finish the job," Russell said. "He said that he had accepted half of the money, and if he didn't finish it Peggy would have to pay it back."

Russell looked anxiously at King. "I told him he was crazy," she said, wringing her hands. "I said those women weren't going to do anything but get him in all kinds of trouble. I said he wasn't going to end up with either one of them, or any money, or anything else."

"What did he say?" King asked.

"He said no one would ever know. He said he had to finish it."

At this point you felt sure he was serious? King asked.

Yes, Russell nodded. She said she got to thinking about what White had told her and it suddenly started to click into place. This was a good weekend to do it, she said, because it was not White's weekend to have his kids; they were going to be with their mother, his ex-wife,

Cheryl Frost. "It's going to leave him free and clear," Russell added.

King drummed his fingers on the desk, considering what to do next. Turning to Russell, who was nervously chewing her lip, he asked her why she decided to contact him.

"I'm scared," she admitted. "In my own mind I want to say that I know that this guy I've known for six or seven years can't be capable of doing this, but desperate people do desperate things, and I just don't know where James's head is anymore. I'm scared for him, for me, for my kids, because the man is in and out of my house all the time. Coming in to talk to you is probably one of the scariest things I've ever had to do in my life, but my conscience won't let me sleep. I haven't slept for days."

King nodded slowly. "Thank you," he said. "Thanks for coming in. Let me take care of it now."

As soon as Russell was gone, King picked up his phone and dialed an extension within the sheriff's office. "Stop what you're doing," he briskly told the deputy who answered, "and run the name James Dennison White through the computer. And let me know as soon as you get something back."

A few minutes later King was handed a single sheet of paper. On it were the bare facts of the brief criminal history of James Dennison White, aka James Howell. Born March 4, 1951, in Memphis, Tennessee, White had a very brief rap sheet. According to the record, his single transgression was a conviction in Birmingham in August 1976 on a drug charge. Two months later, while he was still being held in the local jail, he escaped. For the next five years he was listed as a fugitive, finally surfacing in the summer of 1981 in Arkansas. After being returned to Alabama, White spent most of the next ten months in a prison near Montgomery. He was released on May 27, 1982.

King shook his head. To the detective, this record

hardly indicated that White had potential as a hit man. He had no record of violence at all, at least not in Alabama, and no recorded scrapes with the law since he had been released by the Department of Corrections ten years before, almost to the day. But King knew he could not afford to take a chance. Again he reached for the phone. Seconds later he was talking to an operator at the Huntsville Police Department.

"Listen," he said after he was switched to an investigator named Bud Parker, "I've got a story I think you might be interested in."

As concisely as he could, King related to Parker what Russell had told him, adding, "She believes White has been paid to commit the murder and may be planning it right now."

It was all very vague, Parker thought. From what King had told him, the only thing Parker had to go on was that someone, supposedly a physician, *might* be a murder target at an indefinite time, possibly in the near future. Nothing else was known about the apparent intended victim except that he was married to a woman who had a twin sister who taught school in a tiny town many miles away. By the same token, the alleged hit man could be anywhere, perhaps even in his trailer home in Vincent.

"I'll do what I can," Parker said, sighing, "but I'd appreciate it if you'd keep working on it from your end, too, and if you can get anything more definite, get back to me immediately."

"Okay," King agreed, breaking the connection. A few hours later, confident that there was nothing else he could do, the detective drove home and went to bed.

In Huntsville, Investigator Parker, who had become enmeshed in his own pressing problems with lawbreakers, was leaving for the night as well when he remembered the call from Shelby County. Oh well, he told himself, there's nothing I can do about it this time of night anyway. It'll have to keep until tomorrow.

* * *

In his house up Garth Mountain from the police station, Jack Wilson slept fitfully, his mind racing with last-minute details he would have to take care of before he and Betty flew to New Mexico on Saturday. Jack's uneasy sleep was disturbed by a noise; someone was knocking on his door. Popping up in bed, he saw his stepson Trey standing in the doorway.

"What time is it?" he asked groggily, turning on the light.

"Almost two," Trey replied.

"Is something wrong?" Jack asked, suddenly alert.

"No," Trey replied. "I just wanted to ask you if it was okay if my friend and I left now for Florida."

Jack knew that Trey had been planning to attend a youth camp over the Memorial Day weekend, but he recalled that the original plans did not call for a two A.M. departure.

"Sure it's okay," Jack replied, "but why are you leaving at this ungodly hour?"

Trey shrugged. He had just finished his exams, he said, and he and his friend had decided they might as well get an early start.

"Okay," Jack said, switching off the lamp. "Have a good trip and drive carefully."

Wide-awake at that point, Jack lay in bed and listened to the sound of the departing vehicle as Trey and his friend drove down Boulder Circle and turned onto Chandler, the noise of the engine audible for a long time in the still night.

Jack thought about their unexpected departure briefly, then mentally shrugged. Who was he, he laughingly told himself, the reigning Huntsville eccentric, to call anyone else's actions strange?

Unable to sleep soundly after his conversation with Trey, Jack dragged himself tiredly out of bed a little after five. By the time he showered and dressed to go to the office, it was not yet six, long before Betty normally got up. He didn't bother to wake her to tell her about Trey's departure. He would tell her later, he decided. It wasn't exactly an emergency.

Walking outside, Jack was touched by the beauty of the morning. The sun was just climbing over the mountain behind him, illuminating a cloudless blue sky. The temperature was a comfortable 63 degrees, and there was a gentle wind blowing at his back. This has really been a gorgeous spring, he told himself, inhaling deeply.

FIVE

WHITE HAD MET PEGGY SHORTLY after Cheryl said she was leaving him, White recalled. He had taken Cheryl's departure hard. Of all his wives, White was most attached to Cheryl, and her decision to divorce him had come like a kick in the groin.

After the divorce, he began feeling lonely and frustrated. He started drinking more and popping more pills, the same self-abusive behavior that had gotten him into trouble before. What he needed, he had felt, was someone to be nice to him.

In an effort to make ends meet—he had basically been out of work since he hurt his knee on a construction job many months before—he had been doing some freelance carpentry work at the Vincent elementary school, doing odd jobs for his daughter's teacher. Since he spent considerable time at the school, he got to know several other teachers as well, including a pretty brunette whose name he soon learned was Peggy Lowe. A few days after he met her, Peggy pulled him aside and told him that she needed some shelves built in her classroom. Would he be willing to take on the job? White immediately said yes, both because he could certainly use the money and because he was attracted to this petite, cheerful teacher, a woman who always seemed to have a smile for everyone.

While he was sawing and hammering in her classroom, White began pouring out his life story to Peggy. He told her about how his mother and father had not been married when he was born, and how that had caused him considerable embarrassment throughout his early life. He resented his father when he was a boy, but later, as an adult, he adopted his name, Howell, for several years. In the end, though, he had gone back to his mother's name, White.

Although IQ tests would later show that he was of average intelligence and far from incapable of learning, White never liked school and had dropped out in his mid-teens when he was halfway through junior high. For the next couple of years, he worked at a series of low-paying, low-skilled jobs, until he was old enough to join the military. After he finished basic training, the Army sent him to Germany, but he had not been there long before the war in Indochina began heating up and he was transferred to Vietnam.

Vietnam had been a nightmare, he told her, and when he got back, he was a psychological wreck, suffering from a mental disease called Post-Traumatic Stress Disorder. Over the years, he had been in and out of a string of veteran's hospitals seeking treatment for substance abuse and recurring psychological problems. Military records would only partially bear him out on this. Although he *did* have a long history of treatment in a veteran's hospital, and there was a mention of PTSD in his hospital file, it was not clear if this was an actual diagnosis or something a doctor wrote down as an avenue to be explored. Apparently, the Army decided that White's psychological problems did *not* stem from his time in uniform, and he was never granted a service-connected disability. That is, the Army never compensated him financially for any injuries, mental or physical, he may have suffered during his service.

The reasons for his severance from the Army were

equally obscure. Even though he was rotated back from Vietnam before the time his tour normally would have ended, and he was separated from the service soon afterward, his discharge was an honorable one and his record showed no history of violence.

When he got back from Asia, White told Peggy, none of the hospitals and none of the doctors had been able to do a lot for him, at least not to the extent that he showed any permanent improvement for the conditions for which he had sought help: substance abuse and mental confusion. The divorce from Cheryl didn't help, he said, and as a result of the inner pain he was suffering from the breakup, he had again resumed his habits of heavy drinking and taking drugs, including a powerful psychoactive medicine called lithium.

When Peggy asked him about his marital history, White told her he had been married three times. His first marriage, he said, had been when he was barely twenty-one. It didn't last long, he admitted, and neither did the second one. They both ended unhappily, White related. The third marriage, though, the one that had just ended, had held together for nine years, which was a real record for him.

When she asked him how many children he had, White grinned and held up his right hand with all the fingers extended, including the nub of his amputated digit. "Five!" he said proudly.

Peggy Lowe was not only pretty and a good listener, White determined, but she was sweet, gentle, and kind as well. And even more important, he believed she took an interest in him as a person. She treated him as a man, a person with whom she might like to become romantically involved. He had known her for several weeks, he recalled, before he discovered that she was married.

When his work at the school ended, Peggy showed no sign that she wanted the relationship to end. They continued meeting and talking on the telephone, sometimes in conversations that went on for hours. Aware that he needed work, Peggy also hired him to do a job at her house, and she was always giving him things that he could either pass on to his children, like clothes that her children couldn't wear anymore, or that he could sell at one of the local flea markets.

White was grateful for the continued contact, because by then he'd decided that he was in love with her, the unattainable lady he had been searching for all his life. Although she would later deny that a romantic relationship existed between the two, phone records would show that scores of calls were made between White's trailer and Peggy's home.

On Friday, May 22, after putting in a productive morning, Jack Wilson went home about one for a quick lunch with Betty, then returned to his office to clear the decks for the vacation scheduled to start the next morning.

Betty did some last-minute clothes shopping and stopped to have a prescription refilled at a pharmacy near Jack's office. She then went back home to pick up a bank bag containing the contributions from the previous night's party, which she dropped off at Tim Morgan's campaign headquarters.

Checking out of the Ramada Inn, White returned to K mart and bought two quarts of motor oil and a can of carburetor cleaner. Limping out to his truck, which was sitting in a corner of the parking lot, he popped the hood and added the lubricants. Then he climbed in the cab and settled down to wait.

According to what he told investigators later, it was almost two-thirty before a black BMW pulled up alongside him with a dark-haired woman at the wheel. As White watched, the woman got out of the car and headed his way, walking behind her vehicle. Just before she got to his truck, she stopped and bent over, putting fresh knots in the laces of a pair of shiny new gym shoes imprinted with bright flowers. White stared at the shoes, certain he had never seen anything like them before, certainly not on a middle-aged woman.

Straightening up, the woman walked around to the passenger side of her vehicle and opened the door. Motioning to White, she commanded him to get in. "But crouch down on the floor so no one can see you," she commanded.

Gripping the plastic bag that he had brought with him, the one containing the twine and the gloves, White complied. Two minutes later, White said, the car was maneuvering up Drake Avenue toward Boulder Circle.

Jack got home about four-thirty to an apparently empty house. Deciding there was one more thing he wanted to do before he and Betty departed for Santa Fe, he rummaged around in the garage until he found a metal baseball bat belonging to Trey. With the bat in one hand and a campaign poster for Tim Morgan in the other, Jack strode outside and pounded the sign into the ground. Satisfied with his work, he went back in the house, where, as was his custom, he removed his shoes and left them by the door.

Nancy Nelson looked at her watch. Where the heck was Betty? she asked herself impatiently. A slim, comely, brown-eyed blonde with an accent as soft as an April shower, Nelson was a relatively new member of Betty's chapter in the twelve-step program, having been in the group only since the previous February. However, in that brief time, she and Betty had become close friends, frequently seeing each other socially as well as at AA-sponsored events. They had even shared a room during a statewide AA meeting at Guntersville State Park the previous weekend.

Nelson had talked to Betty on the phone early in the afternoon, telling her she was going to get off work sooner than she had expected and suggesting they have dinner together before the speaker meeting began at eight. Nelson was going through what almost all new members of any twelve-step program experience: a period of terrible insecurity, self-doubt, and lack of confidence. Betty was not only Nelson's friend, she was her sponsor in the program, which meant that Nelson relied on Betty heavily for support. Until then Betty had never let her down, but her tardiness caused Nelson's anxiety to increase by the minute. Many people may not have been troubled by the fact that an expected companion was late for an appointment, but it bothered Nelson considerably. She was still at the stage in her recovery that things like punctuality took on an importance far out of proportion to what they would under more normal circumstances. Besides, being late was very uncharacteristic of Betty, who usually was as precise as the six o'clock news.

"That sounds good to me," Betty had replied when Nelson proposed an early dinner, "but I've got some shopping I need to finish first."

"Okay," Nelson had said, "do what you have to do and I'll meet you at the hall between five and five-thirty."

Now it was almost six, and Betty still had not shown up.

Some fifteen minutes later Betty finally arrived, roughly an hour past the agreed-upon meeting time. "I got held up," she said by way of explanation. "Let's go eat."

Nelson looked at her friend in surprise. Although Betty was usually immaculately clad for all of the program meetings, especially the gatherings that featured a speaker, she had arrived for that night's session wearing sweat pants and a knit top, garb that was not appropriate at all for Mr. Steak, where Nelson had figured they would go for dinner. But instead of the usual restaurant, they climbed into Betty's second vehicle, a black BMW, and drove to a nearby McDonald's.

Over a burger and fries Betty told Nelson about Tim Morgan's fund-raiser the previous night, pointing out that the party had raised almost eight thousand dollars for the lawyer's campaign.

Nelson nodded disinterestedly, then changed the subject. "Are you getting excited about your trip tomorrow?" she asked.

"Oh, God, yes!" Betty exclaimed. "This will be the first time in a long time Jack and I have been away together."

"What are you going to do out there?" Nelson inquired. "Anything special?"

Her friend grinned and leaned forward. "Jack has promised he's going to talk dirty to me," Betty said, giggling like a schoolgirl. "And I can't wait."

Nelson blushed, embarrassed by the sudden and unexpected intimacy. "I think we'd better get back to the hall," she stammered. "The speaker's meeting is going to start pretty soon."

Betty threw back her head and roared, delighted at her ability to shock. "Okay," she said, "let's go."

When the meeting was over at nine, Nelson said good night to Betty and fellow AA members and went home. Betty remained for several minutes, chatting with other members before she, too, got in her car and drove home.

Kathy Seija, a psychologist who lived with her husband and their thirteen-year-old son two houses from the Wilsons', was watching television that Friday night when she was startled by a sudden, violent pounding on her door.

"My God," she said to her son Andy, "what's that?"

When they opened the door, Betty was standing on her stoop, crying and shaking, nearly hysterical.

"It's Jack," Betty blurted before Seija could ask her what the problem was. "He's hurt. I think he was attacked by a burglar and I think he may still be in the house. Please help me."

Seija threw her arms around Betty and led her inside, calling to her husband to dial 911.

The call was clocked in on the emergency line at precisely nine-thirty. The dispatcher, speaking calmly and clearly, ordered an ambulance to 2700 Boulder Circle and then notified the closest officer to the scene, Jim Donnegan, who was on patrol about eight miles away.

"There's a burglary in progress at that address," the dispatcher told Donnegan. "There's an injured victim and the perp may still be in the house."

Squealing to a stop in front of the Wilsons', Donnegan quickly checked the building. Walking around the house first, Donnegan noted that there was a light on in the garage and the front door was ajar. Right arm extended, pistol in hand, Donnegan ventured carefully into the house, mindful of the dispatcher's warning that a burglar might still be inside. Glancing in the rooms on the ground level and finding them empty, Donnegan proceeded cautiously up the stairs. Before he could get all the way to the top, he noticed a woman's purse and two pink plastic garment bags lying on the steps, apparently where they had been dropped. Beyond the items, through the banister that bordered the stairwell on the top level, Donnegan could see a form. Moving closer, he determined that it was a man sprawled on his back. Since he was expecting the worst because of the dispatcher's warning, the officer was not surprised to see that the man was surrounded by a pool of blood.

Following department policy, he warily backed down the stairs and went outside to summon the paramedics in case the man was still alive. Nervously, he waited for reinforcements to arrive in case the attacker was hiding inside. Soon afterward, police ascertained that there was only one person in the house: Jack Wilson. And he was dead.

SIX

AMONG THE PLATOON OF INVESTIGA-
tors swarming to Jack and Betty's house as soon as it was
discovered that a murder had taken place were three
men who would play prominent roles in events that followed: Bud Parker, the detective that Don King had
talked to some thirty hours earlier, Glen Nunley, and
Mickey Brantley, an ex-Marine who would direct the investigation. Nunley was the first to arrive.

A dark-haired veteran of thirteen years with the HPD,
Nunley jumped into the nitty-gritty that accompanies any
homicide investigation, chronicling details of the scene
and trying to keep out of the way of the team of crime
scene specialists who were turned loose after Wilson was
formally declared dead. While Nunley moved methodi-
cally through the house, sketching the layout of the
rooms and noting anything that seemed out of place,
technicians took pictures, dusted for fingerprints, and
catalogued samples of material that might prove valuable later, both in narrowing down the list of suspects
and helping to convict the killer or killers.

Brantley made a quick check of the house to be sure
the teams were working smoothly, then trotted down the
street to the Seija house, where he found Betty collapsed
in a tear-dampened heap, crying for her husband.

"How is Jack?" she wailed as Brantley walked in. "How's my husband? Is he okay?"

An unflappable, athletically built, sandy-haired veteran investigator who works on weekends and in his spare time as a free-lance preacher, Brantley told Betty as gently as he could that Jack was dead.

As soon as she calmed down from her fit of sobbing following that news, Brantley asked her to tell him as concisely as possible how she had come upon his body.

She explained that she had been to an AA meeting, as she almost always did on Friday nights, and had returned home at the usual time, expecting to find Jack either in bed or doing some last-minute packing for the vacation they were scheduled to begin the next day. Not noticing anything amiss, she was walking upstairs to her bedroom, carrying the purchases she had made earlier in the day, when she saw Jack lying in a pool of blood at the head of the stairs. She dropped everything in her hands, she said, and dashed out of the house through the front door. There was a light on at the Seijas', so she ran there and asked them to call the emergency number.

"It was a burglar," Betty sobbed. "Jack must have come home and caught him going through the house."

Noting how distressed Betty appeared, Brantley decided that he was not going to be able to get many details from her in her current condition. "I understand you're upset," he told her, "but I'd like to talk to you some more later. Where will I be able to reach you?"

Betty looked confused. "I can't stay in my house," she said tearfully. "I guess I'll go to my sister's."

"Who's that?" Brantley asked softly.

"Gedell," Betty replied. "Gedell Cagle. Her husband is Euel Dean Cagle."

"They live here in town?" Brantley asked.

"Yes," Betty replied. "Not far from here."

* * *

Investigator Nunley peeked over the shoulders of the crime scene team as they examined Jack's body. The physician, the investigator scribbled in his pad, was wearing a pair of beige casual slacks, a striped polo shirt, and socks without shoes. He was lying on his back with his right arm next to his body and his left arm extended. His feet were in the doorway to Betty's bedroom, but the bulk of his body was in the hallway. His hips were twisted as if he were trying to roll over, and his head was turned to the left. A metal baseball bat, later measured at thirty-four inches long, was lying on the floor nearby. "Possibly the murder weapon," Nunley noted, since even to a non-medical eye it was obvious that Jack's head was badly battered. He also noticed what appeared to be two stab wounds in the doctor's stomach. Although he looked around the area carefully, the investigator could not find a knife.

An autopsy report would later outline Jack's wounds in gruesome detail. The frail physician, the pathologist would report, had been struck on the head with the bat a total of nine times. Six of the blows had been powerful enough to fracture the skull and cause serious surface wounds up to two and a half inches long. In addition, he was hit on the back and the right shoulder hard enough to break the shoulder blade. Jack had been conscious enough to try to defend himself from the blows, because both bones in each forearm were broken, and his hands were fractured in three places.

The pathologist also confirmed what Nunley had suspected regarding stab wounds. The autopsy showed Jack was knifed once just below the right nipple, with the blade of the weapon slipping between his fifth and sixth ribs and plunging three inches into his liver. The second knife wound was a little lower, about three inches above the navel. In that case, the blade went through the abdominal wall and the pancreas, severing two major veins. Either set of wounds—the blows from the bat or the blade—would have proved lethal, the pathologist determined. However, because the amount of blood around the body and in the abdomen was relatively small compared to what it would have been if he'd been stabbed first, the pathologist deduced that Jack was initially beaten with the bat and was already near death when he was stabbed.

After Jack's body had been moved to the lab and the crime scene technicians had returned to their laboratory, the detectives held a conference to pool their information and plot their strategy.

Bud Parker spoke first, telling the others about the strange call he had the day before from an investigator in Shelby County, explaining how the detective had said a woman called him and told him that a friend of hers had contracted to kill a doctor in Huntsville. "And that's what we've got here," he pointed out. "A murdered doctor."

"But you said a contract killing," Brantley interjected. "The victim's wife says this was a burglary. Besides, this doesn't look like what we normally get with a hit."

He wasn't so sure about the burglary, Nunley added, pointing out that the house was not in disarray and there were no indications that it had been explored by anyone looking for valuables. No drawers had been emptied, no closets searched—none of the usual things that were found at the scene of a burglary.

Maybe the victim came home before the burglar had time to do that, Parker suggested.

Nunley hesitated. "Maybe," he conceded. "But I don't think so." There were, he said, a number of valuable objects, including expensive silverware, jewelry, fur coats, and several pieces of readily hockable electronic equipment, that were left untouched in either unconcealed or highly visible locations. In Trey's bedroom, the investigator added, he had found a shotgun and a pistol, either of which would have been snapped up by a burglar because those were items that could be readily sold. "They weren't hidden either," Nunley added. The shotgun was next to the bed and the pistol was in an open compartment in the headboard.

"How about cash?" Brantley asked. "Did you find any?"

"No," Nunley admitted. "The victim's wallet was lying next to his shoes. There wasn't any money in it, but it had several credit cards inside."

"Well," Brantley asked, "what *did* you find that might be suspicious?"

Nunley flipped through his notebook. There was a green ski mask with gold and red stripes that was on Jack's bed, he said.

"Any hairs in it?" Brantley asked.

Nunley shrugged. "We'll have to wait for the lab report."

Brantley nodded. "What else?"

In Betty's bedroom, Nunley reported, there was an empty pistol box.

Brantley's eyebrows went up. "Empty?" he asked.

"Right," Nunley nodded.

That was strange, Brantley opined. "Didn't you say there were two weapons in plain sight in the downstairs bedroom?"

"Yep," Nunley said. "A shotgun and a pistol."

"But this upstairs box was empty?"

"Right," Nunley repeated. "Except for some wadcutters," he added, referring to the type of cartridge commonly used for target practice, so called because the projectile is flat on the end and it makes a neat, round hole in a paper target.

Brantley looked puzzled. "That's weird," he said. "Anything else?"

"Yeah," Nunley replied. "The telephone cord in Jack's bedroom had been cut."

Brantley was surprised. "That right!" he said, more an exclamation than a question. "That doesn't sound like a burglar to me."

"It sure doesn't," Parker said, adding that he was still worrying about that call from Shelby County. He couldn't help feeling it had a lot to do with the Wilson murder. It was just too much of a coincidence, he felt, that one day he got a call tipping off a possible murder of a doctor, and the next day a doctor gets killed, even if it didn't appear to be a contract killing.

"Why don't you get back to that detective in Shelby County," Brantley suggested. "See if he's found out anything else or if there's anything he didn't tell us that might help."

"Okay," Parker agreed. "What else?"

Brantley sighed. "The usual," he said. "Keep after the lab people and see if they found any fingerprints or anything else that might help. Go through the house with a fine-tooth comb. Talk to the neighbors. Friends. Employees. Did he have any enemies? See if there was a will. Try to find out if there was a motive."

"What about the doctor's wife?" Nunley asked.

"I need to talk to her again," Brantley reported. "She was pretty upset tonight. I'll give her a chance to get herself together. By the way," he added, "were there any kids besides the one who lived here?"

"Yeah," Nunley added. "A bunch. They each had kids by previous marriages. But they're all grown. Some of them have families of their own."

"Find out about them," Brantley commanded. "See if they've ever been in trouble or if they would have any reason to be involved in something like this. I'm beginning to get the feeling this wasn't a random burglary," Brantley said. "It feels like an inside job. Let's find out everything we can about these people."

However, before they could quit for the night, there was one more task that needed to be taken care of. The investigators needed to check to see if there were any clues outside the house that might help the investigation.

While one team crisscrossed the yard and the immediate vicinity, the department's search dog was summoned. An officer had discovered a clearly defined walking trail that ran behind the house and down the mountain. Since that was a possible escape route for the killer, the dog was led down the path in hopes of picking up the scent of someone who may have been in the house. The walkway apparently was heavily used, especially by homeowners taking their pets for walks. The dog, despite its training, may have been more interested in what other canines had trod the path, particularly if one had been a bitch in heat, than in singling out a particular human odor. The dog's handler later said that the animal also may have been troubled, as are humans, by an allergy triggered by the pollen that flies in the spring. In any case, the dog search was inconclusive: nothing of substance was found.

One by one, in the following hours, the technician reports came in. To the investigators' disappointment, they were mostly negative. The fingerprints they found belonged only to family members, and they'd been unable to find any clear evidence that anyone who did not belong there had been in the house. Except for one thing. The single bright note came with the report on the ski mask. Stuck to the garment's fabric was a single human hair that later would prove to be alien to anyone who lived at 2700 Boulder Circle. While in itself it could not lead to a suspect, it could be matched with the hair of a particular suspect, once one was found, and either eliminate that person or tie him or her to the scene.

SEVEN

IN A TOWN THE SIZE OF HUNTSVILLE, THE murder of a prominent physician was big news. Jack Wilson's death was the lead item with the local media that weekend and for many weeks afterward. News coverage jumped off to an enthusiastic start on the morning after the incident, Saturday, May 23, when the *Huntsville Times* ran the story of Wilson's killing in the upper right corner of the front page, the spot customarily reserved for the most important article of the day. In the largest type on the page, the headline read, DOCTOR IS FOUND MURDERED.

Because the story did not break until late, details were skimpy. The reporter, Maureen Drost, quoted police as saying that the crime was reported by Jack's wife, who found her husband's body in the upstairs hallway of their home at nine-thirty on Friday night. The story did not mention Betty's contention that she believed that her husband had been killed by a burglar.

Drost quoted an unnamed police official as saying authorities "were not ready to release the cause of death," so no information was given on the type and extent of Jack's wounds. The coroner, citing a disinclination to get on "the bad side" of the HPD, told the reporter such

information would not be released until after an autopsy
had been completed.

Lacking details of the crime or from the crime scene,
the reporter filled in with some bare facts about the victim: Jack had been fifty-five years old—he had celebrated his birthday only seventeen days before—and was
a native of Chicago. He was a graduate of the University
of Tennessee's medical school in Memphis, and he in-
terned at Charity Hospital in New Orleans. Finishing
there, he performed his residency in ophthalmology at
the University of Alabama medical center in Birmingham, and opened his practice in Huntsville in 1968.

Although its initial report was abbreviated because of
deadline pressure, the newspaper would add to its background on Jack in the next few days. Combining that
with what they were able to discover on their own, investigators began to get a clearer picture of the murdered
physician.

The portrait that emerged had a well-lit foreground
showing eight seemingly well-adjusted members of
America's upper-middle class, apparently very ordinary
people, not unlike those who would probably be found
anyplace in the country. But since the investigation had
come about as a result of Jack's murder, the spotlight
shone first on him. And nothing investigators found indicated that Jack was a candidate for murder.

A product of a poor family, Jack appeared to be the
classic example of how anyone in this country can be
successful if he works hard enough. As a youth, Jack
studied hard and applied for medical school, where again
he applied himself and did well. As a professional, he
was highly regarded by his colleagues, his patients, and
even his first wife, Julia, who continued to praise him
even though they had been divorced for fifteen years.

Julia, who never remarried, blamed herself for Jack's
fate, claiming that if she hadn't asked for a separation in
the mid-seventies, Jack's life might never have taken the

path it did, and it may not have ended with him being battered and stabbed to death in his own home.

Between his internship in New Orleans and his residency in Birmingham, investigators learned that Jack had been in the military, a detail that had not been mentioned in newspaper accounts. When Jack finished his internship at Charity Hospital, the war in Vietnam was escalating rapidly and he was certain he was going to be called. Rather than entering a residency program and having it interrupted, Jack volunteered to be drafted. He was trained as a flight surgeon and assigned to a helicopter unit. Although he never went to Vietnam, he saw service in Germany and France before being sent to California and, eventually, to Fort Benning, Georgia, just across the Alabama state line. According to Julia, Jack loved the military and probably would have made it a career if he had not been increasingly troubled by an ailment that had dogged him since medical school, an illness diagnosed as Crohn's Disease.

A chronic condition manifested by inflammation of the intestinal tract, Crohn's Disease symptoms include periodic attacks of abdominal cramps, which are usually accompanied by severe diarrhea. For about three-fourths of the people suffering from the malady, it gets progressively worse. As time goes by, the sufferer's bowel functioning deteriorates, and this can lead to complications such as peritonitis or intestinal obstruction. Once it gets to that point, surgery usually is called for. This is what happened with Jack: the disease progressed until it necessitated his discharge from the Army, and then to where it threatened his everyday health. Eventually it became necessary for him to undergo an operation called an ileostomy. Surgeons removed most of his large intestine and created an opening in his abdominal wall called a stoma. A tube was then inserted into the stoma connecting his small intestine to an external container, which collected material that his system, minus a sizeable hunk of his large intestine, was unable to process. The container is called an ostomy bag, and once the operation was performed, Jack was doomed to wear one for the rest of his life.

As he drew closer to the completion of his residency, Jack and Julia began looking around for a place to settle down and open a practice. They selected Huntsville, which by then was growing rapidly and building its reputation as a high-tech center. At that time, many of the original 118 scientists who had been brought to Alabama from Germany were still alive and active in the burgeoning U.S. space program, which helped give the city a cosmopolitan feel that the Wilsons embraced.

Jack, Julia, and their three children, Perry, Scott, and Steven, moved to Huntsville in July 1968, five months before Apollo 8 made the first manned flight around the moon, and exactly a year before Americans landed there —flights propelled by rockets developed in Huntsville. It was an exciting time to be in the place city boosters call "America's Space Capital," and to live less than a mile from the man who had much to do with the development of American rocketry, Werner von Braun.

When Jack, then in his early thirties, opened his practice, he was the fifth and newest ophthalmologist in the city. Gradually at first, and then rapidly—so quickly in fact that it surprised even him—Jack's practice expanded. New patients, hearing about the strange little eye doctor with a weird sense of humor and an over-abundance of compassion, flocked to his office. Few were disappointed in what they found. Jack proved not only to be a good doctor, but one who was understanding of his patients' financial condition. If a patient obviously did not have the ability to pay, Jack would offer to open a "hundred-year" payment plan, or direct that the bill be settled in home-baked cookies, preferably oatmeal with raisins.

What really bonded his patients to him, though, was

his offbeat sense of humor. In no time Jack became a legend in Huntsville, renowned for his wisecracking and his buffoonery.

He not only imprinted his prescription blanks with his own caricature, but with other clever and very undoctorly aphorisms, such as referring to himself as "The World's Greatest Eyeball Doctor" and "The Best Eye Doctor in the Known Universe." On the blank on which the cartoon appeared, in the spot where a name was to be written, Jack had inserted "Lucky Patient," and in the area where the prescription was to go were the words, "Totally awesome elixer [sic]—cures most all ailments." His humor was better than his spelling.

One of his letterheads identified his practice as "The World Eye Center" and the practitioner as a "Specialist in Expensive Surgery and Optometric Referral." Centered at the top of the stationery was a drawing of the globe, under which was Jack's slogan: "Covering the World with Avidity," which, depending on the reader's interpretation, could mean either "eagerness" or "greed." It was typical of Jack to leave the definition in question. At the bottom of the page was another of Jack's catchphrases: "No Cataract Too Small."

He papered the walls of his office with adages from Murphy's Law and cartoons clipped from magazines. One of his favorites came from *Playboy*. It depicted a deranged-looking man in a white smock leaning over a patient. "I'm an insane eye doctor," the caption read, "and I'm going to kill you right now."

Despite his fondness for printed humor, Jack's real love was practical jokes. One of his favorite subjects, since he had gone to medical school in Memphis and felt a kinship to the singer, was Elvis Presley. To commemorate what would have been the rock and roll great's fifty-fourth birthday in 1989, Jack inserted a small ad in the local newspaper. Sandwiched among the movie notices was an official-looking pronouncement he wrote himself.

It read: "Dr. Jack Wilson . . . announces the closing of his office from . . . 11 A.M. til 12:30 P.M. on January 26 . . . for THE ANNUAL EYE EXAM OF ELVIS PRESLEY." Then he added the admonition: " 'THE KING' requests the cooperation of his fans to keep this a private occasion."

The ad caused quite a stir locally and proved so successful that Jack drew up another one for the next year and added another prescription blank to his repertoire, identifying himself as "Elvis' Personal Eye Doctor."

One of his greatest triumphs, though, centered around a large, thoroughly tasteless print of a stallion that had attracted his attention. Either because he did not recognize how truly hideous the print was or because he thought it was humorous, Jack hung it in a prominent spot in his office.

In the mid-eighties, when he moved to larger quarters, his office staff begged him to get rid of the print. Rather than throwing it in the trash, Jack had a small plaque made to attach to the bottom of the frame carrying the words, "On loan from the private art collection of Dr. Jack Wilson." He then took the print to the office of another ophthalmologist and his best friend, Dr. Sam Hutson Hay, and hung it in the waiting room.

When Hay evidenced a lack of enthusiasm over the exhibit, Jack went to a local judge and conspired to have a warrant issued for Hay's arrest for "stealing an art object." The next day a perplexed Hay appeared in court in response to the official-looking document. As is common in courtrooms, a bailiff appeared at the appointed hour and beseeched everyone in the room to stand for the entrance of the judge. Taking the judge's place, however, was Jack, who swept into the courtroom in a robe three sizes too large for him. Dispensing of the case quickly, "Judge" Jack found Hay "guilty" and ordered him to get rid of the print because its continued display constituted "indecent exposure."

Usually, though, his jokes were less involved and, occasionally, more subtle. One of his favorite pieces of clothing was a garish necktie decorated with tiny Santas, which Jack delighted in wearing at odd times throughout the year "just to see if anyone noticed." If any of his patients commented on the out-of-season decoration, Jack would caution them they "needed their eyes checked."

His staff also remembered:

- The Halloween he instructed all the women workers to show up for the day costumed as hookers.
- The elderly woman who, a respectable period after undergoing cataract surgery, had asked Jack if she could remove the dark patch. "Don't you dare!" Jack had told her sternly, slapping his hand on the counter. "If you do, you'll drop dead."
- How Jack, a devoted fan of Western novels, would decide that on a particular day he was going to be one of Louis L'Amour's characters, and ordered the staff to call him by that name for the entire day.
- The female patient who Jack convinced to ask the receptionist, deadpan, if it was usual for someone to have to "unbutton her blouse" for an eye exam.

In addition to his humor, Jack also was legendary for his frugality.

Whenever he could, he bought used rather than new equipment, and he shopped regularly at discount stores and the commissary at the nearby military base, a facility he was entitled to use because of a veteran's disability that was awarded him after his discharge as a result of his disease. He stocked his office refrigerator with inexpensive sodas that tasted like medicine but were cheap.

For years, until it was destroyed in a tornado, he drove a Mercedes. But unlike Betty's, which was shiny and new, Jack's was old and dented, a vehicle that he had bought from Brenda Cerha after her second husband, Vlad, committed suicide. When he had to replace it, even though he had millions in the bank, he selected a four-year-old Japanese import in bad need of a paint job and a new engine.

He saved "recyclable" envelopes, scratching out the previous address and writing in the new one.

And once, when Betty came into the office sporting a sparkling new President's Edition Rolex for which she had paid eight thousand dollars, Jack got so upset when he learned the cost that he had to take a cold shower.

While few people ever saw it, Jack had a serious side as well. One of those who caught glimpses of what the ophthalmologist was like when he wasn't clowning around was the stockbroker Bobby Cummings.

One evening long before Jack's murder, he and Cummings were sitting on the Wilsons' deck enjoying a pleasant Southern night. The air was heavy with the smell of honeysuckle, and the crickets were so shrill that the men had to speak loudly to carry on a conversation.

For some reason, Cummings recalled, the talk turned to death.

"I'm not afraid of dying," Jack had said, "but what scares me is the *way* I might die."

"Is there any good way?" Cummings had asked.

"Some are better than others," Jack replied without the hint of a smile. "I don't want to die violently," he added. "I don't want to go in a car accident or be murdered."

Cummings remembered this conversation months later, early in April 1992, only a couple of weeks before Jack's death, when he ran into Jack at the funeral of a mutual friend.

One of the things that Jack hated were large, ostentatious funerals. "I think they're silly; they're archaic," he confided in Cummings. "It's not natural for people to spend that much money and make such a big deal out of it."

"What are you going to do, Jack?" Cummings had asked, half in jest.

"I'm going to donate my body to science," Jack replied.

After the church service, when most of the bereaved went to the cemetery for graveside rites, Cummings and Jack slipped away to a coffee shop. Over slices of apple pie, Cummings mentioned Jack's investments and suggested that the ophthalmologist buy more real estate.

"Why would I do that?" Jack had asked. "I like municipal bonds."

"Real estate will make you more money," Cummings had advised.

Jack stared at his friend. "All money will do for you is buy you a pretty wife," he said softly.

EIGHT

AT THAT STAGE OF THE INVESTIGATION, Brantley and his team of detectives had no idea why anyone would want to murder Jack Wilson unless it had indeed been a random killing or was somehow involved with a family scandal they had not yet uncovered. It was when they started delving into Betty Wilson's past that the picture of the all-American family began to fall out of focus. When they looked beyond the obvious and started examining the background they came away with a whole new perspective.

The first thing to arouse investigators' suspicions was a seemingly innocuous statement passed on to Bud Parker by Shelby County Detective Don King. Within hours of the discovery of Jack's body, Parker was back on the phone to King asking for more details on his conversation with Janine Russell.

"That's all I know," King said after going through his interview with Russell in more detail than he had provided during their original conversation.

"Did your informant ever say the name of the twin sister in Huntsville?" Parker asked.

"Nope," King replied. "I got the impression she didn't know it."

"Well," said Parker, "that might be a crucial issue now. Can you track Russell down and ask her?"

King promised he would get back to the Huntsville investigator. But when he called a few hours later, he still did not have a name.

"No identification, huh," Parker commented. "Damn, I wish I knew who that sister is. Were you able to find out anything at all about the sister or about Peggy Lowe?"

"Well," King drawled, "I got one thing. I checked the records and got Peggy Lowe's date of birth. Will that help?"

"At this stage anything will help," Parker said. "You got it handy?"

"Yeah," King said. "Just a sec."

Parker could hear paper rustling over the phone, then King came back on the line. "Here it is: DOB seven, fourteen, forty-five, Etowah County."

"Etowah? Isn't that Gadsden?" Parker asked.

"Yeah," King replied.

There was a pause, then Parker exploded. "Holy shit!" he exclaimed. "We may be on to something. Let me check." Flipping furiously through his notebook, the investigator found what he was looking for. "Listen to this," he told King excitedly, reading from his notes: "Betty Wilson . . . born July fourteen, 1945 . . . Gadsden."

Both men were silent, then Parker broke the hush. "Bingo!" he said. "They're fucking twins!"

Parker could hardly wait to tell Brantley about the connection. "What do you think?" he asked enthusiastically when he had outlined what he'd learned.

Brantley chewed his lip. "That's *very* interesting," the investigator conceded. "But it's just a start." As Parker's face fell, Brantley pointed out that while it certainly sounded fascinating in light of what else had occurred, it still failed to bring any evidence to bear against either Peggy or Betty.

"All we have so far," he explained, "is the word of a woman we've never seen or talked to, claiming that this Peggy Lowe and her twin sister, whose name we now discover is Betty Wilson, *maybe* conspired to murder Jack Wilson."

"But at least it gives us something solid to go on," Parker argued, reluctant to surrender his excitement.

"You're right about that," Brantley agreed. "But let's take this one step at a time. I want to talk to Betty again, and I think King needs to have another conversation with Janine Russell. And then what we need to do is find this James White. Does King have any idea where he is?"

"He's working on it," Parker said. "He said he wasn't at home the last time he went to his trailer, but that was before we discovered the Peggy/Betty connection."

"Let's ask him to go out there and try again," Brantley commanded. "In the meantime, let's see what we can find out about Betty Wilson."

Betty Gay and Peggy Joy were the youngest of Nell and O. L. Woods's four daughters, coming along a decade after the oldest sister, Gedell, and some five years after Martha. They grew up in an unremarkable home in a quiet, working-class neighborhood in what was known as East Gadsden, across the Coosa River from the main business district of the city, virtually in the shadow of plants owned by Republic Steel and Goodyear Tire & Rubber, which at that time was the largest tire-producing facility in the world.

Even though they were twins and bore a strong physical resemblance to each other—they were about the same height and build and both had dark hair—they were not identical, not in their looks or in their personalities. They were close and looked to each other for support and reassurance, but increasingly as they grew older, they developed different sets of friends and different interests.

After they graduated from Litchfield Junior High in East Gadsden in 1961, they went on to the city's only white secondary school, Gadsden High. There, their differences became more pronounced. Peggy, who was widely regarded as the prettier, friendlier, and more outgoing, with intelligent dark eyes and a winsome, ever-present smile, proved to be one of the more popular girls in her class. Of the two, she seemed to have the sunnier personality, always cheerful and bubbly. In the spring of 1962, less than a year after the twins enrolled in the school, Peggy was crowned queen of Gadsden High, an honor so rare for a sophomore that no one could remember the last time that had happened. As if to prove it was not a fluke, she repeated the feat two years later. Before she graduated in 1964, Peggy was chosen to the school's beauty court all three years, was homecoming queen, shone as a vocalist in two school choirs, and was active in a group called Future Business Leaders of America.

Betty, on the other hand, was moodier, more serious, and more independent. A pixielike girl with sparkling dark eyes, she was more caustic than her sister. Peggy may have laughed more, but Betty had the sharper wit. Betty, too, was more interested in current events than Peggy, and seemed more eager for adventure. Although the high school yearbook also listed the Future Business Leaders of America among her credits, Betty ran for and was elected to the student council. While she was a member of the Pep Club, she balanced that with an early interest in health care by being active in the school's Red Cross program. She also showed a flare for acting and was a member of the Dramatics Club.

While Peggy exuded the image of the girl next door, Betty became known as something of a rebel, choosing among her friends those in the school who showed a tendency to strain against the current mores. In the vernacular of the day, she was a "beatnik," affecting the type of clothing now known as "grunge," and running with a crowd characterized by the more conventional class members as "fast."

Despite Betty's apparent independence, those who knew both girls generally agreed that Peggy had the stronger personality and was the dominant member of the pair. Betty, although demonstrating a proclivity to go her own way, often deferred to Peggy and tried to follow her lead. Some said she was jealous of her sister and seemed determined to prove her superiority.

A few weeks after graduating from high school in 1964, Peggy married her high school sweetheart, Kenneth Godfrey. Seemingly intent not to let her sister get a step up, Betty scheduled her own wedding. On October 24, four months and three days after Peggy's ceremony, Betty exchanged vows with Grover Talmadge "Sonny" Taylor III.

Neither marriage lasted very long. By 1967 Peggy and her husband had divorced and she had remarried a pudgy, unassuming music teacher named Wayne Lowe. They settled down in a farmhouse on the edge of a large lake east of Birmingham and had a daughter, Stephanie, who they raised along with Peggy's children by her first marriage, a daughter named Angie and a son, Blake. By the spring of 1992 Angie was twenty-five, Blake was twenty-three, and Stephanie was fifteen. From all outward appearances, the Lowes had a happy, solid marriage and were moving into middle age with a large degree of financial and emotional security.

Betty's history, however, was quite different. Although her first marriage lasted a little longer than her twin's— until 1969—it ended acrimoniously and with a twist unusual for the time and place.

When Betty decided she wanted a divorce, she simply packed up the bedroom and living room furniture and shipped it to Huntsville, abandoning her husband and three young sons. Following behind the moving van in the couple's ten-year-old Volkswagen, she quickly found an apartment and enrolled in nursing school at nearby Calhoun Community College. Back in Gadsden, a judge listened to Sonny Taylor's description of Betty's actions and swiftly signed a legal order awarding Taylor permanent custody of the three boys, a very unusual judgment in the Deep South of the sixties. At the time, the oldest boy, Bo, was four, Dink was two, and the baby, Trey, was only ten months. For more than a decade after that, Betty's contact with her children was all but nonexistent. Although the boys would occasionally come to visit her and her new husband, Jack Wilson, they did not have any sustained contact with their mother until after they had graduated from high school. In the meantime, in an apparent attempt to buy their affection, Betty presented Bo and Dink with new cars on their sixteenth birthdays. When Trey turned sixteen, however, there was no set of keys beside his plate at the breakfast table. Pleading temporary poverty because she had recently opened a boutique and had sunk most of her available cash in the new venture, Betty told Trey that she was unable to supply him with a new vehicle as she had done for his brothers. The lapse caused a rift between the two that took several years to heal. Ironically, once that rupture was smoothed over, Betty's relationship with Trey proved stronger than hers with the other two boys, each of whom lived with her only a short while before going out on his own. Trey, on the other hand, was still living with Jack and Betty at the time of Jack's murder.

During the seven and a half years between her divorce from Taylor and her marriage to Jack, Betty lived the life of a sexually liberated woman. After she received her R.N. degree, the twenty-nine-year-old Betty went to work at what then was known as Huntsville's Medical Center Hospital. According to statements to a reporter

from those who knew her at the time, Betty built a reputation as a competent nurse and was "popular with the
doctors." Others who knew her in that era characterized
her "popularity" in more earthy terms: her nickname
among the male medical staff was "Blowjob Betty." A
former hospital department head told the *Huntsville
Times* that her goal seemed single-minded: "She . . .
made it plain that she wanted to marry a doctor." In
1977 she found her physician.

That year, when Jack was forty and separated from
Julia, his wife of eighteen years, he began dating Betty,
who was then thirty-two. They married a year later, eight
days before Betty's thirty-third birthday. At that time,
Jack's three sons ranged in age from eleven to seventeen,
and Betty's, who were living with their father in Gadsden, were thirteen, eleven, and nine.

Up until then, as a single woman, Betty's sex life technically was no one's business but her own. Although her
marital status changed in 1978 after she married Jack,
she continued living the lifestyle of an unmarried
woman-about-town. In 1981, only three years after her
marriage, Betty confessed to Jo Ann Chiri, a woman who
worked with Jack as an ophthalmologic assistant, that
she was having an affair.

"Does Jack know?" Chiri asked, horrified.

"Of course," Betty had replied easily. "I got drunk and
told the sawed-off little twit."

Although it went on apparently unnoticed by others
except those who knew her well, Betty also developed a
dire drinking problem. It became so severe in more recent years that Betty herself decided to seek help
through Alcoholics Anonymous, an experience that
seemed to have radically changed her personality. One
of her former close friends said Betty took the AA tenets
seriously and apparently remained true to her vow to
stay sober, but in the process she became a lot less fun.

"She was always saying or doing something funny

when she was drinking," the friend said, "but once she sobered up, she became much more serious and difficult to get along with."

Betty's other problem was sex. In an interview with investigators after Jack's murder, Betty readily admitted to having long-standing sexual liaisons with at least a half-dozen men, including the risk manager for the city of Huntsville, who also happened to be black, a juicy tidbit that set tongues wagging all over town. After that affair became public, the man resigned and moved to California.

Although gossip later focused heavily on Betty's admittedly active sex life, those who knew her painted a picture of a much more complex personality, a woman with widely divergent mood swings and contradictory behavior patterns.

When she wanted to, it seemed, or when it suited her purposes, she could be sweet, loving, and thoughtful. After Jack had his ileostomy and was going through a difficult recovery, Betty literally moved into his hospital room, sleeping on a cot next to his bed and nursing him tenderly until he recuperated enough to go home. Not long afterward, though, she announced how repelled she was by the fact that he had to wear an ostomy bag and went to no great lengths to hide her revulsion.

Although Betty and Chiri also had an up again/down again relationship because of Chiri's loyalty to Jack, Betty could also be extremely nice to her. Several years before Jack's death, when Chiri was hospitalized for a tonsillectomy, Betty volunteered to nurse her as she had Jack.

After Jack's murder, Betty called Chiri and asked if they could meet at Jack's office so she could begin straightening out the paperwork. While they were shuffling through file folders and stacks of documents, Betty looked up at Chiri. "Jo Ann, will you please be my friend?" Betty asked her plaintively.

Yet, not many hours later, at the memorial service for Jack, Betty nudged Chiri and pointed with her chin at one of the detectives assigned to the case. "Doesn't he have a cute ass?" Betty whispered.

Although Betty said many damaging and hateful things about Jack, she apparently was not one to speak ill of someone behind their back. Many of the names and remarks Betty made to others about her husband, she also made to his face. Chiri recalled several times when Betty, during her infrequent trips to the office, would pass Jack in the hallway or in the lab. She would look coldly at her husband, Chiri said, and tell him: "You make me sick."

If anything, those who knew her said later, Betty's frankness was exceeded only by her vanity and her extravagance.

The day she turned thirty, a friend of hers told a reporter, Betty went into a fit of depression "and cried for a week." Soon after that, she embarked on a long-term program of cosmetic surgery that included, over the years, face lifts, nose reconstructions, a tummy tuck, an operation to make her cheekbones more prominent, and a breast enhancement. "You name it," said one woman who knew Betty well, "and she's had it."

After she married Jack and no longer had to work, her main preoccupation, friends said, was spending money.

"She had an engagement ring with a three-carat diamond, apparently which she bought herself with Jack's money," one friend said, "and a half-dozen fur coats."

When she made up her mind that she wanted something, Betty nagged Jack until he bought it for her. "One time," Chiri recalled, "Betty came in to the office and told Jack that she absolutely *had* to have a set of earrings she had seen, a pair of gold disks inset with emeralds. 'Life will not go on without those earrings,' she told him. The next day Jack ordered them for her. They cost five thousand dollars."

It was the same, said a friend, with the house on Boulder Circle. Jack and Betty had been living in Jack's condo when Betty found the Boulder Circle home during a house-shopping tour. According to the story the friend told the *Huntsville Times,* Betty stomped into the office and demanded that Jack buy the house. When he demurred, she threw a tantrum, screaming and yelling until he finally agreed.

In more recent years, Jack kept a tighter rein on Betty's spending. Or at least he tried. Despite his remonstrations to curb her extravagances, Betty usually found a way around her husband's prohibitions. One of Betty's favorite ways of securing ready cash, one friend said, was to go to the grocery store and write a check for $150 to pay for three or four dollars worth of merchandise, putting the difference in her purse and moving on to the next store. Even with Jack watching the monetary outgo more carefully, Betty never seemed at a loss for cash or evidenced any restrictions on her credit card charges.

Betty's opinion of herself, not unexpectedly, was much more grandiose than those of others. In preparation for her twenty-fifth high school class reunion, she composed an autobiography for the reunion yearbook that covered most of a single-spaced typewritten page. Listing her occupations as grandmother and part-time model, Betty launched into a long list of accomplishments that she claimed included two college degrees and a cum laude diploma in her nursing school class. She also served, she said, as director of nursing at the federal Centers for Disease Control in Atlanta. Among her civic duties, she claimed membership or administrative positions in the Art Museum, the Madison County CPR Board, the Council for Human Relations, and the scholarships program for the medical auxiliary. Over the years, she added, she had "traveled extensively around the world," enjoyed "gardening, entertaining, and cooking," and felt "snow skiing was her best outdoor sport." Her summary briefly mentioned Jack, her three sons and two of her stepsons (one was omitted), her daughter-in-law, and two grandchildren. "But," she wrote, "my best friend is as always, my twin Peggy."

Peggy's summary in the reunion book was two lines long. On the first was her name and on the second her address.

NINE

NANCY NELSON COULD HARDLY BELIEVE it. Betty, who had always been so much in control, was falling apart before her eyes. When Nelson learned about Jack's murder on Saturday morning, she made a few calls and found out that Betty was staying with her brother-in-law and sister, Euel and Gedell Cagle, a couple with whom Betty normally had only limited contact. Since Gedell was more than ten years older than Betty, they had not formed a close relationship when they grew up in the same home in Gadsden. Also, Gedell's husband, Euel, usually called by his middle name, Dean, was a retired federal civil service worker and basically conservative, certainly not the type who would develop close ties to a rebel like Betty or a bona fide eccentric like Jack. Betty was on speaking terms with them, but the couple was not part of what she considered her inner circle.

As soon as she discovered where Betty was, Nelson had grabbed her purse and car keys and rushed to the Cagle home to see if she could comfort her friend. Although she knew that Betty had been through a traumatic event—she herself had lost a husband years before—Nelson was not prepared for what she found.

When she walked into the Cagle living room, Betty

was crumpled on the couch, sobbing uncontrollably. Her chest was heaving and she was gasping for breath. Peggy was sitting next to her, holding her hand. And, while Peggy was crying, too, she seemed to be managing her grief much better than her twin sister.

"Jack . . . used to . . . laugh . . . at me," Betty wailed, taking in huge gulps of air between groups of words. "I . . . always left a . . . light on . . . I . . . just knew . . . we . . . were . . . going to be . . . burglarized."

A dagger of fear and sympathy stabbed through Nelson. Oh God, she thought, I wonder if she's going to hyperventilate. Moving quickly to her side, Nelson took Betty in her arms and began trying to calm her. It took the four of them—her and Peggy, Gedell and Euel—the entire day to bring her back to a semblance of normalcy. By evening, though Betty was still crying copiously, she was no longer hysterical.

Once her friend had settled down, Nelson began wondering about Betty's reaction. Was there something strange going on? she asked herself. Grief over the unexpected death of a spouse was one thing, she thought, but Betty's behavior went beyond what she considered ordinary. Was Betty putting on an act? She wondered if Betty was trying to cover something up, then felt guilty about having such thoughts. But they kept coming back, and she found it harder to banish them from her mind. I wonder, she asked herself just before she fell into an exhausted sleep, if there was really a burglary at all? Maybe, Nelson thought, Jack committed suicide and Betty doesn't want anyone to know. At that time, Nelson and everyone else except investigators and Jack's killer, knew nothing about the nature and extent of Jack's wounds.

Earlier in the day, Brantley had tried to interview Betty more closely than he'd been able to at the Seija's house the night before, but abandoned the idea when he was told how badly Betty was reacting to her husband's death. "Let's do it tomorrow," he had suggested to Euel Cagle. "Will you ask Mrs. Wilson to meet me at police headquarters, and I'll try to get it over with as soon as possible."

"Sure," replied Cagle, a taciturn, soft-spoken Gary Cooper type. "I'll see that she gets there."

Betty showed up on schedule on Sunday, seemingly having adjusted to confronting her grief. Although she had to pause occasionally to wipe tears from her eyes, she calmly answered the investigator's questions about her background and her life with Jack.

"Were either of you having an affair?" Brantley asked —a routine question to a person whose spouse has just been murdered.

"Jack wasn't," Betty replied, "at least not that I know of."

Brantley picked up on the implications of the answer. "Were *you*?" he asked pointedly.

"Yes," she said forthrightly. "Several."

Although Brantley had been an investigator long enough to cease being surprised at many things, he was more than slightly taken aback by what Betty told him.

She and Jack had separate bedrooms, she explained, and had not had sexual relations with each other in a long, long time. On the other hand, she said, she and Jack had an "arrangement," and she often had men spend the night in the house.

"How would you meet these men?" Brantley asked.

She met them in various ways, she said, but mostly through Alcoholics Anonymous.

Brantley could not restrain his curiosity. You'd just bring them home? he asked.

Yes, Betty replied. After the meetings. And they would sleep over.

Brantley scribbled furiously in an effort to keep up as Betty reeled off a list of names of the men with whom she had liaisons, even though he wasn't sure how this information fit in with the investigation. Despite the fact that Janine Russell's story apparently tied Betty to the death of her husband, Brantley had not yet given up on his original hunch that Jack may have been killed by someone within the family, someone other than Betty, perhaps by or because of one of the sons. Within forty-eight hours he would discard this theory entirely, but at the time it still seemed to make sense.

"How was your husband's relationship with the children?" he asked.

"Good," Betty said.

"All of them?"

"Yes," she replied, "all of them."

"And what about yours?" he persisted.

"Mine was good too," she said. "I got along with all of them."

Brantley paused, not sure exactly where to go next. As far as he could tell, Betty had answered his questions honestly and completely. There was not much else he needed to know.

"Oh," he said to Betty, "one more thing before you go. Did Jack leave a will?"

"Yes," Betty replied, "but sometimes he would change it."

"Could you get me a copy?"

"Sure," Betty replied. "I'll drop it by later."

When Betty had gone, Brantley turned to Investigator Harry Renfroe, who had been sitting silently at his side during the session. "She seemed cooperative enough," he commented.

Renfroe nodded. "Are you considering her a suspect?" he asked.

Brantley pondered the question. "Noooo," he said slowly. "Not at this stage. I still want to know more about the dynamics of the family. That's still bugging me, the relationship between Jack and Betty and all those kids."

"What about this guy James White?" Renfroe asked.

Brantley stiffened. "That's a good question," Brantley replied. "What about him? What the heck is Shelby County doing down there? Don't they know how anxious we are to question that guy?"

Renfroe rolled his eyes and shrugged, a motion that said, You know how it is in those small, rural counties.

"Let's build a fire under 'em," Brantley commanded. "And let's get a copy of that will."

Jack's testament, when they had a chance to study it later, provided no surprises for investigators other than the fact that it was a near-perfect example of Jack's reputation for frugality. Rather than pay a lawyer to draw up his will, Jack had simply borrowed a similar document from his best friend and used that as a template, filling in details of his own family in the appropriate blanks, an act he admitted in a typewritten addendum. In its entirety, including the insert, the will was nineteen pages long and was dated January 8, 1991, almost seventeen months before his death. Although the addendum was signed, notarized, and slipped into the body of the will, it was not independently dated.

The main beneficiary under the will was Betty, to whom Jack bequeathed the bulk of his inheritance. The value of the entire estate was not mentioned in the will, only his wish that $600,000 be set aside in what he called "the family share." That amount was to be split equally among five of the six children who made up his and Betty's combined families, plus Betty.

When Jack and Betty were married on July 6, 1978, each brought three sons into the marriage. Jack's children by his first wife were Scott and Stephen, plus a child of Julia's, Kenneth Perry, whom Jack had adopted many years ago. Betty's sons were Bo, Dink, and Trey.

In the will, Jack specifically excluded his adopted son, called Perry, except for one dollar. He had previously been given a trust fund, Jack noted, so it was not necessary to make him a major beneficiary. By the same token, Jack specified that his first wife, Julia, also be bequeathed only one dollar.

He directed that the larger part of the inheritance—all except the $600,000 set aside as "the family share"—be referred to as "the marital share," and commanded that it all go to Betty. Once the will was probated and the value of the estate was settled, it appeared that Betty would inherit some $6,240,000, excluding interest. This would become an issue in itself in light of later developments.

Despite his attempts to prod Shelby County investigators' efforts to find James White, it was Tuesday, May 26, four days after Jack's murder, five days after his name had been given to Don King, before there were any results. The reasons for this have never been made clear; White himself said he was making no attempt to hide since he did not know he was being sought. In fact, he said, on Sunday, probably about the time Betty was being interviewed by Brantley and Renfroe, while Peggy remained with her sister and brother-in-law, White appeared at the Lowe house on Logan Martin Lake. Peggy's husband, Wayne, apparently was out on the lake testing a boat he had recently purchased. Undismayed by the fact that the occupants were away, White entered the garage and poked about. Several minutes later, as he was leaving, he ran into a neighbor who was trimming her shrubs along the fence that separated her house from the Lowes'. Stopping his truck abreast of the woman, White amiably told her that he had been collecting a ladder and brushes he had left at the Lowes' when he did some painting for them earlier in the spring.

"I've got another job," he told the woman, "and I

needed the material. When Wayne comes home, please tell him I was here." With a wave, he drove away, leaving the neighbor to ponder the peculiarity of the encounter.

On Tuesday, Don King tracked White down at his trailer and confronted him with what Janine Russell had said. Obviously nervous, White was sufficiently evasive in his answers to make King suspicious enough to take him back to the sheriff's office for further questioning. Late that afternoon, he called Brantley. "I think you'd better get down here," King told the Huntsville investigator.

"I'm on my way," Brantley replied.

Hanging up, he turned to Renfroe, giving him the gist of his conversation with King. While he went to Shelby County to talk to White, Brantley said, he wanted Renfroe to schedule another interview with Betty.

Earlier that day, although investigators did not learn about it until much later, Betty, along with a friend named Gene Montgomery, had been to see Jack's accountant. Acting on his advice to set up a separate bank account so her operating funds would not be encumbered by the legalities that stem normally from a person's death, Betty withdrew $85,000 from her and Jack's joint account and opened a new one in her name. She also emptied her house of her furs and jewelry and a number of other valuable items, taking them to a friend's for safekeeping.

Renfroe was getting ready to call Betty to ask her to come to headquarters to answer a few more questions when his phone rang. It was Betty.

"There was something I forgot to tell you when we were talking the other day," she told the surprised Renfroe.

"What's that?" he asked.

Betty gave him a name, explaining that it was another person with whom she had an affair and had forgotten to mention in the previous interview.

Renfroe thanked her for the information and said he
was about to call her when she rang. "Can you meet me
to go over a few more things?" he asked.

Betty hesitated only slightly. "Sure," she said. "I'll
come down right now."

When she was seated across from him at his desk,
Renfroe brought her up to date on the investigation.
Brantley was on his way to Shelby County, he told her, to
talk to a man named James White, who reportedly had
been paid to kill Jack Wilson. "He said he was paid by
you and your sister, Peggy," Renfroe told her. "What do
you know about that?"

"What did you say his name was?" Betty asked.

"James White," Renfroe repeated. "James Dennison
White."

"I don't know him," Betty answered, shaking her
head.

Renfroe told her he was a handyman who lived in
Vincent and knew her sister.

"Oh!" Betty said, brightening. "You mean 'Mr. Carpenter.' "

Renfroe looked puzzled. "Who?" he asked.

"The man who works for Peggy," Betty said lightly.
"He was going to build an island in my kitchen and fix
my screen door."

Elaborating, she explained that she had arranged
through Peggy for White to do some work at her house,
as he had for her sister.

"Have you ever met him face-to-face?" Renfroe
asked.

"No," Betty replied, explaining that she had called
him and tried to set up a meeting but he had not shown
up. But before she had left her house on Friday, she left
a message for him detailing the work she wanted done.
She had left the message on the door in an envelope
addressed to "Mr. Carpenter."

Renfroe eyed her skeptically. "Did you pay James White to murder your husband?" he asked abruptly.

"No!" she replied indignantly.

"Well, why would he say you did?"

"I don't know," Betty replied.

"Have you ever paid him for *anything*?" he asked.

"No!" she shot back.

Renfroe paused to consider the situation. At that point he was operating only on information he had received from Don King. Brantley had not yet arrived in Shelby County to interview White personally. Until someone from the Huntsville PD actually talked to White and confirmed what Russell and King had said, Renfroe felt unable to push the issue too forcefully.

"If you don't mind," he politely told Betty, who had turned sullen and uncommunicative, "I'm going to ask your sister to come down and answer a few questions too."

A half hour later Renfroe, out of Betty's presence, repeated to Peggy the same information about James White that he had given to Betty.

"You mean that this Mr. White has said that Betty and I paid him to kill Betty's husband?" Peggy asked.

"That's right," Renfroe said. "Do you know him?"

Peggy said she had met him at school, and, when she found out that he was having financial and psychological problems stemming from a recent divorce, she decided to help him by being sympathetic and offering him work. "We must have talked thousands of times on the phone," she said.

In response to a question from Renfroe, Peggy said she had last seen White on Tuesday, May 19, three days before Jack's murder. On that day, she said, her daughter had suffered an allergic reaction to some medication she had been given for a bad cold and she had to rush her to the emergency room to be treated. When she and her daughter returned home late that afternoon, White was at the house loading some boxes in his truck. The boxes held some clothing that she had collected while cleaning out her closets, which she had offered to White, thinking his children might be able to use it.

"And that's the last contact you've had with him?" Renfroe asked.

"Well," Peggy said after a pause, "he called Wednesday to see how my daughter was."

"Are you having an affair with him?" Renfroe asked.

"No!" Peggy replied emphatically.

"Any sexual contact at all?"

"No!" she said emphatically. Setting her jaw, Peggy told the investigator that she did not want to talk to him anymore.

Renfroe shrugged, knowing there was nothing further he could do. Telling Betty and Peggy they were free to go, the investigator left them with a warning.

"Investigator Brantley is on his way to Shelby County to talk to James White," he said, "and when he gets back, we may want to talk to both of you again."

Nodding grimly, in unison, Betty and Peggy left.

TEN

BRANTLEY ARRIVED AT THE SHELBY County Sheriff's Office about five-thirty on Tuesday and immediately closeted himself with White. After an interrogation that went through the night and into the next morning, the handyman admitted murdering Dr. Jack Wilson. The confession, however, was hardly a coherent document. In his rambling, often inconsistent narrative, White led the detective down one path and then another. Alternately pugnacious and meek, sly and self-serving, White tried to evade direct answers, groping instead for excuses and exits. "I was drunk," he claimed at one point. "I was on drugs," he said at another. Often his remarks were much more obscure: "I don't know . . . I don't remember . . . I don't want to talk about that."

He bounced from one subject to another, often contradicting himself. His dates and times were a jumble, and he claimed to have only a vague recollection of some events. At first he denied that he was ever in the Wilson house. Then he conceded that he was there, but it was only because he was looking for something to steal. Then he denied taking anything. He said Jack came home unexpectedly and surprised him while he was still inside. Then he said he had been there waiting for Jack to come home. He said Jack attacked first, coming at him with a baseball bat, and all he did was defend himself.

But bit by bit, as it got closer to dawn, his evasions grew less effective and he yielded on more points. Confronted with a series of seemingly minor details to which he had admitted, he had to surrender to a larger one. Eventually White acknowledged that he was boxed in. "Okay," he said at last, staring over Brantley's shoulder at the wall.

Brantley looked at White and realized that he was a defeated man, all of the fight gone out of him. "Okay what?" the investigator asked.

"You're right," White whispered. "I killed Dr. Wilson."

Brantley, looking rough around the edges himself after ten and a half hours of dogged questioning, exhaled slowly.

"Why?" he asked.

White continued staring at his hands; he wouldn't meet Brantley's eyes.

"Betty Wilson paid me to do it," he whispered.

Brantley slumped in his chair, exhausted, and more puzzled than when he had begun the interrogation. While he felt all along that White had something to do with the killing, the handyman's assertion that Wilson's wife was the prime mover behind the doctor's murder caught the detective totally by surprise. Rubbing his red-rimmed eyes, which felt as though they had been dusted with topsoil, the husky ex-Marine sighed. One thing at a time, he told himself. Let's get this scumbag locked down and see where it goes from there.

At four-ten A.M. on Wednesday, May 27, some four and a half days, roughly 108 hours after Jack's murder, White was charged with capital murder in connection with the ophthalmologist's death. In Alabama the penalty for capital murder is death by electrocution or life in prison without parole.

From a prosecutorial point of view, White's statement was a decidedly imperfect document, littered as it was with inconsistencies, evasions, denials, and assertions that could not be proved or disproved. But it *was* a confession; it was enough to form a basis for a formal accusation against White and open the door to more interrogations. It was incomplete and full of holes. It left as many questions as it answered. But it was a beginning; it gave investigators a map to follow in a continuing effort to tie up the loose ends.

Brantley took White's contradictions in stride. He had learned over the years that virtually every guilty person he had ever interrogated began by trying to minimize his or her own involvement, proffering rationalizations and excuses that they later admitted had been lies from the very first. To Brantley, the details were unimportant at that stage. He knew White was going to continue giving him different versions of events until he recognized that it was senseless to try to maintain such a stance. Then he would tell the truth. Or a close approximation of it. In the meantime, the significant thing was that White had admitted relatively quickly his participation in a series of events leading to Jack's death.

After his admission, White was led away to a cell and Brantley found a motel. By mid-morning, after about four hours of sleep, Brantley returned to the jail to pick up White for the long drive back to Huntsville. But before he could leave Shelby County there were a few things he wanted to take care of. One was to make sure there was a formal statement from Janine Russell. At Brantley's request, King brought Russell back to the sheriff's office and asked her to repeat for the record everything she had told the detective the previous Thursday.

Glancing uncomfortably at the recorder that was humming quietly on King's desk, Russell went through her story one more time. The interview consumed exactly thirteen minutes. When it was finished, King took the tape to a secretary and asked her to transcribe it, then send a copy to Brantley.

Brantley, meanwhile, had one more stop he needed to make before taking White to the Madison County Jail. On the way back, he detoured to White's trailer house to search for evidence he hoped would irrefutably link the handyman to Jack's murder.

There was the footwear he had on the evening of the murder, White said, pointing to a pair of boots. Brantley looked closely, observing a dark spot on one of them that he thought might be blood. The boots went into a bag, but laboratory tests on the spot later proved inconclusive.

After going through White's closet, Brantley was puzzled because he could not find any obviously bloodstained clothing. Given the violence of the attack on Jack and the way the walls had been splattered with his blood, Brantley was certain that White must have been splashed with blood himself. Oh well, he said to himself, if it isn't here, it isn't here. I can ask him about that later. Just to be safe, the investigator collected White's meager wardrobe and loaded it up so it could be examined more closely by forensic experts.

Disappointed with what he had found inside the trailer, Brantley's spirits lifted considerably when the search extended outside. In White's truck the investigator found a slim book entitled *The Sleeping Beauty and the Firebird*. Flipping through it, Brantley frowned. As best as he could determine, it had something to do with an opera or a ballet. What the heck was White doing with *that*? he asked himself, reckoning, probably correctly, that White had not read *any* book in years, much less one about such an esoteric subject. Before dropping it in an evidence bag as well, Brantley noted that the book had come from the Huntsville Public Library. That should be easy enough to trace, he thought.

What Brantley considered to be the prize catch, however, was a .38 caliber Smith & Wesson revolver that was hidden beneath a loose board in the wooden porch of a shack adjoining White's trailer. Brantley opened the cylinder and was not surprised to find it loaded. Dumping the cartridges in his hand, the investigator stared. "Wadcutters!" he said aloud, remembering the pistol box with wadcutter ammunition that crime scene members had found in Betty's bedroom.

Turning to White, Brantley asked him where he had gotten the weapon.

"Mrs. Wilson gave it to me," he said. "I was supposed to use it to kill her husband."

Brantley studied the disheveled and exhausted-looking prisoner. "Well, why didn't you?" he asked.

"I don't like guns," White said. "Never have since Vietnam."

Brantley shook his head and tagged the weapon as another piece of evidence. We'll have to go into that in more depth later, he told himself.

White did not know it at the time, and may not have cared if he had, but the news of his suspected involvement in the murder of Dr. Jack Wilson preceded his arrival in the city. The May 27 *Huntsville Times* announced his arrest in its one-star edition, the first one on the street, under the headline, SHELBY COUNTY MAN IS ARRESTED IN WILSON MURDER. Although the story ran in the newspaper's top news spot, hard information was scarce and the article provided little more than White's name, age, and address, along with some background on the murder. The two-star edition, which ran off the presses a few hours later, fleshed out the original report somewhat and included a mug shot of White staring wide-eyed at the camera, looking as if someone had just jabbed him with a cattle prod. Although it hinted at the possibility that White's arrest might not be the only one made in connection with the killing, it did not mention either Betty or Peggy, or speculate about a motive.

However, the announcement, as brief as it was, elated Euel Dean Cagle, the twins' brother-in-law. Even before he opened his morning paper, Cagle's telephone was jangling with callers informing him about White's arrest. Ecstatic over the news, Cagle hurried down the hall to the room where Betty and Peggy were sleeping and banged excitedly on the door. "Wake up!" he announced joyfully. "I have great news for you."

Betty had been staying with the Cagles since the night of the murder, and Peggy had driven up early the next morning. There had been a memorial service for Jack the afternoon before, but neither Betty nor Peggy seemed in any hurry to leave the Cagles. In the end, Jack's wish that his body be donated to a medical school could not be carried out because of the autopsy. Medical schools, it seemed, had no use for a cadaver that had already been dissected. As a result, as soon as the service was completed, Jack's body was cremated.

Without waiting for them to answer his knock, Cagle pushed open the door, anxious to share with them the information that police had arrested a man in connection with Jack's murder. "They found somebody," he blurted excitedly. "They arrested a guy for killing Jack."

The twins' reaction to his disclosure caught Cagle by surprise. Instead of sharing in his jubilation, Betty and Peggy looked as if they could care less. Peggy turned her head away and stared out the window, while Betty put her hands in her lap and stared at her nails.

When neither woman responded, a puzzled Cagle backed out of the room. "I'm going to go tell Gedell," he said, referring to the twins' sister. "There's coffee on. Y'all come on out when you're ready."

Five minutes later the twins, looking gloomy and fearful, strolled hesitantly into the kitchen, filled their coffee cups, then wandered into the living room where Cagle and his wife were sitting. No one spoke. While Cagle watched, puzzled, Betty and Peggy sipped their coffee, then rose as one, walked across the hall to the bathroom, and closed the door. They stayed inside for more than fifteen minutes, then emerged as silently as before.

Determined to try to get to the heart of the matter, Cagle decided to break the hush.

"Did either of you girls know this James White?" Cagle asked.

"I do," Peggy replied softly. "He did some work for me."

Turning to the other twin, Cagle asked Betty, "How about you?"

"I knew him indirectly."

Again, as if exchanging messages on some secret band only they could tune in, Betty and Peggy moved as one. Turning abruptly, they retreated to their bedroom and closed the door. A few minutes later they emerged fully dressed. "We have to go out for a while," Betty said, leaving Cagle confused.

He may have been even more puzzled if he had talked that morning to Jack's long-time assistant, Jo Ann Chiri.

Trying to comply with Betty's request to help her through a difficult period, Chiri had stuck close to Betty the entire previous day, and was at her side at the funeral home where the memorial service was held. While they were waiting for the service to start, Chiri turned to Betty and, in an effort to be helpful, she asked yet again if there was anything she could do to help. "How about having your house cleaned?" she asked as delicately as she could. "I mean, seeing that the carpets are scrubbed and all."

"Oh, don't worry about that," Betty had said indifferently. "Where Jack was killed there was a hardwood floor."

Shocked by Betty's apparent callousness, Chiri bit her tongue and did not reply.

By the time Brantley and White arrived at the Madison County Jail it was mid-afternoon on Wednesday, certainly not too late, the investigator figured, for another question-and-answer session. There were still a lot of holes to be filled in White's story, and Brantley was anxious to get the case wrapped up.

One thing that White did *not* do at the session in Shelby County was implicate Peggy. Yet Janine Russell, in recounting what White had told her, had been very explicit about Peggy's involvement. Later that afternoon White would outline what he claimed was Peggy's role in the plan that led to Jack's death. Asked why he had not mentioned her the first time, White looked embarrassed. He loved her, he said haltingly, and he had wanted to protect her as long as he could.

Some thirty hours later, Brantley went looking for the twins. His first stop was the Cagles, since that was where Betty had told him she was staying. He arrived there only to be told by the twins' sister, Gedell, that Betty and Peggy had gone to visit one of Betty's friends, a local entrepreneur who lived in a condominium complex not far from Jack and Betty's house.

A little after four in the afternoon on Thursday, May 28, six days after Jack was murdered, Brantley and Harry Renfroe knocked on the man's door. When he belatedly answered the knock, the investigators asked brusquely for the twins. Waved inside, they emerged a few minutes later with Betty and Peggy in handcuffs. A news photo that got prominent display later showed the four of them approaching Brantley's car. Peggy was wearing a simple black and white polka-dot dress, and Betty was clad in a man's long-sleeve dress shirt with her friend's monogram on the pocket. The detectives took them to police head-quarters, a ten-minute drive away, and booked them with capital murder.

ELEVEN

ROY MILLER IS NO BRIGHT-EYED IDEAL-
ist searching for a cause. Neither is he an ambitious
young defense attorney seeking a high-profile client in
hopes that the publicity will propel him on the path to
money and celebrity. He is a shrewd, experienced, somewhat cynical lawyer who looks like a disheveled bank
teller and sounds like a profane Andy Griffith.

Born on a farm in backwoods Alabama, Miller grew
up working in the fields—"a white nigger in the cotton
patch" by his own description—and dreaming of something better. Smart enough to realize that education was
his ticket out of poverty, Miller enrolled in a small junior
college in the tiny northeastern Alabama town of Boaz,
with plans to become a teacher. He got his degree from
Jacksonville State College and was teaching science at a
junior high school in Birmingham when he figured prac-
ticing law might be a better way of trying to earn a living
than trying to keep twelve-year-olds interested in the
laws of physics. After several years of night courses, he
got his degree from Cumberland Law School, passed the
bar, and went to work for the district attorney's office in
Gadsden, the city where Betty and Peggy were born and
grew to adulthood. Two and a half years later he left
Gadsden and went to work as an ADA in Huntsville, a

job he held for almost a decade. During that period, he prosecuted forty-five accused killers, including three charged with capital murder.

Eventually, like many who get their start in district attorneys' offices, Miller figured it would be more lucrative to switch sides and become a defense attorney. With no regrets, he turned in his resignation and opened a small office across the street from the courthouse on Huntsville's "lawyer's row."

Miller, like all criminal defense attorneys, is called upon from time to time to represent an accused criminal who has no funds to hire a lawyer on his own. While this is a task that goes with the territory, there is enough flexibility in the system to allow some lawyers a degree of choice about their clients. When Miller got the call from the court administrator's office asking him if he would defend an accused murderer named James Dennison White, Miller knew just enough about the case from what he had read in the newspapers to be disinterested. Although he had pretty much convinced himself that he was going to reject the request, Miller agreed to go see White before making a final decision. What he found made him change his mind.

The first time he saw White, the accused killer was sitting on the edge of his bunk in his cell, gripping his hands between his knees and rocking back and forth. As Miller approached, White looked up with unfocused eyes and screamed, "Get my lithium to me."

Although he had asked repeatedly for his medication, White was denied both the lithium that officers had confiscated when he was arrested—the label on bottle it was in was not consistent with the type of drug it contained—and treatment for drug or alcohol abuse.

Not one to be taken in by jailhouse theatrics, Miller studied White carefully. "He was in pain," Miller said later. "He wasn't faking it. He may have been a liar and a thug, maybe even a killer, but I didn't think he deserved that kind of treatment."

After talking to White and reading the statements he had already made to investigators, Miller perceived there was only one way he was going to be able to help.

"Listen," he told Brantley and acting district attorney Mo Brooks, "I know you want those two women. And the only way you're going to get them is to cut a deal. I'll get my client to testify against them if you'll back off the capital murder charge against him."

Brooks looked at him coldly and shook his head. "We don't make deals with killers," he said sharply.

"Okay," Miller replied astutely, knowing in the end that they would come around to his way of thinking, "but y'all think about it and let me know."

A week later Brantley called. "Let's talk," he told Miller.

When the two were seated in the investigator's office, Brantley made an offer. "We'll give him life without parole," the detective suggested, promising that the prosecutors would not seek White's execution.

Miller shook his head. "Not good enough," he said.

"What do you have?" Brantley wanted to know.

Miller grinned. "I ain't going to tell you that," he said, "but I will tell you this. I promise you we can corroborate everything that White says: times, dates, places, phone numbers—everything."

The arrangement, agreed to by Brantley and subsequently approved by Brooks, called for White to testify against Betty and Peggy in return for a reduction in the charge against him from capital murder to murder. That would mean White, who would get a life sentence on the murder plea according to the agreement, would be eligible for parole at about the turn of the century. Technically, the capital murder charge could be reinstated against him if he refused to testify against the sisters, or if his testimony deviated from what he told investigators.

But that was not likely to happen. In essence, White's confession minimized the case against him while strengthening it against the twins. The Brantley/Brooks agreement virtually guaranteed that White would never be executed for Jack's murder. At the same time, though, it cleared the way for prosecutors to seek the death penalty against Betty and Peggy.

Although Miller and White went over the handyman's story again and again, there were two things in the confession that nagged at Miller, a pair of concerns that the lawyer could not reconcile in his own mind. One was the mystery surrounding the clothes that White had been wearing on the night of the murder. They had never been found. While several garments would later turn up under very questionable circumstances, it was never proved that they were White's clothes, or that they had any connection to the killing. The second issue was that White denied that he ever stabbed Jack. Miller could not understand why his client would admit to so much else and yet be so adamant about that one point. In the end, it was never definitively resolved, but neither did it matter. It may simply have been that White was a lot more cunning than Miller and others gave him credit for. A close examination of White's confession shows that he implicated himself only to a point; his admissions as to what *he* did stopped short of what would have been needed to convict *him* of capital murder. Although he admitted hitting Jack with the bat, he claimed it was self-defense. That underlined the subtle distinction between murder and capital murder. It meant the difference between a life sentence and death in the electric chair *for White,* but perhaps not for Betty and Peggy.

The story that eventually evolved, the one that White would later relate in a courtroom, went like this:

He first met Peggy when he was doing work at the Vincent elementary school. She asked him to do some work for her and was very friendly, so friendly in fact that he initially thought she was single.

They began talking on the telephone as well as at school, and eventually she began telling him about her personal life. One night several months after they met, either late in 1991 or early in 1992, they were chatting on the phone when she unexpectedly blurted out that she loved him. She said that she and Wayne had not slept together in five years and she was very unhappy in her marriage. "I wish something would happen to Wayne," he quoted her as saying. He said he understood her statement as a joke, and quipped that he had "connections" and that maybe something could be worked out.

One day not long after that, Peggy suggested to White that he might want to go boat riding with Wayne. When he asked her why he would want to do that, she replied, "Because boating accidents happen."

Not long after that discussion, Peggy told him that she had "a friend who had a problem she wanted to resolve." Gradually, White said, the focus changed from getting rid of Wayne to getting rid of a man in Huntsville.

He told Peggy he would do the job for twenty thousand dollars, a price that was later reduced to five thousand because he was in love with her. "Late in April," he said, "Peggy called and said she had the money."

White admitted taking an advance payment of $2,500 and using the money to pay some overdue bills and back child support. While he had been uncertain of dates and times in his first sessions with investigators, White later nailed them down specifically.

On the morning of Friday, May 15, he said he consummated his relationship with Peggy. Wayne was at work and her daughter, Stephanie, was at school when he went to her house. She was wearing white shorts and a blouse tied at the waist. They began kissing and petting and then went upstairs, where they made love on her bed. It was the first and only time they had sex, he added.

The following day, Saturday, May 16, he drove to Guntersville State Park, near Huntsville, to pick up some expense money from Betty, who was attending an annual conference sponsored by AA. He got to the park after ten that night and was stopped by a guard at the gate who told him that he could not get in because he was not a guest. Frustrated, White said he called Peggy, who suggested he keep trying to get Betty by telephone. Eventually he talked to her and she told him she would put some money in a book and have it delivered to him at the gate by a security guard. When he got the book, *The Sleeping Beauty and the Firebird,* two one-hundred-dollar bills were tucked into the slot where the library card usually goes.

He said he then went to a nearby convenience store, where he filled his truck with gas, bought a case of seven-ounce Budweisers and a bottle of over-the-counter caffeine pills. Gulping fifteen of the tablets and washing them down with beer, he drove to the Wilson house in Huntsville, but there was a blue pickup parked in the driveway. Disgusted, he drove back to Vincent.

Soon afterward Betty called him. "What the fuck is going on?" he quoted her as saying.

He told her about her son's truck being in the driveway and asked her if she wanted "both of them killed."

"No," he said Betty told him. "I don't want my son killed."

Soon after that, he said, Peggy told him that she had talked to Betty, who insisted that the "job" be done before May 24. Quoting Peggy, he said the murder had to be committed before then because Jack and Betty were going on a trip and Betty "couldn't stand the thought of spending a week in a hotel room with Jack."

Stalling for time, he told Peggy he could not fulfill the contract because he didn't have a gun. On Wednesday, May 20, Peggy called him and said, "We have the tool and the equipment to do the job."

Late that afternoon, he drove to a deserted parking area on a small earthen dam across an arm of Logan Martin Lake. He was sitting in his truck when a black BMW pulled up. Betty was driving and Peggy was sitting in the passenger seat. The car stopped a few feet away, White said, and Peggy got out and walked over to him, clutching a sweater. She leaned in his cab through the passenger window and extended her arm. Opening her hand, she let a pistol, which had been concealed inside the sweater, fall out onto the passenger seat. "Be careful," he quoted her as telling him. He took the pistol back to his trailer, wrapped it in a frayed brown towel, and hid it under the porch.

Later that evening, he said, Betty called him and told him that the best place for the "assassination" was at Jack's office.

Once he got there, he felt there were too many people around, so he begged off until the next day. He met Betty at a fast-food restaurant so she could give him some additional expense money. He then went to a discount store where he bought several items, then checked into the Ramada Inn for the night.

The next afternoon, Friday, Betty picked him up from a parking lot near Parkway City Mall and took him to her house, where she left him to wait for Jack.

Although he expected Jack to be home within thirty minutes, it was much longer before he arrived. While he waited, he paced nervously around Jack's bedroom, further unnerved by a telephone that rang every few minutes. Under a spur-of-the-moment plan he worked out with Betty, she would call the house, and if the "job" had been done, he was to pick up the receiver and then hang up without saying anything. The ringing telephone, he decided, was Betty calling to chart his progress.

Finally Jack came home, White said. When he confronted the ophthalmologist, they wrestled before White "grabbed something or other" in an attempt to subdue the frail physician. Swinging the weapon, which he later described as a baseball bat, White said he hit Jack and "kept hitting him until he turned me loose."

After Jack quit struggling, White started to follow his original plan to escape through the woods, but changed his mind when he saw how many houses there were in the neighborhood. Instead he went back into the house to wait for Betty to return. When she did, he asked her to take him back to his truck. Snuggling down on the floor in the back of her BMW, he covered himself with two garment bags that were on the seat for the short ride down the mountain to his truck.

After she dropped him off, he climbed into his vehicle and began the drive back to Vincent, stopping only for cigarettes, beer, and more motor oil. He found his younger brother and his girlfriend waiting for him at his trailer, eager for a night on the town. Shoving aside his memories of the evening, White and the couple went drinking.

On Sunday, May 24, White said he went to the Lowes' house to pick up the $2500 that was still due him. Peggy had promised him the money would be in a box in the garage, but when he searched for it, he couldn't find it. When he was leaving, he said, he ran into one of the Lowes' neighbors and stopped briefly to chat.

That, essentially, was where his story ended. When he spun this tale in a calm, matter-of-fact voice in a courtroom many months later, White concluded with the words: "I feel very bad. I know I've done a serious crime and I need to be punished."

This version of events, at least, is what White claimed was the absolute truth, even though a number of people voiced serious reservations about the handyman's veracity. Disregarding the misgivings expressed by Betty's and Peggy's attorneys—that either woman would have anything to do with a loser like White—other, less biased observers pointed out that White had no history of violence, that he was, in fact, a very unlikely murderer. None of the skeptics, however, could offer a solid reason why White would confess to a crime he did not commit. It would prove to be one of the great conundrums of the case, a puzzle that was never satisfactorily answered, even though Betty's lawyers would proffer a theory. To believe it, however, would require an even greater leap of credulity than it would take to accept White's word as the final one.

TWELVE

THE MAIN REASON BRANTLEY AND Brooks had agreed to the deal with White, as Miller had felt sure they would, was because *with* his testimony, the chances of convicting Betty and Peggy were much better. *Without* his testimony, the cases against the twins were undeniably weak.

From the beginning Betty appeared to be the easier target. Investigators had little trouble finding witnesses to talk about how badly Betty treated Jack. But treating someone badly is a long way from murder, and there were only two people who could bond Betty with an alleged plan to have her husband killed: White and Peggy. Brooks and Brantley knew it would be a waste of time to try to convince Peggy to testify against her sister. So that left White. In the end it would be his word against hers, a seemingly uneven contest. He was a convicted felon, a man with a long history of substance abuse and marital difficulties that pointed toward mental instability. And no matter what others said about Betty's personal behavior, she still was the wealthy widow of a respected eye doctor, with no criminal record and no known criminal associations. Connecting her to a murder plot would be difficult no matter what White said, especially when there was nothing to link the two. Despite a diligent search, investigators had not been able to come up with a single witness who saw White and Betty together, indeed who could tie the two together definitively in *any* way.

On one hand, investigators had a man who admitted killing Jack Wilson. On the other, the man also claimed he was hired to commit the murder by the victim's wife, and that his go-between was the wife's sister. The only way a prosecutor could build a bridge between the murder and the two women was to use the testimony of the killer. Roy Miller knew this and used it to his client's advantage. He was selling White's testimony, and the price was a reduced sentence. Brantley and Brooks were not happy with the situation, but they felt they had little choice.

After carefully checking White's story, Brooks and Brantley believed they could build a credible case against Betty. But tying Peggy to Jack's murder was going to be harder. Although Peggy admitted befriending White, she insisted that the relationship had always been platonic and superficial. She emphatically denied ever having sex with him, much less joining him in a conspiracy to murder her sister's husband.

Again the key was White. If his testimony could convince a jury that Betty hired him to kill Jack, it might not be unreasonable to expect that his testimony would convince another jury that the *only* connection White could have had to Jack Wilson was through the victim's sister-in-law. The way Brooks saw it, a deal with White was inevitable if he hoped to also rope in Betty and Peggy.

While this was the apparent line of reasoning that provided the main impetus for the arrangement, it was not the only factor. Brooks had to keep reminding himself that the case against White, without his confession, also was incredibly thin. So thin, in fact, that unless he confessed before a jury, the prosecution might fall on its face. If prosecutors went after White, they would have to fall back on physical evidence to convict him. And significant physical evidence was almost nonexistent. The single hair recovered from the ski mask that had been found on Jack's bed was pronounced by crime lab experts as belonging to White. Plus, Betty's pistol had been found hidden under his porch. But those items related only to White's presence in the house and did not directly connect White to Jack's *killing*. White's fingerprints were not on the bat or anywhere else in the house. Using the hair and Betty's claim that the pistol had been stolen, prosecutors may have been able to make a good case against White for burglary, but Brooks wanted him for murder. By working out an arrangement with the admitted killer, Brooks felt he was guaranteeing at least one murder conviction—White's—while possibly putting the noose around Betty's and Peggy's necks as well.

The argument for *not* making a deal was the perception that White would be escaping with a sentence that was far too lenient than what he deserved for brutally battering the well-liked ophthalmologist to death. Public sentiment against a deal was strong, and it proved to be a profound factor in the political race Brooks was running against Tim Morgan for the district attorney's seat.

Still another factor Brooks had to consider was one that may have been overlooked or underestimated by the public. Unlike White, whose free, court-appointed lawyer was aggressively promoting his client's offer to plead guilty, Betty and Peggy indicated from the beginning that they intended to put up a well-financed, forceful defense, denying everything that White said and refuting investigators' attempts to tie them to Jack's murder. One of the first things Betty did after her arrest was hire a well-known attorney.

Huntsville, like most medium-sized cities that also serve as regional centers, has a relatively large and active group of attorneys who work exclusively in criminal defense. But instead of turning to one of them, Betty's first choice was Charles Hooper, a member of a prominent local firm that specialized in civil, not criminal law. Hooper's then-current area of expertise was personal injury, the kind suffered in automobile accidents, *not* injuries that result in murder. On the other hand, Betty's choice of a lawyer was not as implausible as it seemed on the surface. For twelve years before he joined the civil firm, from 1975 to 1987, Hooper had been an assistant in the Madison County District Attorney's Office. During that span, he had prosecuted some two hundred accused criminals. One of his more prominent cases involved a man named John Paul Dejnozka. Thanks to Hooper's aggressive prosecution, Dejnozka, labelled the "Southwest Molester" by the local news media, was convicted of assaulting eighteen Huntsville women and sentenced to 830 years in prison.

During his time as a prosecutor, Hooper built up a vast reservoir of knowledge about criminal law and courtroom procedure. But none of his experience was as a criminal defense lawyer. At the time, Betty may not have appreciated the subtle difference.

Despite Hooper's background, Betty's decision to pick him to head what soon became a defense *team* raised a number of eyebrows in Huntsville's legal circles. The reasons for her decision have never been made clear, but even her critics have not been able to deny that Hooper has been totally dedicated to his client. Once he took over her defense, he dropped all other duties and devoted all his time to Betty. Some referred to that dedication as an obsession and questioned whether, in the end, it did more harm than good. In any case, his commitment to her was total. During the nine months between the time Betty was arrested and she was brought to trial, Hooper visited his client in her jail cell an average of forty-two times a month, sometimes staying with her for seven or eight hours at a stretch. At one point he and Betty taped paper over the window in her cell door in an attempt at privacy. They removed it only after the sheriff issued a direct order to tear it down. Hooper also tried unsuccessfully to convince the sheriff to waive the rules to allow Betty to keep a cellular phone and a word processor in her cell and let him bring in dinners of lobster and other exotic foods.

Since Hooper could not defend both women, he brought in another lawyer to represent Peggy. Like Hooper, Marc Sandlin was a former prosecutor. Unlike Hooper, he had never practiced anything but criminal law.

Sandlin was fresh out of the University of Alabama Law School in 1978 when state officials decided to split the judicial district that then included Madison and Limestone counties. In a political move incomprehensible to anyone but a native Alabaman, the completely inexperienced Sandlin, a native of Athens, the seat of Limestone County, was named acting district attorney for the new district. At the time, he had never seen, much less participated in, a criminal trial.

However, he proved to be a quick learner; in a matter of months he had adjusted to his new role with amazing alacrity. One courtroom regular likes to tell the story about Sandlin's prosecution, not long after he became D.A., of a hapless young man charged with writing worthless checks. The youth pleaded guilty to the charge, and when he came into court for sentencing, the judge and Sandlin sped through the procedure, mumbling in legal terms that left the defendant confused. When the proceeding was over in a matter of minutes, the bewildered youth, who had been unable to track the swift-paced action, turned to Sandlin and asked, "What happens now?"

Sandlin looked at his watch. "Well," he drawled like a cynical veteran, "I'm going to lunch and you're going to jail."

Sandlin ran unopposed for the Limestone County district attorney's seat in an election in 1980, but decided two years later that he had had enough of being a prose-

cutor. He resigned and moved to Huntsville, a half
hour's drive away and the seat of Madison County, to
open his own practice and specialize in criminal defense.
For him, involvement in a capital murder case was not an
unusual role. In his fourteen years experience in the field
of criminal law, Sandlin has prosecuted five persons
charged with capital murder and defended a half-dozen
others.

However, Sandlin's tenure as Peggy's lawyer was remarkably short, a situation that turned out to be of little
consequence since he then joined Hooper to help plan
Betty's defense. Before Betty went to trial, three other
lawyers would join the team, including one of the country's foremost defenders, and Sandlin would be shoved
into the background. But in those first few days after the
charges were filed against the twins, his role was prominent and it was he who engineered Peggy's release from
jail.

Within hours after Peggy and Betty were arrested,
Hooper and Sandlin began working to have them freed
on bail, arguing that it was unnecessary to keep the two
women behind bars while the legal process wound
toward a trial because they were esteemed members of
their communities and it was unlikely that they were going to flee. Besides, they said, the women were innocent.

"They have absolutely no knowledge of what [White]
did," Hooper told the *Huntsville Times*. "There has been
no contact between [White] and them."

Sandlin also dutifully pronounced his faith in Peggy.
"She came up here to bury her brother-in-law and con-
sole her sister," he said with a hint of outrage, "and she
finds herself arrested for the most serious charge there
is."

A week later Peggy was released on $150,000 bond
after members of her church in Vincent put up their
property as a guarantee that she would abide by a court
order to appear at the proper time. However, bail was

denied to Betty after Brooks argued strenuously against Hooper's request.

Soon after Peggy was freed, she hired a pair of lawyers, one from Huntsville and one from Birmingham, to take over her defense. Later her case would be formally separated from her sister's and a different judge would be named to hear the charges against her. Also, their trials would be held in different cities, and different prosecutors would be appointed.

Typically in murder trials in state courts there is no doubt about who will be prosecuting the accused: the job falls to the local district attorney's office. In this case, however, the situation was muddled by two factors: the forthcoming election for district attorney, and the amount of publicity the murder was attracting.

As the summer wore on, Jack's murder never strayed from Huntsvillians' minds, thanks to aggressive news reporting of events and issues surrounding the killing. One day, the stories would deal with the tribulations of White, Betty, or Peggy: their fight to be released on bail . . . grand jury sessions . . . statements by Hooper and Sandlin . . . a public airing of White's confession. The next day, the emphasis might be on some other issue relating to Jack's death: interviews with those who knew the principals . . . background articles on the twins . . . a court order for a psychiatric examination for White. More commonly, though, the noncrime stories that filled the newspapers and airwaves during that period dealt with the battle over Jack's multimillion dollar estate.

Ten days after Jack's murder, an attorney representing Jack's three sons filed suit to stop the settlement of his estate pending Betty's trial, arguing that Alabama law prohibited her from inheriting if she were to be convicted of her husband's death, even though Jack had designated her in his will as administrator and chief beneficiary. Circuit Court Judge William Page, who would later be named to preside at Peggy's trial, seemed to agree, since he appointed a Huntsville bank as special administrator until Betty's guilt or innocence could be established.

Two weeks later the three Wilsons—Stephen, Scott, and Perry—filed a second suit in an attempt to force Betty to return some seventy thousand dollars she withdrew from her and Jack's joint account soon after his murder.

At that point Betty countersued, claiming that she was entitled to half of the couple's joint assets regardless of any possible verdict in a criminal court, because Alabama is a community property state and she is legally entitled to her share without conditions arising from her own legal status. Even if she were to be convicted—and she would not, her lawyers contended, because she was innocent—she qualified for a one-half share of the property she and Jack had. Her request subsequently was denied, but the issue continued to make headlines when she appealed to the Alabama Supreme Court.

One by-product of these events was the creation of an apparently irreparable break within the extended Wilson family. On one side were Jack's three sons and their mother, Jack's first wife, Julia. On the other side were Betty and her three sons: Bo, Dink, and Trey Taylor. If the Wilsons won this battle, Jack's sons would inherit his six million dollar estate. If Betty prevailed, she would get the bulk of her money and, presumably eventually, her three sons would benefit.

It is, perhaps, a reflection on modern mores that although the Wilsons—that is Jack and his children and Betty and her children—were legally a unit, the reality was that they were anything but unified. Betty's three sons, for example, had very little contact with their mother and even less with Jack until they were in their late teens, which meant they had not been significantly exposed to her influence. By the same token, the Taylor youths had little contact with Jack, except for Trey, who was still living with Jack and Betty at the time of the murder. Trey also worked part-time for Jack in the opthalmologist's office.

By the spring of 1992 the boys, except for Trey, were out on their own. At some time in the not-too-distant past, each had lived for at least a few months in the Wilson household, but almost invariably each had moved out because they found it increasingly difficult to get along with Betty.

Scott was the only one of Jack's three sons who was married. At twenty-nine he was working as a crane operator and living in Huntsville. He and his wife, Heather, had two children, a daughter and a son. The older Wilson youth, Perry, who was thirty-one at the time of the murder, was working as a car salesman in Birmingham; and Jack's youngest son, Stephen, then twenty-five, was studying law at the University of Alabama in Tuscaloosa. He dropped out of law school after a year, however, and moved to San Francisco with his girlfriend, taking a job as an accountant.

Of Betty's three sons, Bo, at twenty-five the same age as Stephen Wilson, had moved back to Gadsden and was working for his father in his crane service. Trey, twenty-three, was living with Betty and Jack. Only Dink was married. He worked as a driver for Coca-Cola, and like Scott, also lived in Huntsville. The twenty-seven-year-old Dink, and his wife, Carla, had two children, a boy and a girl, roughly the same age as Scott and Heather's children.

Although Betty enjoyed bragging about her grandchildren and how well she treated them, she seemed to heavily favor her son Dink's children over those of Jack's son, Scott. Heather Wilson, Scott's wife, recalls, not without some bitterness, how Betty decorated her refrigerator with snapshots of Dink's son and daughter, while pictures of her two offspring could hardly be found in the house. She also remembers how, soon after her oldest child, a daughter, was born, Betty volunteered to keep the infant while she went back to work. The arrangement was quickly terminated, however, when Heather discovered that Betty was neglecting to feed the baby, insisting instead that the infant be content with a bottle of water in place of the normal formula. "It was obvious," Heather said, "that Betty did not care for me and my children. If we visited with Jack, it was away from the house."

Ironically, the person from Jack's and Betty's past who Betty seemed to get along with best of all was Jack's first wife, Julia. Although Julia stopped short of referring to Betty as a friend, she said Betty was always friendly to her whenever their paths crossed, which was not infrequently in a city as small as Huntsville. "I think," Julia mused long after Jack was murdered, "that Betty was nice to me because she didn't like Jack."

Inescapably, because at its core Huntsville remains a small Southern town, despite the influx of "Yankee" engineers, technicians, and scientists, the dynamics of the Wilson family were not secret. After Jack's murder, tongues wagged freely and the interrelationships of Wilson family members made great grist for the city's gossip mill, which was already abuzz with stories about Betty's relations with her husband and other men. Given the dynamics of the city and the southern traditions that lay just below the surface, it was perhaps inevitable that another area would be affected as well: the political one, specifically the dogfight between Brooks and Morgan for the district attorney's chair.

The controversy began in mid-June, less than a month after Jack's murder and only days after his three sons filed their first suit dealing with their late father's estate. Brooks, in an effort that seemed politically motivated, announced that a private law firm would assist his office in Betty's prosecution. Not coincidentally, the lawyer from the firm who would be working with the D.A.'s office was Joe Ritch, who also represented Jack's three children. When Brooks announced his plan, the *Huntsville Times* headlined the story, WILSON SONS TO ASSIST PROSECUTION, which implied not only that Jack's children had already made up their minds about their stepmother's guilt, but were throwing their weight behind the man they thought would convict her, rather than the candidate whom *she* had supported. It was very shrewd; very Southern.

The situation grew more tense a few weeks later when Betty fired her counterbarrage, instructing her lawyers to publicly accuse Brooks of misleading the grand jury, which was considering whether to indict her. They also said Brooks "lied" to the public about the terms of the agreement with White.

Brooks responded angrily, heightening the tension further, claiming the accusations from Betty's lawyers were aimed more at wrecking his election attempt than in righting any alleged irregularities. Sandlin and Hooper were Morgan supporters, Brooks pointed out, who wanted to see *him* elected, because if Morgan won the race, Sandlin and Hooper would be facing him in the courtroom rather than Brooks. This would be a double advantage for Betty, Brooks claimed, because Morgan was not as strict a law-and-order prosecutor, and more importantly, Betty was a Morgan supporter.

Unable to resist the temptation to respond, Morgan publicly joined the fray. He admitted that the Wilsons and Betty's lawyers had contributed financially to his race, but he added that most of the lawyers' contributions came *before* Jack's murder. Then, compounding the controversy, he attacked Brooks for trying to make Jack's death a topic in the bid for votes.

The issue grew so heated that the *Huntsville Times* felt compelled to address it in an editorial chastising both candidates for their behavior. "The time to talk about the political implications of the Wilson case is after it has been resolved," the newspaper opined. "Both Brooks . . . and Morgan . . . ought to refrain from any public discussion of the case as a campaign issue."

In the fall election, Morgan defeated Brooks, giving rise to another complication. As a friend of both Jack and Betty, and a beneficiary of their financial and moral support, Morgan decided that he would not be able to prosecute Betty. The question then became, who would lead the charge against the widow?

In the meantime, the judge assigned to Betty's case, Thomas Younger, granted Sandlin's and Hooper's request for a change of venue. Their motion, one of some four dozen that had been filed on the twins' behalf since they were charged, contended that the case had received so much publicity in Huntsville that Betty could not get a fair trial. Younger, whose treatment of reporters was a throwback to the officials who ruled during the days of the civil rights demonstrations and who regarded reporters as a major menace to society, readily agreed. The local news media had indeed been overly assertive in covering the story, Younger decided, so much so that in his view it would not be possible to select an unprejudiced jury in Huntsville. This led to another question: Where would the trial be held?

It was an unusual circumstance. A woman was in the Madison County jail awaiting trial on charges that she hired someone to kill her husband. But there was no one in Madison County to prosecute her, and her judge had ruled that she could not be tried fairly in her home city.

The problems, however, were not insurmountable. In short order the acerbic Younger decreed that Betty would be tried in Tuscaloosa, a usually sleepy city in the southern part of the state, which was home to the University of Alabama. At about the same time, the state attorney general appointed a prosecutor. Handling the case against Betty would be the district attorney from Limestone County, a baby-faced former Green Beret named Jimmy Fry.

Fry, who succeeded Sandlin as the chief legal officer in the county immediately to the west of Madison, had a reputation as a low-key but highly effective prosecutor. In his decade as D.A., he had prosecuted thirty-one accused murderers and sent twenty-nine of them to prison, a remarkable ninety-four percent conviction rate. Six of those convicted had been charged with capital murder, including two women. One of them, Betty Jo Green, received three life sentences for killing her former husband and former sister-in-law and trying to kill a one-time fiancé. The other, Jackie Sue Schut, was convicted of killing a woman and kidnapping her sixteen-day-old son, then abandoning the infant in a cotton field, where he surely would have died if he had not been found in time by a passing farmer. She got life on the murder charge and twenty years for taking the baby.

THIRTEEN

MICKEY BRANTLEY HEFTED THE HEAVY
file containing the details of the investigation of Jack
Wilson's murder onto Jimmy Fry's desk just before
Christmas 1992, seven months after Jack's murder. By
the way lawyers and judges measure time, it was virtually
the last minute. Betty's trial was scheduled to start in
Tuscaloosa in late February, a scant eight weeks away by
the calendar, considerably less when down time for the
forthcoming holidays was subtracted.

The rotund Fry, whose reputation for courtroom expertise is exceeded only by his legendary fondness for
fried catfish and hush puppies, buried his head in his
hands and groaned. "We don't have much time, do we?"
he asked, peeking through his fingers at the mountain of
material that Brantley had lugged over from Huntsville.

"Nope," replied the laconic investigator.

"Well," Fry said, straightening his shoulders, "I guess
we'd better get on it."

Because the crime occurred outside his jurisdiction,
Fry had not put his own imprimatur on the investigation.
All he knew about the case up until the time Brantley
walked into his office on the ground level of the Limestone County Courthouse was what he had read in the
newspapers or heard on radio or TV. The investigation,

instead, had been directed and carried out by people who had shaped it in their own unique way, aiming toward their own idea of how the material would one day be presented in court. If it had been his investigation from the beginning, Fry might have done things differently. But the trial was looming, and he had no time to worry about what he might have done. For the most part, Fry was going to have to live and work with what had already been accomplished.

Brantley, Renfroe, and other investigators had already talked to dozens of witnesses and collected a huge stack of documents, such as records from the telephone company, banks, military hospitals, and Jack Wilson's files. Fry's first job was to organize the material and put it in a form that he felt comfortable with. Then he had to go through witnesses's statements one by one, searching for inconsistencies, weaknesses, or hidden strengths. Buckling down with Brantley and his own staff, which included a single assistant district attorney and an investigator, Fry began shaping the approach he would use in the courtroom.

Working seven days a week, taking time out only for Christmas and New Year's, Fry and his team reinterviewed more than seventy potential witnesses, talking to some of them two or three times. By the end of January, with the trial only three weeks away, several things were apparent.

It was a given, the district attorney told his small group, that the weakest *and* the strongest element in the prosecution's case was James White. "He's a wretch," Fry cautioned, "and we have to face up to that." But White also was the hub around which the rest of the case revolved. If Fry could convince the jury to look through the confessed killer's faults and unsavory characteristics, focusing instead on the positive aspects of his testimony —claims that could be substantiated by documents or supporting statements from other witnesses—he would be a long way toward proving the state's allegations and securing a conviction. But as a witness, White was a huge and important question mark. No one, least of all Fry, could predict how he would react under the pressure of an intense cross-examination. He might fall apart completely, becoming so confused and rattled that his testimony would be reduced to mere blubbering. Another equally unpleasant possibility was that White might react aggressively, turning hostile toward Betty's lawyers and trying to shout them down. In the end that could be just as damaging to the prosecution as if White collapsed. The jury, Fry knew, would not look upon White positively if he showed undue belligerence or, worse yet, flew into a rage on the stand. Admittedly, White was a more stable person in late January 1992 than he had been when he was arrested more than eight months previously, if only because he had dried out in jail. Fry figured one reason White's early statements were so inconsistent was because his brain had been clouded by alcohol and drugs. With the long period of enforced abstinence that had come about as a result of his incarceration, Fry hoped his star witness would show more constancy in the witness box than he had in his first interrogations.

White was the linchpin of the prosecution's case, the district attorney's team agreed, because none of the other witnesses would have such a dramatic tale to tell or were as ideally situated to describe events that led to Betty's alleged involvement in Jack's murder. Fry would love to call Janine Russell, but he knew that prospect was dim. While her information had been invaluable in breaking the case, she more than likely would never be able to tell her story in a courtroom because it constituted what legal authorities call "hearsay," that is, it involved events that Russell herself did not witness. The only thing she could testify to firsthand was what White had said. And White was not on trial.

Another important witness that Fry would like to call

was Brenda Cerha, the fellow nurse who had been Betty's best friend. That relationship had collapsed, Cerha alleged, because she had refused Betty's request to help her plan Jack's murder. The defense team had a good idea of what Cerha would testify to, and had already asked Judge Younger to refuse to allow her to take the stand on grounds that the events which she was expected to describe had taken place too long before Jack's murder to be relevant. According to Cerha, she and Betty had their falling out in March 1986. Even if Betty *had* been planning Jack's murder, the defense lawyers asked, making no concession that allegation was even remotely true, why would she wait more than six years to go through with it?

The hang-up was that Younger had not yet decided if he was going to let the jury hear Cerha's story, and her testimony was not something the prosecutor was going to be able to bank on.

Although the list of potential witnesses that Fry dutifully turned over to the defense team, as required by law, had more than three-score names, the number of witnesses Fry actually planned to call was far fewer. Several of those on the list, such as Brenda Cerha, were questionable, while others were considered backups in case Fry felt that additional testimony was required to hammer home a point. Many of those, too, were minor witnesses, persons Fry planned to call simply to underline a specific detail or to testify to a single event, such as the type of shoes Betty was wearing on the day of the murder.

The closer it got to trial, the more Fry worried that his case was going to hinge almost entirely around James White, because it was him, and only him, who could directly implicate Betty. As far as Fry was concerned, it was not an ideal situation, but he had to play with the cards he had been dealt.

But it was not only his own case that Fry had to worry

about; he also had to be concerned about what Betty's legal team was planning.

In the weeks immediately preceding the scheduled start of the trial, Fry watched apprehensively as the defense team grew from two to three lawyers, then almost doubled to five. I hope this thing gets into court pretty damn quick, he thought, before Betty hires a whole *army*.

The most prominent addition to her team, the one whose presence caused Fry the most unease, was a Georgia lawyer named Bobby Lee Cook, a man whose name is usually mentioned when criminal law specialists talk about the top defenders in the country.

Reputed to be the model for Matlock, the TV lawyer, Cook is a drawling, charming, excessively polite relic of the Old South, a self-made lawyer who took and passed the bar without benefit of a law degree in the days when that was still possible. Over the years, he has been involved in a number of high-profile cases, both civil and criminal, including cases affecting some of the country's top personalities. His list includes members of the Rockefeller family; Andrew and Thomas Carnegie; former Carter administration heavyweight Bert Lance, and Tennessee financier C. H. Butcher, Jr. While his roll of white-collar clients is impressive, it is Cook's other client list that caused Fry his most anxious moments: those defendants—men and women, blacks and whites—accused of crimes of violence, especially murder. During a career that has spanned almost half a century, the sixty-five-year-old Cook estimates that he has participated in more than three hundred murder trials. While he modestly claims that he has not kept a detailed tally, he figures that ninety percent of his clients have been exonerated.

Once Betty heard about Cook, she went after him as resolutely as University of Alabama recruiters court hot athletic prospects. Because of his fame as a cross-examiner almost without peer, Betty was anxious for him to grill White, who she realized would be the most damaging witness against her. After considerable negotiation, Cook agreed to join the team and to question White if he also was allowed to make one of the closing arguments. In actuality, his role proved to be considerably more far-reaching.

The other additions to Betty's legal team were Joseph Colquitt, a professor at the University of Alabama law school, and Jack Drake, a sandy-haired, sharp-faced, forty-seven-year-old Tuscaloosan with ambitions to be a federal judge. Drake, regarded in some circles as one of the top appeals lawyers in the state, built his reputation through a series of successful suits against the state of Alabama going back almost a generation. In the seventies Drake represented a number of prisoners and patients at state mental hospitals who claimed they were not receiving acceptable treatment because the state underfunded their programs. His actions led to widespread reforms, which helped seal Drake's rank as a top-notch civil rights lawyer.

Colquitt and Drake were added to the team for specific reasons. The professorial Colquitt was hired as an expert on legal technicalities; Drake was recruited to watch for issues for a possible appeal and to help with selection of a jury, since he knew just about everyone in and around Tuscaloosa, a city of some 75,000, which seemed even smaller when the academic community was excluded.

Unlike the prosecution, the defense was not required to furnish its opponents with a list of potential witnesses, although court records showed that Betty's lawyers had subpoenaed more than a hundred persons. Many of the names reflected in the documents were the same as those on Fry's list, while others were unique to the defense. One name that caused Fry to lift an eyebrow was that of Ann Morgan, the wife of the newly elected Madison County District Attorney. The defense apparently

planned to call her to testify that Betty had been in the
Morgan campaign headquarters on the afternoon of the
murder at about the time that White claimed that Betty
was with him.

The defense also had a surprise witness, a stocky, bespectacled man named David Williamson, who made his
living selling sports memorabilia, mainly photographs of
highlights in Alabama sports history. Although Fry had
seen his name on the subpoena list, it meant nothing to
him. When he eventually took the stand on the fifth day
of the trial, Williamson's testimony would directly contradict an important part of White's description of events
that immediately preceded Jack's murder.

Since Fry would be the only one taking an active role
in the courtroom for the prosecution, there was no need
to work out a plan distributing tasks for the trial. Fry,
who nevertheless would get research help from his own
staff and Brantley, would present the state's opening and
closing statements, conduct direct and cross-examinations, and argue points of law with Judge Younger.

His style customarily is low-key, and he did not plan to
deviate from that during Betty's trial, preferring a soft-
spoken approach to the aggressive, abrasive strategy that
would be adopted by the defense. When talking to the
jury, Fry used a we're-all-just-country-people-in-this-to-
gether tone, which fit well with the mostly blue-collar
panel chosen to hear the case.

The defense, on the other hand, devised a completely
different and considerably more complicated game plan.
Cook, whose forte was the dramatic statement, often relied on theatrics to make his points, letting his voice rise
and fall like a Shakespearian actor, flailing his arms and
gesturing extravagantly, pointing a long, bony finger
toward heaven in the manner of a skilled revivalist. Using quiet sarcasm like a scalpel, Cook's aim was to evis-
cerate Fry's main witnesses, especially White.

In contrast to Cook, who never abandoned his South-

ern Gentleman persona despite the intenseness of his
probing, Drake and Hooper fell enthusiastically into the
bad guy role. Utilizing a tactic that has proved effective
for a succession of Alabama football teams—the maxim
that the best defense is an aggressive offense—Hooper
and Drake tried to browbeat the prosecution witnesses
with intimidation and fright. Taking turns conducting
cross-examinations, Hooper and Drake frequently
leaped out of their chairs, screaming at Fry's bewildered
witnesses. But a courtroom is not a gridiron, and what
works for the Crimson Tide and the Auburn Tigers
might not necessarily translate into legal strategy, especially when many of the opponents are soft-spoken para-
digms of Southern womanhood. Worried that a
strenuous objection would only call the jury's attention
to a particular issue, Fry bit his tongue and sat quietly
during the defense attorneys' vicious attacks, hoping that
Hooper and Drake would seal their own fate and come
across to jurors as a pair of insensitive bullies.

Judge Younger also sat silently during most of the defense excesses, as he did during practically the entire
trial, peering Buddhalike through tinted glasses over the
top of the high desk, his bald head barely peeking above
the surface. Even when the opposing lawyers voiced objections, Younger seldom reacted palpably, preferring a
nod of the head or a whisper to a vigorous audible response, often leaving everyone in the courtroom, including the lawyers, uncertain as to what his decision, if any,
had been.

The judge, who has a reputation for being tough and
outspoken when sitting in his own courtroom, was mild
and retiring in Huntsville, seemingly afraid to say anything that might provide fodder for an appeal. In Tuscaloosa the only group Younger was inflexible with was the
media. Apparently angry because of the way his hometown news agencies had covered the case in its early
days, Younger announced before the trial began that the

press would not be allowed any privileges in Tuscaloosa, including guaranteed access to the courtroom, seating, or reentry. Using the excuse that there were not enough seats to accommodate both prospective jurors and the media, Younger closed the courtroom entirely during the jury selection process, leaving the dozen or so reporters covering the trial to pace up and down the hallway outside. And once the trial began, newsmen had to follow Younger's strict rules regarding admission to the courtroom.

In many high-profile cases, the judge works out an arrangement with reporters to string an audio, and sometimes a video, line from the witness stand to an empty room nearby so newsmen do not have to take seats inside the courtroom, which otherwise could be allocated to the public. But Younger refused to even consider such an operation. Reporters, Younger decreed, would have to stand in line with other spectators if they wanted to get inside. That meant not only to get *into* the courtroom, but to *stay* in the courtroom. Once inside, a reporter would not be able to leave when Younger called a bathroom break for himself and the other court personnel. Anyone who left the room had to return to the end of the omnipresent queue. Because of the unusual nature of the case, spectators flocked to the trial and began lining up at a metal detector through which everyone had to pass as soon as the courthouse doors opened at six-thirty. For Huntsvillians, to get to Tuscaloosa in time to secure a seat meant rising well before dawn to make the two and a half hour drive, or staying overnight in a Tuscaloosa motel. By lunchtime, when deputies cleared the courtroom and locked the doors, there was already a line for the afternoon session.

FOURTEEN

EARLY RISING TUSCALOOSANS INTENT ON exercise opened their doors on February 23, 1993, and walked outside into a gloomy, humid, and chillingly cold dawn, a rude introduction to the beginning of a between-seasons day that was too cold for spring yet not cold enough for what passes for winter in south-central Alabama. Many of them popped back inside for an extra sweater before continuing their morning constitutionals. Others just said to hell with it and went back to bed for another thirty minutes sleep. However, there was no extra sleep that day—nor would there be for several days to come—for those involved in the trial of Betty Wilson.

Already at the courthouse by the time it was light enough for passing drivers to turn off their headlights, were the newly empaneled jurors who had been selected from a panel of one-hundred-plus veniremen summoned one day earlier for possible jury duty. The jurors did not know it, but it was nine months to the day since Jack was murdered.

The day also marked the beginning of a new court term for Tuscaloosa County, which meant that five other courts, in addition to the one in which Betty would be tried, would be in session that week, three criminal and two civil. Because Betty's trial was expected to draw huge crowds, it was assigned to the largest courtroom in the five-story building that occupied an entire square block on Greensboro Avenue in the heart of Tuscaloosa's tiny downtown. A ten-minute drive to the east is the University of Alabama campus, with its graceful old oaks and broad, green quadrangles. Near the center of the campus is the university's School of Communications, whose building was made famous in 1963 when Governor George Wallace made his futile stand in the doorway in an attempt to prevent the entry of the university's first black students.

The courtroom where Betty would be tried occupied a corner spot on the third floor with enough benches to hold about 125 spectators. And, because it was a capital murder trial, it got top priority in jury selection. To speed up the process and help weed out those not qualified to serve in a capital case or who judged themselves unwilling or unable to pronounce a death sentence, prospective jurors had been asked to fill out a form containing fifty-four questions composed jointly by the prosecution and defense. The questionnaire covered the basics, such as name, age, and occupation, and went on to more esoteric subjects such as philosophical attitudes toward the death penalty, and specifics such as opinions about Betty's guilt or innocence.

Flipping through the completed forms, Prosecutor Fry and his lone assistant district attorney, Kristi Adcock, separated them into three stacks, categories that the prosecutor referred to as "stars," "maybes" and "go-to-hells." The "stars" stack contained the forms filled out by those whom Fry would fight to keep on the final panel; the "go-to-hells" were those whom he would not voluntarily accept under any conditions. Included among those in Fry's "stars" pile was a retired orthodontist.

Not relying entirely on the forms, Fry had done some preliminary checking on the prospective jurors as soon as he had received the list of names from the Tuscaloosa

County Clerk of Court. What his investigator had uncovered about the orthodontist was that he had an intense dislike and distrust of lawyers. Some months before, the retired dentist and a Tuscaloosa lawyer had gotten into a shouting match on a golf course over whose turn it was to tee off. The argument escalated into a physical confrontation, and the dentist had broken the lawyer's arm in the ensuing fight. In retaliation, the lawyer had sued the dentist.

Fry wanted that man on the panel in the worst way, hoping he would take one look at the battalion of lawyers surrounding Betty and be inclined to listen to the outgunned underdog: him.

On the other side of the room, Betty's lawyers were going through a similar process. When they got to the orthodontist's name, Sandlin, Hooper, and Cook glanced at Drake, the local expert. "Let's get him on the jury," Drake said, thumping the dentist's questionnaire. "From what I know about him, he wouldn't vote to convict *anybody*."

In remarkably quick order, the jury pool was trimmed, pruned, and cut until a final group of fourteen remained: twelve jurors and two alternates. Except for one rail-thin black man in his early twenties, it was an older group. Three of the remaining thirteen were in their mid-thirties, four were in their forties, and six were in their fifties or older. The two women on the panel, one white and one black, were in their sixties. The majority of the jurors were blue-collar workers, including one who labored in a coal mine. Two members of the panel were self-employed. One was a teacher and four were retired, including the orthodontist.

As soon as the panel had been sworn, Fry sauntered over to the waist-high rail separating the jury box from the rest of the courtroom like the sheriff in a Western movie approaching the saloon bar: head and shoulders back, chin up, confident and relaxed.

"Jack Wilson was a good man," he began in a conversational tone, letting his eyes roam over the twelve men and two women who sat in padded chairs, gazing back at him expectantly. He paused, allowing his words to sink in and giving the jurors time to take their measure of him. "Jack Wilson was a good man," he repeated, lowering his voice almost to a whisper. "A loving and devoted husband. And he died outside his wife's bedroom in a pool of his own blood."

The purpose of the opening statement is to allow each side to give the jury a synopsis of its case, explaining in detail what it expects to establish during the trial. The lawyers' statements are not evidence and do not have to be proved; they are merely guidelines designed to give jurors an overview of the situation before they get involved in the details of testimony. At the end of the trial, the lawyers go through roughly the same procedure again, outlining what they think they *have* proved and what they think the other side *has not*.

Fry spent as much time in his opening remarks schmoozing with the jurors as he did in outlining his case. Since much of what he was going to be bringing up in the next few days would have to be taken on faith, because there was little hard evidence to support Betty's involvement, he wanted to get the jury feeling friendly toward *him*. Once he forged a bond with jurors, he felt, they would be more receptive to his arguments and his witnesses.

His background, he said, had been much the same as theirs. Like them, he had been brought up in rural Alabama, and his parents, like theirs, placed a lot of emphasis on traditional values. In that place and time, when fundamentalist Christianity was the predominant religion and peer pressure carried considerable weight, marriage was a sacred state, and anyone who violated the wedding vows was playing with fate because the punishment could be severe. In this particular case, he said,

Betty had not only defiled her vows through numerous acts of adultery and by showing monumental disrespect for her husband, but she was accused of plotting his murder. "That is going to be the bottom line for y'all," he drawled. "Did she hire someone to kill her husband?"

Pausing to let his words sink in, Fry paced the length of the box and again turned to the jurors. "Why would she do that?" he asked rhetorically. "The answer is simple."

Twisting to face Betty, who was sitting across the room, sandwiched between Sandlin and Hooper, he pointed a thick finger. "There," Fry said loudly, "is a vain woman. A woman obsessed with her own image and with having *things*, things like a Mercedes convertible and a BMW. She didn't want more," he said, his voice rising almost to a shout, "she wanted it all!"

Turning to face the jurors again, he spoke in a subdued tone, shutting off his indignation like flipping a switch. "This case is like a triangle," he said. "James White is on one side, Betty Wilson is on another. And on the third side is Peggy Lowe."

He outlined what he expected to prove about the White/Peggy relationship, and how that was transformed into a White/Betty relationship. He explained White's claim that he received money and a pistol from Betty, and how Betty had driven him to her house late on the afternoon of May 22, 1992. "James White was left there to wait for Jack Wilson," Fry said. "Waiting for the express purpose of killing him."

Still later, he said, Betty came home and expected to find her husband dead and White gone. "James White was supposed to go through the neighbors' backyards and work his way back to the main road. But he decided that wasn't a good idea, so he waited for Betty to come back."

At that point, Fry said, mindful that his witnesses were going to testify about Betty's comings and goings that afternoon, she did not have any choice but to help White escape.

That, he said, was his case in a nutshell, an abbreviated overview of what he hoped to prove over the next few days. But before he sat down, there was one more point Fry wanted to make. Aware that White was the most vulnerable of his witnesses and a somewhat disreputable person to boot, Fry wanted to put as much distance between himself and the murderer as he could, hoping that by doing so he would at least partially defuse the inevitable defense attack on White's character and credibility.

White, Fry pointed out, was not going to testify against Betty because he had an attack of conscience and felt it was the right thing to do. "James White was *allowed*," Fry said, emphasizing the word in an attempt to show that he had been caught up in spite of himself, "to plead guilty to Jack Wilson's murder in exchange for his testimony."

The prosecutor knew he was going to have to go into that issue in more depth later, that if he didn't explain the mechanics of the deal White had worked out with Brantley and Brooks, the defense would. The prosecutor was anxious to explain his position in the arrangement before Betty's lawyers had a chance to put their own spin on it. However, he also was reluctant to make things any more complicated for the jury than he had to at that stage. He wanted them to think about the White/Betty/Peggy triangle and how it led to Jack's murder without going down the side road that led to White's motivations in turning against the two women. With an over-the-shoulder glare at Betty, who was sitting grim-faced and pale, surrounded by members of her legal team, who loomed over her like bodyguards, Fry returned to his seat and leaned back, waiting for his first courtroom glimpse of the celebrated Bobby Lee Cook.

* * *

A tall, slim man with receding reddish hair and a sparse paper-white goatee, Cook opted to take a formal stance in his first remarks to the jury. Although he could legitimately claim rural roots that went as deeply as Fry's, he was hindered in using that approach by his reputation. In New York or Chicago or San Francisco he could get away with playing the part of the country lawyer. In Tuscaloosa he was stamped as a city slicker, and as such he was required to act more sophisticated.

Instead of walking over to the jury box to get as close to the panel members as he could, Cook stopped at the lectern that stood in the aisle halfway between the prosecution and defense tables. Sitting six feet behind him, staring at his back, was Betty. She wore her dark hair in her favorite pageboy style and was clad in a stylish gray-and-black-checked, tailored suit, and a white blouse buttoned to her throat. Her hair, which was streaked with bands of red the color of dried blood, had been set that morning by a hair stylist she had imported from Huntsville specifically to help her prepare for her daily court sessions. Her face, as usual, was chalk-white, but the starkness was relieved by a pair of round, dark-framed glasses that helped set off her wide chocolate-colored eyes, her most attractive feature. In subsequent court sessions, she appeared more plainly dressed, taking the advice of her lawyers, who reminded her that she wasn't there to be a fashion plate. The plainer she looked, they said, the better she would appear to the unpretentious, working-class jury.

Where Fry's speech was characterized by the same thick drawl spoken by the jurors and almost all of the witnesses, the lawyer from tiny Summerville, Georgia, spoke in the clipped tones of the outlander. And where Fry was given to understatement and quiet humor, Cook relied heavily on dramatics and extravagant gestures. When it suited his purposes to summon outrage, he really *sounded* and *looked* outraged. And when he wanted to cut up a witness or an opposing argument, he wielded a verbal rapier as sharp as a Wilkinson blade.

As Fry had done with White—smearing him with a certain amount of tar so the jury would not get the impression that he was to be regarded as a model of virtue —Cook did with Betty, to a more limited extent. "She is not a sainted person," he confessed to jurors. "She has her faults. She was an alcoholic. She has admitted she has had affairs. But," he cautioned, "that is not what she is charged with."

The reason Betty was on trial, Cook pointed out, was because she had pleaded not guilty to the accusations that she had conspired to have her husband murdered. "It is her contention that she is, *in fact,* not guilty, that she did not enter into an agreement or complicity to kill Jack Wilson. She is not guilty not by some technicality or loophole," Cook said, "but she is not guilty as a *fact."*

Pushing his gold-framed half glasses up on his nose, Cook glanced at the notes he had been holding in his left hand. Reading from the sheets torn from a yellow legal pad, Cook gave jurors a brief biography of Betty, detailing how she had come from a working-class family in Gadsden, how she had met and married Jack Wilson, and how, even though they were married, each had gone their own way. "It was never an intimate relationship with Dr. Wilson," Cook said, pausing to make sure he had the jurors' attention.

Despite this unusual arrangement, Cook said, the marriage was a solid one. Although they had differences, there existed between them a bond based on a common belief in humanitarianism. "Betty and Jack Wilson had one thing in common," Cook said. "They both liked to help people."

One thing defense lawyers had agreed upon before the trial began was that none of them would try to attack Jack. They felt that he was too well-known and too popular, and that any attempt to smear him might backfire with disastrous consequences. Instead they took a more positive approach. Rather than picking at Jack's faults, Betty's legal team would contend that Betty's innate altruism may have been her downfall. Her contact with White, they would argue, was not an attempt to plan a murder, but an honest effort by her to help a desperate fellow alcoholic.

Having planted the idea in jurors' minds that Betty may have been a victim rather than a victimizer, Cook launched into the anticipated brutal attack against White.

Eight months before Jack's murder, Cook said, attempting to throw a cloud of doubt over White's credibility, White had made another of his numerous trips to a veteran's hospital, where he complained to doctors that he was experiencing hallucinations. "He said he was hearing voices," Cook proclaimed, "but he said he couldn't understand what they were saying. Yet," he added ominously, "the state's whole case is predicated upon the believability of James White."

A veteran of World War Two, Cook scoffed at White's claims that he was psychologically damaged by his service in Southeast Asia. "James White was screwed up *before* he went to Vietnam," he said. "He was discharged because of character and behavior problems. He shirked his duty and deserted his post," a charge White later denied. Once he was back in the United States, Cook told the jurors, White was convicted of selling drugs, and then he escaped and became a fugitive.

"James Dennison White," Cook thundered, "is now and has been for twenty-five years a pathological liar. He is not," he added with the hint of a smile, lowering his voice, "someone you would want to buy a used car from."

White, Cook said, in a more serious tone, had suffered over the years from a host of psychological problems and had attempted suicide a dozen or more times. He had used drugs ranging from amphetamines and alcohol to LSD and marijuana. Leveling his index finger like a pistol, Cook pointed at the jury box and shouted: "He has even engaged in sexually abusive behavior with his *own daughter.*"

Pausing to let that sink in, Cook continued in a quieter voice. "And that," he said, "is only a little bit about the state's star witness."

In the case involving Betty, Cook said, White had given seven or more different statements about events. "And in each of these statements he has lied and contradicted himself. *All* of his statements are conflicting, and many of them make no sense at all. Still," the defense attorney added in a whisper, "in order to return a conviction in this case, you have to believe *everything* James White says."

It was a theme the defense would return to time and again: White was known to have lied about some things, therefore everything he said had to be considered a lie. It was a disingenuous argument, but it was the glue that held the defense case together.

FIFTEEN

BEFORE THE TRIAL STARTED, FRY HAD determined how he was going to lay the case out for the jurors, dividing his planned presentation into four major sections. First he was going to concentrate on White and the murder plot, the phase Fry referred to in his own mind as "the man and the plan." It was the most delicate of the four steps because it encompassed White's introduction to the jury. Although he worried that the panel members would take an instant and deep-seated dislike to the witness and might convince themselves to reject anything he said, Fry knew he had no choice; White was the core of the prosecution's show.

Since there was nothing he could do to improve White's personality or gloss over his background, Fry knew he had no choice but to bring White before the jury as soon as he could, lead him through his story, throw him to the defense—which was waiting like a pride of lions for the chance to attack—and move on to more credible and presentable witnesses.

To set the stage for White's appearance and to give jurors the chance to adjust to what, to them, were strange surroundings, Fry scheduled the appearance of three persons he did not anticipate would be controversial to lead off the prosecution's case: Patrolman Jim

Donnegan, who had been the first officer at the murder scene; Investigator Glen Nunley, who had worked with Brantley from the beginning; and Dr. Joseph Embry, the pathologist who had performed the autopsy on Jack. Fry decided to hold Investigator Brantley until later, knowing that he would be one of the defense's major targets, and because he wanted to deal with White before kicking another hornet's nest.

There were a few uncomfortable moments when the jurors, unaccustomed to dealing with the consequences of violent crime, heard Embry describe in clinical detail the nature of Jack's wounds, and again when they got their first glimpse of pictures of Jack's battered body. However, the tension was shattered a few minutes later when Jack Drake rose to cross-examine the pathologist.

"Isn't it true that contract killers usually shoot their victims?" Drake asked, attempting to throw early doubt on the prosecution's contention that White had been a hired killer.

"Not in Alabama," Embry shot back, drawing a stress-breaking guffaw from both the jurors and spectators who had jammed the courtroom. It was the first time, but it would not be the last, that a prosecution witness capitalized on questions from the aggressive defense lawyers, effectively turning the tables with quick ripostes that often drew laughter and, in one instance, applause.

For the most part, seemingly saving their strength for the forthcoming clash with White, the defense attorneys began their cross-examinations on a relatively benign note. That position would change dramatically as the trial wore on, possibly on orders from Betty herself. Drake and Hooper would become increasingly antagonistic, until their attacks on some witnesses seemed gratuitous, bordering on the cruel.

The opening statements and the testimony from the three non-disputatious witnesses, as Fry had hoped, consumed the opening day of the trial. That meant he could call White as the first witness the next day, when he, White, and the jurors would be fresh. By then, he hoped, jurors would be feeling more at home in the courtroom and would be open-minded about White.

Before White could be called, however, there was one preliminary requirement that had to be the fulfilled. After Judge Younger dismissed the jurors for the day, sending them back to their motel, where they would be sequestered for the duration of the trial, he asked that White be brought in. Standing before the bench, almost at military attention, White responded to a series of questions from the judge designed to verify the voluntary nature of the testimony he would be called upon to deliver the next morning.

"I wish to waive my constitutional rights [against self-incrimination] and testify," the nervous-looking prisoner declared.

Judge Younger nodded curtly, a signal for sheriff's deputies to step forward and escort White back to the cell where he was being held pending his appearance as a witness.

When the jurors filed back into their box the next morning, White was already seated in the witness chair, having been led in moments before by deputies, so jurors would not see him arrive in chains. The person they saw contradicted the mental impressions they had formed of what White would look like based on their interpretations of the lawyers' opening statements and Embry's testimony about the viciousness of the attack against Jack.

Expecting a burly, mean-looking man—the type of person who could beat a small, frail victim nearly to death with a metal baseball bat—jurors were somewhat taken aback by their first view of the self-admitted killer, probably the first real murderer most of them had seen in the flesh. In contrast to their expectations, the man staring back at them from just a few feet away was small, mostly bald, and seemingly inoffensive. Clad in a white jail jumpsuit with a vee neck through which graying chest hair protruded, White raised his bushy eyebrows expectantly, as if he anticipated the questions to come from the jurors rather than the lawyers. For several moments the courtroom was deathly still as the jurors and White took their measure of each other. The spectators, many of whom had been standing in line since seven that morning to ensure seats for the session that formally began at eight-thirty, watched in fascination, enthralled by the drama unfolding before them. Jammed into the narrow benches on the side of the rail, called the bar, that divides trail participants from the onlookers, were members of Betty's and Jack's families—carefully sitting on opposite sides of the room—retirees, housewives, friends of the Wilsons who had driven from Huntsville for the proceeding, University of Alabama students playing hooky from classes, local lawyers and law students anxious to see Bobby Lee Cook in action, a dozen reporters and writers, including two from national television networks who were working on screenplays based on the case, and just plain curious Tuscaloosans drawn to the courtroom by the publicity the trial had received and the fact that watching a trial was high drama in a city where the most exciting event is commonly a sports contest at the university.

Wearing a funeral-black suit, glaring white shirt, and a dark tie with a vague, subdued pattern, Fry began lobbing questions at White. Moving gently at first, the prosecutor first asked White about his background.

"Yes sir, that's right," White replied politely in a voice that was surprisingly deep and resonant for a man of his relatively small statue. "Yes sir, I do . . . Yes sir, I did . . . Yes sir, that's correct . . . Yes sir, I am . . ."

Gradually Fry picked up the pace and broadened the depth of his interrogation, eliciting from White details about how he met Peggy Lowe, how he fell in love with her, and how he decided that he would do anything he could to maintain the relationship.

"She said she was very dissatisfied with Wayne," White related. "She told me that she and her daughter had discussed renting an apartment and moving out, but it would mean a reduction in their lifestyle."

Eventually, he said, Peggy began talking about how "she wished that something would happen to Wayne."

And how did you respond to that? Fry asked.

"I told her that I had connections," White replied, glancing quickly at the jury box. "I told her I might be able to work something out."

Over a period of weeks, he continued, Peggy's talk about her dissatisfaction with Wayne lessened. Her main topic of conversation instead focused on "getting rid of a man in Huntsville."

What did you tell her then? Fry inquired.

"I told her I knew someone who would do it for twenty thousand dollars."

As the discussions continued, White said he learned that the person Peggy had been talking about was her sister, who was married to a physician in Huntsville. But, he said, Peggy told him that her sister was almost broke and was unable to pay the twenty thousand dollars that White had mentioned. Because he felt such emotion for Peggy, White told her he would drop the price to five thousand dollars.

And what happened then? Fry interjected.

"Late in April," White replied, "Peggy called me and said she had the money."

The prosecutor paused momentarily. At this point he was entering a new phase of the questioning, one in which the emphasis would shift from Peggy to Betty, and he wanted to give the jurors time to make the mental transition. In Alabama, unlike in many other states, jurors are allowed to make notes during the trial, jottings which they can use as reference points later during deliberations. During White's testimony so far, Fry had been watching the jury surreptitiously to see how they were reacting to his star witness. With no little amount of self-satisfaction, he noted that they seemed more enthralled than repelled by White. Some of them were watching the confessed murderer's performance in gape-faced amazement, having forgotten the notebooks and pens clenched in their hands. A few of the others were taking sporadic notes, and one juror—Tommy Ford, who worked as director of ticket sales in the University of Alabama sports department—was scribbling furiously. A former journalism student who worked as sports editor of the student newspaper when he was an undergraduate at Alabama, Ford had reverted to form.

With minimal urging from Fry, White explained how, in late April, he had accepted a down payment of $2500, which was given to him in a thick stack made up of three one-hundred-dollar bills and the remainder in twenties. He used the cash to pay some overdue bills and catch up on his child support.

A little more than two weeks later, on May 15, a Friday, Peggy summoned him to her home on the southwest shore of Logan Martin Lake. She had called in sick and was at home alone. Wayne was at work and their daughter, Stephanie, was at school. He kissed Peggy and she responded. One thing led to another, and a few minutes later, he said, he found himself in Peggy's bed. "She was wearing white shorts and a top tied at the waist," White testified. "Underneath she had on pinkish-purple underwear."

The next day, Saturday, May 16, White made the two and a half hour drive to Guntersville State Park south of Huntsville to meet Betty and collect some additional expense money, since he had already spent the twenty-five hundred he had received weeks before. By the time he got to the park, however, it was after ten. The gate was closed for the night and the guard would not let him inside so he could search the parking lot for Betty's BMW. Peggy had told him that Betty, who was attending an Alcoholics Anonymous meeting at the park lodge, would leave two hundred dollars concealed in a library book he could retrieve from the backseat of her car.

Frustrated at his inability to get inside the park, White backtracked down the highway until he found a convenience store with a pay telephone. He called Peggy and asked her what to do. "She told me, 'Keep calling Betty's room,' which I did." When he finally reached Betty, he testified, she told him to go back to the gate and she would have a guard deliver the book to him. "And that's what I did," White said.

Three days later, the following Tuesday, Peggy's daughter suffered an allergic reaction to some medication she was taking and Peggy had to rush her to the hospital. Although she recovered sufficiently to return home that night, Betty drove to Vincent the next day, Wednesday, May 20, to check on her niece and visit with Peggy. It was that evening, White said, that he met the two women at the small dam not far from the Lowe's house and Peggy gave him Betty's pistol.

The day after that, Thursday, after receiving a call from Betty, who told him that the best place to murder her husband was outside his office early in the morning, White drove to Huntsville and lay in wait for Jack. But White felt there were too many people around so he called it off after telephoning Betty, who was still at Peggy's house in Vincent. During the conversation, he told her he needed some more money, so she returned to Huntsville and met him in a fast-food restaurant at lunchtime to give him an additional one hundred dollars.

The next day, after spending the night at the Huntsville Ramada Inn, White drove to the Parkway City Mall and waited for Betty to pick him up. She arrived in her BMW at two-twenty, White said, and pulled up next to his truck. She got out of her car and walked to his vehicle, circling behind her car. When she got to the back of the BMW she stopped, bent over and tied her shoes, which White noticed were new and decorated with a flower design. At her insistence, he crouched on the floorboard in the passenger seat and she drove him to her house, where she gave him an additional forty dollars ("I didn't know what that was for") and told him to wait for Jack to come home.

She had let him off in the garage, White said, so he entered the house and walked up the stairs to the top floor, where he went into Jack's bedroom to wait for the eye doctor to come home. "She said he would be home in about thirty minutes," White said. "She was going to call, and if the job was complete I would pick up the receiver and hang up. She also told me to make it look like a burglary, but I didn't take anything."

When the half hour passed and Jack had not yet arrived, White said he began getting extremely nervous, especially with the telephone ringing every few minutes. "At that point, I almost left," he said.

Did you have any weapons with you? Fry asked.

White nodded. "I had some rope in my pocket, but I don't remember carrying a knife."

It was two and a half or three hours after he arrived before Jack finally came home, White testified. When he did, he came upstairs, saw White, and the two began to wrestle. "I grabbed something or other and hit him until he turned me loose. When he stopped struggling and didn't move anymore, I left."

White said his original plan was for him to exit by a trail through the woods behind the house, work his way back down to the main road, and return to his truck. But when he got a good look at the neighborhood, he thought he would be too exposed on the trail so he returned to the house to wait for Betty to come back.

When she did, he asked her to drive him back to his truck.

"I got in the backseat and covered up with some clothes bags that were there," he testified. "I don't remember any conversation with her." When they arrived at the mall, White got in his truck and headed back to Vincent, stopping along the way to fill up with gas and buy beer, cigarettes, and oil.

According to the plan, White added, Peggy was supposed to bring the last $2500 that he was owed back from Huntsville after the funeral and leave it in a box in her garage for him to pick up. But when he went to the Lowe house on Sunday, two days after the murder, the money wasn't there. That afternoon, a deputy from the Shelby County Sheriff's Office came to the place where he had found a temporary job cooking in a barbecue restaurant and told him they wanted to talk to him. Two days after that, on Tuesday, May 26, Brantley arrived to begin questioning him about Jack's murder.

Fry exhaled slowly. So much for that, he thought, relieved that White had gotten through his recitation without any major problems. But the prosecutor was only halfway home; a lot depended on the way White handled himself during the cross-examination. If he could survive a thorough pounding by the expert Cook and still appear credible, Fry would be satisfied. He did not expect the jury to believe everything White had said. The best he could hope for from the jury was that the panel would accept what White had said as fundamentally true. Fry could then use White's testimony as a foundation upon which other witnesses would build. White had been specific about certain times, dates, and places. Fry's job now was to substantiate those details with other testimony. But first White would have to hold up under Cook's grilling. Fry glanced at his watch. It was a few minutes after ten-thirty. The direct examination had taken almost exactly two hours. He knew the cross-examination would take at least twice as long. And until that was over, he would not be able to relax.

SIXTEEN

BOBBY LEE COOK ROSE AND WALKED DE-
liberately to the lectern, shuffling a handful of notes.
Carefully setting the papers down, he rested his hands on
the stand and stared at White for several seconds before
speaking. When he did, it was sharp, forceful, and direct.
"Did you lie?" he barked.

White, who was expecting the worst, replied unhesitat-
ingly, "When I was first questioned, yes, sir."

Cook gave no indication he had even heard the murderer's reply. At that stage, *whatever* White said was irrelevant. Cook knew that if he could get White to cave
in, it would be a long, tedious process, and he was prepared to administer the most severe verbal thrashing he
could if that was necessary to accomplish his goal. Although by nature a polite and gracious man, an old-
school Southerner in every sense, Cook became a different person in the courtroom. When he donned his
defense attorney's hat, he could be cold, fierce, determined, and totally dedicated to his client, even if that
meant destroying whoever or whatever stood in the way,
as long as it was for his client's benefit. White may have
been handled relatively gently by Fry, but he was not
going to receive any mercy from Cook. And he knew it.

Cook began by confronting White with the seven

statements he had made to investigators, pointing out that each new one usually contradicted earlier ones. Because each was different, Cook pointed out, not all of them could be true. Therefore, at least part of the time, he must have been lying, or not telling the whole truth. Carrying this reasoning one step farther, Cook said, pointing at the witness, White could not be believed. Not ever. He was a man who had been lying all his life.

"When you were in Vietnam, you shirked your responsibility, didn't you?" Cook yelled. "You deserted your post and you fled, didn't you?"

"No, sir," White replied.

Ignoring his denial, Cook pointed out that White had lied to jurors a few minutes earlier when he told them that he spent his time in jail working on a high school equivalency certificate.

"You already have that, don't you?" Cook asked.

"Yes sir," White replied, seemingly unconcerned at having an untruth so readily uncovered.

At this point in the grilling, Cook and White were talking at cross purposes. The defense attorney either knew what White's replies were going to be before he asked the questions or the answers didn't matter. He was not interested in eliciting information from the hapless witness, only in making him look like an inveterate liar and perhaps getting so flustered that he would fall apart before the jurors.

White's goal, on the other hand, was to surrender on the irrelevant points while remaining rock-solid about his statements concerning Betty's involvement in her husband's murder. It was a battle of wits, and White was horribly outgunned. The best he could hope for was to survive. But he had to do that; his life depended on it.

At first Fry watched the fight anxiously, fearful that his star witness was going to be torn apart by the skilful Cook. But after the first thirty minutes, the prosecutor began to relax. There was nothing he could do except

Peggy Lowe *(in rear)* and Betty Wilson being led to Huntsville City Jail on May 29, 1992 by Huntsville homicide investigators. (©1993 Dave Dieter/*Huntsville Times*)

Betty Wilson being taken to a preliminary hearing at the Madison County Courthouse. She is being escorted by Deputy R. D. Fitts of the Madison County Sheriff's Department. (©1993 Glenn Baeske/*Huntsville Times*)

Betty Wilson on trial, February 1993. (Courtesy *Birmingham News*)

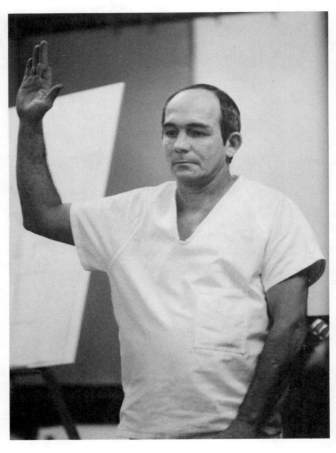
James Dennison White being sworn in. (©1993 Eric
Schultz/*Huntsville Times*)

Defense attorney Bobby Lee Cook during the trial.
(©1993 Eric Schultz/*Huntsville Times*)

Defense attorney David Cromwell Johnson holding
the bat White used to hit Dr. Jack Wilson. (©1993
Glenn Baeske/*Huntsville Times*)

Prosecutor Jimmy Frye holding the gun during the
Wilson trial. (©1993 Dave Dieter/*Huntsville Times*)

Peggy Lowe during her trial. (©1993 Eric
Schultz/*Huntsville Times*)

voice objections to Judge Younger, and he knew that would do little good. So far in the trial, the judge had demonstrated an amazing degree of passivity, which indicated to Fry that he would do little to rein in the defense. Prosecutorial objections, Fry intuited, would do nothing except antagonize the cantankerous jurist. White was a prosecution witness only because he was necessary. Fry had little empathy for him and felt no undue obligation to protect him. White had become a murderer on his own, and he was going to have to suffer the consequences. Fry's job was to convict Betty, not to shield White.

Realizing that the prosecution was not going to object unless he allowed himself to wander totally afield—something he knew he was not likely to do—Cook felt free to attack White with virtual impunity. Part of the reason Cook was able to get away with this was because of the respect with which he was held, both by Younger and by Fry. Also, he had a certain style that seemed to indicate he was doing what he had to do and there was nothing personal in his attack. It was a highly individualistic technique that was extremely difficult to copy. When Hooper and Drake tried to emulate Cook's combativeness, they succeeded only in sounding shrill and spiteful rather than incisive.

In two long strides Cook quickly crossed the distance to the clerk's desk, where items introduced as evidence were being held. Lifting the metal bat that had been found near Jack's body, Cook handed it to White, an action that resulted in a visceral response among jury members, several of whom shuddered at the sight of the killer actually clutching the murder weapon.

"Have you ever seen this before?" Cook asked in a conversational tone, which in itself seemed to heighten the tension.

"No," White said.

Cook's eyebrows shot up. "Isn't that what you took and used to beat this man to a pulp?"

"No," White replied indecisively. Then added, "That is, I don't remember."

"And after you got through beating him, how many times did you stick him with a knife?" Cook asked, shrewdly using the Southernism "stick" instead of the more common "stab."

"I don't remember stabbing him," White replied.

Removing the bat from White's hands, Cook returned it to the clerk's desk and resumed his place at the lectern. For the next thirty minutes he questioned White closely about a plastic bag that was found hidden under a rock at the rear of the Wilson house several weeks after the murder. The bag represents one of the enduring mysteries of the case. Long after he was arrested, weeks after he had worked out his deal with Brantley and Brooks, White told investigators something that he had never mentioned before: that he had changed clothes after he killed Jack and had stuffed his bloodstained garments in a plastic bag, which he hid under a boulder in the yard behind the Wilson house. Following his directions, investigators looked under the rock the prisoner had described and indeed had found a plastic shopping bag. In it were a pair of jeans with a belt in which the name "Cookie" had been tooled, a knife, a short length of heavy twine, and a pair of thin plastic gloves of the type used in hospitals and medical facilities. Although this seemed to settle one issue that had been nagging at Brantley—why he had not been able to find any bloodstained clothing in White's closet—in actuality it raised more questions than it resolved. The clothing in the bag was stained, but because the items had been repeatedly soaked by runoff from summer showers, laboratory tests were inconclusive on the nature of the stains. The same was true for the knife. It was rusty and contained spots that appeared to be blood, but the suspect material was too chemically unstable to determine if it *was* blood, much less if it was Jack's.

There were two things about this discovery that particularly disturbed the defense, issues that Cook would return to several times during the trial. One was why the bag, if it had been there since the evening of the murder as White alleged, had not been found during the initial search of the grounds. Although it had been hidden under a rock, it was not buried and it should have been noticed by searchers if a careful examination had indeed been made. But not only had the bag eluded human searchers, it also escaped the nose of a specially trained search dog. The answer to that, Cook asserted, was simple: the bag had *not* been there when the search was made, he said, implying that it was placed there later. Although White's nickname was "Cookie," which ostensibly heightened the possibility that the belt at least was White's, the jeans were not the right size. When asked if he would put them on for the jury, White demurred, saying that he had gained considerable weight while he had been in jail and could not be expected to be able to wear the same clothes he had eight months previously. He also was unable to explain where he had gotten whatever garments it was that he had worn away from the house, since he did not mention bringing a change of clothes with him when he met Betty at the Parkway City Mall.

But what really seemed to bother the defense even more was White's description of the bag itself. White repeatedly claimed that the bag was one that he knew well, that it was, in fact, the same one in which he had received the initial twenty-five-hundred dollar payment for murdering Jack. It was a white plastic shopping bag with a black design, he contended. However, when Cook produced the bag that had been found under the rock, it was a tan color with red wording on it.

White was never able to satisfactorily account for the discrepancy.

"When did you remember that you had buried the bag?" Cook asked. "Wasn't it two months later?"

"Yes," White replied.

"How many statements had you made and had recorded up until then?" Cook asked.

"At least five," White said.

In that case, Cook asked skeptically, why did it take so long for him to remember?

White shrugged and said he did not know.

Cook stared at him, seemingly pondering his response. Unexpectedly, he leaned forward, as if he intended to grab White by the front of his jumpsuit. "How can we tell when you're lying?" he yelled. "Is it whenever you open your mouth?"

White's face reddened. "All I know," he replied loudly, "is I've made my peace with God."

Jurors were enthralled by the proceeding; most of them had never seen anything like it and probably would never see anything close to it again. Fascinated by Cook's trenchant cross-examination, their initial impression was that he was completely demolishing the state's case because he was tripping White up on so many things.

Painstakingly, Cook began going through the transcripts of White's interrogations, pointing out how he had said one thing one time, another thing hours or days later.

At first, Cook said, White claimed he had been given a hand-drawn map by Betty showing him how to get to her house. Then later he said there was no map. One day he said he got the pistol from Betty and Peggy on May 12 or May 19, then he decided it had been on May 20 because that was a date, according to Cook, which better fit the prosecution's case.

"Well, Mr. Witness," Cook said, refusing to address White by his name, in an effort to depersonalize him before the jury, "let's look at this." Running his finger down the page, he came to the spot he was looking for. "You say here that you drank eighteen beers while you were waiting. If you drank that much, how could you possibly remember *anything*?"

"I do have an alcohol problem," White admitted.

"Well, how much *does* it take you to get drunk?" Cook asked.

"I start getting a buzz after about a case," White replied.

"Let's move on," Cook said, shaking his head.

Flipping pages, the defense attorney came to another item he had highlighted. "At one point," Cook said, his voice rising, "you told police you just went to the Wilson home 'to ramble around' and see if you could find something to steal."

"No sir," White yelled back, "my purpose in being at the house was to murder."

As the day wore on, Cook seemed increasingly desperate to compel White's collapse, either forcing him to recant from the witness stand or to damage his credibility so severely that the jurors would reject his testimony. To accomplish this, Cook's questions ranged further afield than just the murder itself. After some four hours of being pummeled by Cook on top of his two hours of direct testimony, White should have been near the point of disintegration. Instead he seemed remarkably fresh. While Cook had been able to make a little headway by pointing out some obvious minor inconsistencies in White's statements, he had not been successful in drawing out any major retractions.

Seemingly aware that continuing to badger the witness about points in his confession was not going to do much good, Cook's attack became more personal, apparently with the intent of demonstrating that White was a loathsome creature whom the jury should not believe under any circumstances.

"You're just a big liar, aren't you?" Cook screamed at him at one point. "You're trying to save your own neck, whatever it takes. You're trying to place that woman," he said, turning to point at Betty, "in the electric chair or in prison for the rest of her life. You're willing to say whatever is necessary to save your own sorry neck."

To Fry's immense relief, White kept his temper. Except for the one outburst in which he had screamed back at Cook about his purpose in being inside the Wilson house, White refrained from being drawn into a verbal confrontation with the defense attorney, even when Cook again grabbed the bat and waved it in White's face.

"Jack Wilson should have taken this ball bat and beaten *you* to death with it, shouldn't he?" Cook bellowed.

"Yes, sir," White replied calmly.

"Then we all would have been better off," Cook added.

Fry glanced at the jury and saw that they had stopped taking notes. To him that was an extremely good sign, an indication that Cook had gone too far in pounding White. The defense attorney, Fry felt, had passed the place where he was making points with jurors and had reached the stage where the panel members were beginning to feel sorry for the witness. Although the cross-examination would go on for another hour, Fry quit worrying.

Cook's questions bounced from topic to topic, touching here on White's claims to have had sex with Peggy, and there on White's problems with substance abuse. The defense attorney asked White if he had seen any identifying marks on her body, and when White replied that he had not, Cook feigned amazement. "That's strange," he bellowed, "because she's had a hysterectomy that left large scars."

Turning abruptly to White's past, Cook asked the hapless witness if it were true that the only drug-free period in his life was when he was in prison. When White hesitated, Cook bored in. "That's true, isn't it?" he pressed.

White looked down at the floor and mumbled that it was true.

"How many mental institutions have you been in?" Cook asked sharply.

"Six or seven," White replied.

"You were locked up where you probably should have been kept?"

"Yes, sir," White agreed.

"Why were you there?" Cook pursued.

"I was suffering from a nervous condition and I had attempted suicide," White said.

"Have you ever had hallucinations?" Cook asked.

When White replied that he had not, Cook flourished a paper claiming that White had reported to a Veterans Administration physician on August 11, 1991, shortly before he met Peggy, that he had been hearing voices but he did not know what they were saying.

"In 1986," Cook added, "the record says you were homicidal and paranoid."

White shrugged. "They never discussed that with me," he said.

Cook dug into his stack of papers and extracted a page. "In April of 1989," he began, reading from the sheet, "did anything significant happen then with reference to hospitalization or any psychological evaluation?"

White looked blank. "Not to my memory, no sir," he replied.

"Don't you remember," Cook threw at him, "that's about the time that you sexually molested your daughter? Do you deny that?"

White bobbed his head up and down. "Yes, sir," he answered firmly.

However, a few minutes later, Cook revisited the

topic. Holding the sheet at arm's length, he quoted the document's author. " 'Recently,' " he read, " 'Mr. Howell [the name White sometimes used] reported . . . that he engaged in sexually abusive behavior with his daughter while under the influence of alcohol.' Is that you?" he barked at the witness.

"That's me," White replied, "but like I said, I don't remember that," adding, "I was under the influence of alcohol and drugs."

Cook threw up his hands in exasperation. Despite his determination to destroy the state's main witness, the renowned lawyer had actually accomplished little. Although he had been able to demonstrate that White was a totally unsavory person, he made no major dent in the prosecution's case.

Cook had railed at White, insulting his character, his intelligence, and his motives. He had tried sarcasm, using his words like a scalpel to try to slice White to pieces, and he had amply proved that he could outsmart him, leading White into one trap after another. But they were empty victories. In the end, after some five and a half hours of relentless cross-examination, a weary Cook surrendered the witness.

"That's your story and you're sticking to it?" he asked in frustration.

"Yes sir, I am," White replied.

Casting a glance at the jury, which seemed to ask "What else can I do?" Cook returned to his seat wearing an expression that showed he felt he had just stepped into something unpleasant and could hardly wait to wipe his boots.

SEVENTEEN

FRY BREATHED EASIER AFTER WHITE WAS led out of the courtroom in chains and taken to a waiting patrol car for the trip back to Huntsville. His testimony had been the part of the case that had caused the prosecutor the most anxious moments, but once White had made his statements and gone through cross-examination, Fry could concentrate on tying up the loose ends.

For the next two days the prosecutor called a series of witnesses who would corroborate points White had made. Although the defense and prosecution did not know it at the time, this was a turning point for the jury as well. The panel members had been fascinated and repelled by White, and they had been impressed when Cook caught him in a number of minor lies. But their impressions changed considerably when the parade of prosecution witnesses, all of whom were considerably more presentable and reliable than White, substantiated what the disreputable murderer had said.

· White had claimed that Betty had given him two hundred dollars in expense money hidden in a library book, *The Beauty and the Firebird*, at Guntersville State Park. A young library worker confirmed that the book had been checked out by Betty. Park security guards Keith Tucker and Robert Hawkins confirmed that White appeared at the park, just as he said he had. Hawkins, who hand-carried the book from Betty to White, testified that Betty, handing him the book that she retrieved from her car, told him to tell White, "Have a good time and don't lose the book."

· White told the jury that he had received an advance payment of $2500, mostly in small bills, late in April. A shy, well-dressed bank teller testified that White, clutching a large handful of currency, had come into the bank on April 27 to deposit five hundred dollars into his checking account, make payments on two loans, and purchase money orders to pay on his child support, which was considerably in arrears.

· The confessed murderer said that he had met Betty and Peggy at an earthen dam on Logan Martin Lake near Vincent on May 20 so they could give him a pistol which he was to use to murder Jack Wilson. A friend of Peggy's and a reluctant prosecution witness testified that she babysat Peggy's ailing daughter, Stephanie, that evening while Peggy and Betty left the house to drive to nearby Vincent to get two movies and some ice cream. Although they returned with the items they had left to get, the period they were gone coincided with the time White claimed the meeting took place.

· White testified that he met Betty at a fast-food restaurant in Huntsville at lunchtime the day before the murder to collect some additional expense money. While no witnesses could be found who could place Betty and White together at the restaurant, Fry called two employees from a nearby music store who testified that two CDs were charged to Betty's credit card at the store at 11:52 A.M., a few minutes before White said he met her.

· Fry also called a K mart manager who confirmed

that at 12:24 P.M. a customer bought several items in the store and paid for the purchases with a one-hundred-dollar bill, as White said he had.

· The prosecutor summoned Gary Houck, manager of the Ramada Inn, to testify that White checked into the motel when he said he did. Although Fry did not know it, White's presence at that particular motel at that specific time would be an important issue to the defense and would play a major role in supporting Betty's contention that she was framed. At the time, though, Houck's testimony was viewed by Fry as only one more building block in the prosecution's case.

Houck also testified that motel records showed long distance calls were made from White's room to Peggy's home in Vincent. The state, of course, could not prove that it was White who made the calls or, assuming it was he, that he talked to Peggy. Neither could the prosecution offer evidence of what was said, but the fact that the record at least partially substantiated White's testimony would be important to the jury during its deliberations. White also claimed he called Betty that night, but that could not be authenticated because motel equipment did not record the numbers of local calls.

After Houck made his first relatively brief appearance before the jury, Fry's emphasis turned to the day of the murder. To support White's testimony about events that allegedly occurred that afternoon, he called another string of witnesses:

· The manager of a shoe store said he sold Betty a pair of athletic shoes with a flower motif, clocking the transaction at precisely 2:11 P.M.

· The owner of a tanning salon placed Betty in the area where White said she was from about three o'clock to three-twenty.

· A department store manager provided proof that

Betty's credit card was used in his Parkway City Mall store twice that afternoon, at 3:55 and at 4:21.

· A worker in Tim Morgan's campaign office testified that Betty was in the area where White's testimony had indicated at "around" four o'clock.

· A clerk at a pharmacy said Betty came in between 4:30 and 4:45 to have a prescription refilled.

· The manager of a boutique told how Betty had bought a camisole in her shop that afternoon and carried the garment away in one of the store's distinctive pink bags, exactly like the one White had described. The register recorded the transaction at 4:55 P.M.

Testimony from these witnesses, while hardly dramatic, helped Fry make his case against Betty by nailing down specific times and places that supported the prosecution's charges. Late in the afternoon, just when jurors and spectators were beginning to look drained, Fry summoned an attractive blonde whose presence got everyone's attention, particularly the defense's.

When Sheila Irby strode briskly to the witness stand and softly promised to tell the truth, she appeared to be just another well-dressed, carefully coiffed homemaker who probably had to pass up a Junior League meeting to make the trip to Tuscaloosa. But there was a twist to her testimony that none of the previous witnesses had offered. While those who preceded her had testified about Betty's presence at various locations on Huntsville's south side, no one had mentioned seeing White that afternoon. No one, that is, until Irby.

Speaking in a low, shy voice in a drawl thick enough to spread on corn bread, Irby testified that she had seen White walking down Boulder Circle, the street on which the Wilsons lived, at the crucial time of 4:45 or five P.M. on the afternoon of the murder. She was ferrying a group of eleven-year-old girls to a softball game at the time and it was *their* sighting of White that made the incident memorable for her.

When the girls began giggling and pointing at a man who was walking down the street, laughing about how his ears stuck out from the side of his head and about how inappropriately he was dressed for the neighborhood, Irby looked to see who had drawn their attention. Seeing *any* pedestrian in that part of town at that time of day was rather strange, and she was struck by the man's appearance sufficiently to remember the episode when she was questioned later by investigators. He was indeed, as the girls had indelicately pointed out, a decidedly homely man with prominent almost cartoonish features: ears like Ross Perot, very little hair on his head, and he walked with a pronounced limp. Furthermore, he was dressed in the rough clothes of a common laborer, which made him an unlikely-looking pedestrian in the genteel, upper-middle-class neighborhood. The fact that Irby had seen a stranger she later identified as White was significant, but the fact that she also saw Betty in the same area not many minutes later exploded like a hand grenade in the defense camp.

Twenty to thirty minutes after she and the girls had seen the man she was certain was White, Irby testified, she was returning home to change clothes after dropping the girls off at the park, when she almost collided with Betty's BMW. Asked by Fry why that incident made such an impression on her, Irby self-deprecatingly explained.

"At that time, I had my new car only one day," she said, coloring slightly, "and since I have a tendency to hit nonmoving objects, I took the turn onto my street particularly wide. Betty Wilson was coming down Boulder Circle and we almost hit."

"How do you know it was Betty Wilson?" Fry asked.

"I'd seen her around the neighborhood," Irby replied

easily, adding that she not only lived less than a block away, but that she and Betty had gone to the same high school in Gadsden. "She graduated two years ahead of me and she didn't know me, but I knew who she was."

Irby said she had not seen White inside Betty's car, but that was consistent with White's claim that he was hiding behind the backseat with a garment bag pulled over him. She also admitted that she had not volunteered to be a witness, and told her story only after a neighbor gave her name to the district attorney's office.

Irby's testimony noticeably affected the defense team, which had been as surprised as anyone in the courtroom by her tale. Although they knew that Irby was going to testify, they did not know that she was going to provide a valuable, albeit tenuous, link between Betty and White, placing them each a few hundred feet from the Wilson house at roughly the time of the murder. Although Irby's testimony did not actually put Betty and White together, it was close enough to rattle Betty's legal team, possibly propelling them into their first major mistake of the trial. Although Drake and Hooper had been aggressive with other witnesses, Drake pushed his pugnaciousness over the top in dealing with Irby, an action that did not sit well with the jury.

Popping out of his chair and rushing forward as if he were going to jump in Irby's lap, Drake, without introducing himself, began his cross-examination by imputing that she had a grudge against Betty.

"You cooked this whole story up, didn't you?" he yelled accusingly.

Judge Younger, who had been tranquil to the point of dormancy throughout the trial, sprang to the alert. Be careful about what you're saying, he cautioned the defense attorney.

Irby reacted to Drake's verbal attack with disdain.

"And just who are *you*?" she asked contemptuously, giving him an icy stare.

Somewhat taken aback at being questioned by a witness rather than doing the questioning, Drake blurted his name, then added sarcastically, pointing to his chair at the defense table: "I guess you'd like for me to go back over there and just sit down."

Irby didn't miss a beat. "That would be nice," she deadpanned, prompting a roar of laughter and applause from the spectators.

Undaunted, Drake continued his verbal assault. Drake questioned Irby about whether she had been able to pick White out of a lineup and what she had told Hooper about it. "You *did* talk to him, didn't you?" he asked sneeringly.

Irby glared at him intently for several seconds, contemplating his question and his tone before she replied.

"Yes," she answered frostily, "I was *harassed* by Mr. Hooper over the telephone." When she said that, several jurors smiled and Fry quickly covered his mouth.

The exchange prompted Judge Younger to reprimand the defense attorney for the second time, informing him that his tactics were "improper." The judge, however, made no move to back up his warning, and he continued to allow the defense remarkable leeway. A few minutes later, for example, after a recess in which attorneys from both sides retired to Younger's chambers to listen to Hooper's recording of his conversation with Irby, Drake asked for permission to play the tape for the jury. When Fry objected, Younger denied the request, but sat silently while Drake read a transcript of almost the entire conversation.

Up to that point, all of Fry's witnesses had testified about chance encounters with Betty on the day of Jack's murder, meetings that not only showed that she indeed could have been not only where White said she was, but that she was at a certain place at a certain time consistent with the known facts about the circumstances surrounding Jack's death.

Peggy Black, the wife of a Huntsville policeman and a volunteer worker for Tim Morgan, testified how she had been working late in the campaign office on May 22 when Betty Wilson came in. Under Fry's questioning, the woman said she was sure it was five-thirty or a few minutes afterward when Betty came in because Morgan's wife, Anne, had come in only moments before and she had glanced at the clock at that time.

The defense, which was anxious to knock as many holes in the prosecution case as possible, was especially eager to demolish reports of witnesses who were emphatic about events occurring at precise times. The theory was that if the defense could get a witness to admit that he or she may have been mistaken about a specific issue, such as a certain time, the jury might question the witness's reliability about other issues as well.

When Hooper approached the lectern to begin cross-examining Black, he pointed out that the two had grown up together. But the long-standing relationship did not deter him from a determined effort to attack her veracity.

"Could it have been five twenty-five when she came in and not five-thirty?" he asked.

Black shrugged, "It might have been," she conceded.

"In that case," Hooper asked, "could it have been five-twenty?"

Black looked surprised. "No, Charlie," she explained patiently, "five-twenty is not the same as five-thirty." It could have been 5:27 or 5:28, she conceded, maybe even 5:25, but it certainly wasn't five-twenty.

Well, Hooper insisted, if she were willing to back off from her testimony enough to admit that it may have been five minutes earlier than she originally said, why wouldn't she agree that it could have been ten minutes earlier? The debate went on for another five minutes, with Hooper asking her who else had come in the office that day and exactly what time they had been in. In the end, Black refused to yield further.

"In my mind," she said stubbornly, "five twenty-five is the same as five-thirty, but that definitely *isn't* five-twenty."

Hooper's manner with Black was an early indicator of the tone the defense was going to take for the rest of the trial. Taking turns cross-examining witnesses, Hooper and Drake seemed to be in a contest to see who could outnasty the other. Often going beyond the normal boundaries of courtroom combativeness, the two defense attorneys became increasing vicious in their approach. Possibly on orders from Betty, who was paying the bills, Drake and Hopper sprang pugnaciously at each prosecution witness, yelling, screaming, and threatening. Rather than appearing as justice-seeking representatives of an unjustly wronged party, they came across as loud-mouthed bullies, especially since the majority of their targets were women who were obviously nervous and frightened to begin with.

A few minutes earlier Fry had called a woman who said she had seen Betty Wilson twice that afternoon in the area where she would have had to be if White's story was accurate.

When it came time to cross-examine the well-dressed professional woman, the mother of a young child, Drake had only one question, but it was a stinger that had nothing to do with the testimony the woman had offered.

"Isn't it true that you're a member of Alcoholics Anonymous?" Drake asked, apparently intending to imply that an AA member was unreliable and perhaps untruthful.

"Yes," the witness answered, unflustered, "it's something that I'd rather keep private, but I'm not ashamed of it."

"Thank you," Drake said, turning and walking away.

Fry's purpose in calling these witnesses was to create for the jurors' benefit a schedule that traced Betty's movements around the south end of Huntsville from the time Jack came home for lunch until Betty met Nancy Nelson, her AA colleague, for dinner that evening. A chronology was particularly important to Fry because, in lieu of anyone who actually saw White and Betty together, the prosecution's entire case hinged on the plausibility that they *could* have been together.

To make this argument convincing, Fry constructed a timetable showing how the movements of the three principal players—White, Betty, and Jack—interacted. After all of his witnesses in this phase of his case had been called, the schedule looked like this:

Betty	Jack	White
	1 P.M.—Goes home for lunch; returns to his office about an hour later.	
2:11—Buys a pair of Keds at a local store, writing a check for $24.29.		
		2:20 (approximately)—Says Betty picks him up at the Parkway City Mall

Betty	Jack	White
		and takes him to her house.

Betty

3:00—Goes into a tanning salon which she visits regularly and spends less than twenty minutes on the machine.
3:55—Buys three items in the juniors department at a local department store.

Jack

4:00—Prepares to leave his office, going home to pack for his and Betty's vacation trip to New Mexico.

4:21—Buys some Liz Claiborne clothing in the same department store.

4:30—Four youngsters from the Wilsons' neighborhood report seeing Jack in his front yard erecting a

Betty	Jack	White
	Morgan campaign placard, pounding it into the ground with a baseball bat.	
Between 4:30 and 4:45—Stops at a pharmacy in the same building as Jack's office to have a prescription filled.	*About this time Jack is believed to have been murdered, but the time is inexact.*	
		Between 4:45 and 5—Sheila Irby reports sighting a man she later identifies as White walking on Boulder Circle, apparently leaving the murder scene.
4:55 P.M.—Leaves a boutique a five-minute drive from her house, carrying her purchase in one of the store's distinctive pink garment covers.		This is about the time White says Betty smuggled him away from the house in the backseat of her car, hidden under a pink garment bag.

Betty	Jack	White
Between 5:10 and 5:15—Almost collides with Irby on Boulder Circle. 5:25—Seen by a fellow AA member getting into her BMW in a parking lot not far from where White says Betty dropped him off. Between 5:30 and 5:45—Makes a quick stop at the Morgan-for-D.A. office. 6:00—The same AA member who saw Betty at 5:25 sees her again in the same area. Between 6:00 and 6:15—About an hour later than originally planned, meets Nancy Nelson at the AA Fellowship Hall, which is near the spot		

Betty	Jack	White
where she was reported seen at 6:00. She is wearing sweat pants, a knit top, and flowered tennis shoes. They go to McDonald's, return to the Fellowship Hall for a speaker meeting, then go home. 9:30—Discovers Jack's body.		

Despite attempts to discredit the prosecution witnesses with sarcasm and innuendo, the defense made little headway. The only gain Betty's lawyers were able to achieve was with a woman named Linda Vascocu, and that was more in Peggy's favor than Betty's.

A friend of Peggy's and a fellow teacher, Vascocu was living with the Lowes during the latter part of May. Under direct examination by Fry, Vascocu testified that she had been in the Lowe house with Peggy's daughter, Stephanie, on the evening White said the twins rendezvoused with him on the dam at Logan Martin Lake so Betty could give him her pistol.

Rather than delving into this issue on cross-examination, Drake instead elicited testimony that was favorable to Peggy, encouraging Vascocu to tell jurors how Peggy had a reputation for kindness to neighbors in need.

That was correct, Vascocu agreed, confirming that Peggy had sheltered one pregnant, unwed teenager as well as another young girl with a drug problem.

"When she met James White, he looked like a troubled man," Vascocu related, adding that his children were receiving financial assistance and that White had not been able to support them properly. The implication was that Peggy had simply followed her normal practice of helping someone in trouble by being kind to White, who had then stabbed her in the back by making wild accusations against her. The unvoiced corollary was that if White would do that to Peggy, he would do it to Betty as well.

Although Judge Younger refused to let Vascocu answer Drake's question about whether she could imagine Peggy having sex with White, the defense attorney was free to question Vascocu about her impressions of Peggy's marriage. In her view, Vascocu said, the union was a solid one, and the only reason Peggy and Wayne slept in different rooms was because Wayne snored so loudly.

"When I was there," she added with a slight smile, "I could hear him snoring from down the hall even though both our doors were closed."

EIGHTEEN

IN PREPARING HIS CASE, FRY SEPARATED HIS witnesses into definable categories. There were "investigatory" witnesses such as Jim Donnegan, Glen Nunley, and Dr. Joseph Embry, who were called to testify about the technicalities of the search for Jack's killer. There were "place" witnesses whose main function was to substantiate as completely as possible White's testimony about how Betty could have been where White said she was when he said she was there. And there were "character" witnesses whom the prosecutor planned to call to establish Betty's possible motives for wanting Jack murdered.

The "investigatory" witnesses, except for Mickey Brantley, whom Fry was saving for last, testified on the opening day. They were followed by White, who in turn was followed by the series of "place" witnesses. They began with the library worker, Jennifer Michelle Wilson, who testified that the book, *The Sleeping Beauty and the Firebird,* had been checked out by Betty, and they ended with Peggy Black, a volunteer in Tim Morgan's campaign and a childhood playmate of Charlie Hooper, who testified that Betty had been in the candidate's headquarters, which was near the spot where White said Betty dropped him off, at five-thirty or 5:45 on the afternoon of the murder, a time that fit neatly into the state's scenario. Those witnesses began testifying late on Wednesday, February 24, and continued through most of the next day.

Late on Thursday, Fry began calling his "character" witnesses. The first was Joey Luttrell, an accountant from SouthTrust Bank, which had been named special administrator of Jack's estate. According to Luttrell, Jack had his money sunk into a variety of investment plans and funds, some of which Jack himself was the sole owner, and some of which he owned jointly with Betty.

In addition to his practice, which Luttrell valued at $500,000, Jack owned an IRA worth $1.2 million, had $102,000 invested in real estate, $300,000 in limited partnerships, and an additional $330,000 in mutual funds and bonds: a total of roughly $2.5 million. Plus he had slightly less than $4 million invested jointly with Betty: $3 million in a Merrill Lynch account, $360,000 in real estate, $300,000 in mutual funds, and $75,000 in a joint bank account.

Fry had made the point in his opening argument that Betty had not wanted to divorce Jack because she probably would have had to settle for a financial settlement equaling only half of their joint holdings, plus whatever she could negotiate in alimony. While that amount probably would not have been insignificant by almost anyone's standards, since Jack was bringing in an additional $1 million a year, Fry contended it was not enough for Betty. She wanted Jack killed, the D.A. asserted, because she was not content with half. "She wanted it all," Fry had said. By calling Luttrell to define just what "all" of it meant, Fry felt certain he had made a valid point to back up his accusation that Betty planned Jack's murder because she was greedy.

Fry's next witness after Luttrell was Betty and Peggy's brother-in-law, Euel Dean Cagle, the man who was married to the twins' older sister, Gedell.

Straight-backed and proud, as erect as a colonel, Cagle explained in a clear, firm voice how Betty had come to stay with him and his wife on the night of the murder and how Peggy had driven up from Vincent the next day. On May 27, the Wednesday after Jack's murder and the day following his memorial service, Cagle said he was awakened by a telephone call from a friend of Betty's who told him about White's arrest.

"I immediately went into the bedroom where the twins were sleeping," Cagle related. "I woke them up to tell them what I thought would be uplifting news for Betty— to say, 'Betty, they have found the man that has killed your husband.' "

"What did she say or do?" Fry prompted.

"As I recall distinctly," Cagle drawled, "Betty sat up in bed . . . [and] put her hands in her lap. Peggy turned to the window, hung her legs off the bed and didn't say a word to me, neither one of them."

He was "confused" by their reaction to what he thought would be good news, Cagle said. When neither of them responded any further, he left their room and went to wake his wife.

He and Gedell were sitting in the den a few minutes later, he testified, when Betty and Peggy walked through the room, into the kitchen, and then into the living room, where they stayed for several minutes.

"During this period of time did they ask you any questions about who this murderer was?" Fry asked.

"Not a word was spoken about that yet," Cagle replied.

"Where he was from?"

"Not yet," Cagle replied laconically.

"Why he did it?"

"Not yet."

"*Nothing?*" Fry asked, feigning astonishment.

"Nothing!" Cagle replied emphatically.

After they left the living room, Cagle testified tersely,

the twins went into the bathroom, where they remained for about fifteen minutes.

"Did you hear the shower going?" Fry asked, building tension for the jurors' benefit.

"I didn't hear anything," Cagle replied. "I didn't hear any discussion. I heard nothing."

Finally, he added, they came out of the bathroom and returned to the den where he and his wife had been sitting in silence.

"Now, I was curious," he said slowly, in the manner of a master storyteller. "I asked, 'Do either of you girls know this Mr. White?'" Peggy confirmed that she did, Cagle testified, and Betty admitted that she knew him "indirectly."

"Was anything else ever said that morning about Mr. White or the murder?" Fry asked.

"Not from me," he answered brusquely.

"Did [Betty] ever ask you any questions about Mr. White or about what was on television?"

"No."

"Did Mrs. Lowe?"

"No."

The impression Fry wanted jurors to go away with was that Betty and Peggy's behavior had been singularly suspicious, that when confronted with the information about White's arrest, they showed absolutely no curiosity or interest, that they didn't have to ask questions because they already knew everything they needed to know about White. A slow-talking, deliberate man in late middle age —an obviously honest, intense, and sincere witness— Cagle was the perfect vehicle to convey this concept. Fry never asked him if he believed that his sisters-in-law were directly involved in Jack's death, but the tone of his testimony clearly indicated that he did. Whether his wife, Gedell, felt the same way was never made clear because she was never called as a witness, nor was she mentioned again in testimony of others.

During cross-examination Drake succeeded in getting Cagle to admit that the circumstances under which he had delivered the news of White's arrest were unusual and that Betty was under medication at the time, implying that her apparent indifference may have been due more to the effect of the drugs she was taking than to her lack of feelings about the incident.

"Were you present when Peggy was telling Betty . . . 'It's all my fault; if I had not told you that he was a carpenter and could do some work in your kitchen, he would never have come to Huntsville and killed Jack'?" Drake asked.

"I heard it said," Cagle answered, adding that Peggy felt "very guilty" about that introduction.

Although it was late in the day, much past the hour when most judges usually call it quits, Younger showed no sign that he was ready to call a recess. A hard worker who started his sessions at eight-thirty and usually kept going until past six with barely an hour for lunch—an anomaly in a system in which many judges conduct court only four or five hours a day—Younger nodded at Fry, indicating he wanted the prosecutor to call his next witness.

Fry sighed. He had been working fourteen to sixteen hours a day since he was handed the Betty file two months before, and he had witnesses whose testimony he had to go over before he could fall exhausted into his motel bed. On the other hand, he was as anxious as Younger to get the trial completed so he could go home and attack his own workload. "Jo Ann Chiri," he said tiredly, summoning a tall brunette.

Chiri, who listed her occupation as ophthalmic technician, said at the time of Jack's death she had been working for him for sixteen years, since before Jack had met Betty and some two years before they were married.

Soon after Jack and Betty's marriage, Betty came to work in Jack's office, and she and Betty worked at being friends, having lunch together and planning shopping trips to Birmingham. However, she said, the relationship deteriorated, at least from her perspective, when Betty began telling her about her extramarital affairs.

When was that? Fry asked.

Chiri stared at the back wall, searching for a time reference. "It was in the early eighties," she said somewhat hesitantly, about four years after they were married.

"And when was the last time you and Betty discussed her affairs?" Fry asked.

"That was in the mid-eighties," Chiri answered with more assurance.

"Have you ever seen or heard her make unkindly—" Fry began before Drake jumped to his feet.

"Objection!" the defense attorney shouted.

Younger glanced at Fry through his tinted glasses. "Sustained," he whispered.

"Have you ever had a conversation with Betty about how she got money—" Fry tried again.

"Objection!" Drake yelled.

"Sustained," Younger repeated.

Frustrated, Fry examined his notes. "One more question," he said. "Did Betty ever say she wanted to be a widow?"

"Yes!" Chiri answered quickly, preempting Drake's expected complaint. "She told me she didn't want to be divorced, but she wanted to be a well-respected widow. She said if you're divorced you don't live the same, but if you're widowed you get everything."

Despite the seriousness that surrounds any trial, especially one in which a defendant's life is at stake, there are inadvertent and unpredictable periods of comedic relief. No one *intends* a witness's responses to be humorous, least of all the person in the witness chair, but sometimes it just happens that way. In Betty's trial it happened more than once. The first time was with Sheila Irby, who

won the affection of jurors when she refused to be intim-
idated by Drake's bullying tactics. Another such incident
occurred on Friday morning, the fourth day of the trial,
when Fry called a bookkeeper named Brenda McDowell
to testify about Betty's attitude toward her husband.

On direct examination, McDowell's testimony was cir-
cumspect enough. A shy woman in her early fifties, the
bespectacled wife of a prominent Huntsville minister,
McDowell told about the first time she met Betty. It was
soon after she went to work for Jack in the summer of
1990, she said, when she and another of Jack's employees were going to lunch. As they left the building where
Jack had his office, maneuvering across the parking lot,
Betty pulled up in her Mercedes. "The first words I
heard her say," McDowell related, "were, 'Where's
Jack?'"

Betty was in a rage, McDowell said, apparently furious
because she had been waiting at the dealership where
she was having her car serviced for Jack to come get her.
However, he had been called to the hospital to perform
emergency surgery and had forgotten to tell his wife.

Betty launched into a tirade against her husband, Mc-
Dowell said, calling him all sorts of names. "Then she
told us, 'You can give him this for me,'" raising her right
hand with her middle finger extended.

It was, she said, the first of several such instances she
witnessed in which Betty cursed Jack both to others and
to his face.

"Thank you," Fry said, taking his seat, turning Mc-
Dowell over to the defense.

Drake strode briskly to the lectern for the cross-examination, seemingly eager to show that Betty's reaction had
not been untoward or unusual considering she had been
stranded for two hours while waiting for her husband to
pick her up. But as he had with Irby, he came on strong,
too strong for the Southern jurors who still believed in
treating women with deference.

"Have you ever shot the bird to anybody?" Drake asked loudly.

McDowell's eyes widened in surprise. "Certainly not!" she answered primly.

Drake looked incredulous. "Not even like this?" he asked, lifting his left arm so it partially covered his right hand, which he pumped rapidly up and down with the middle finger foremost.

"Absolutely not!" McDowell replied.

"Why not?" Drake asked disbelievingly.

"I consider myself a lady," McDowell said in a deep Southern accent.

But how about your husband? Drake persisted. Haven't you ever been mad at him.

McDowell conceded that she had.

Sensing a victory, Drake pounced. "Well," he said triumphantly, "have you ever called him a son of a bitch?"

McDowell reddened. "Not to his face," she said softly, "and not so he could hear me."

NINETEEN

WITNESS BY WITNESS, FRY CONTINUED building his case against Betty, using the words of others to show her up as rude, crude, cruel, insensitive, disrespectful, and unloving toward her husband. Although the defense would argue later that these accusations, even if they were true, did not make Betty a murderess, the testimony elicited by the prosecutor was designed to leave jurors with the impression that if Betty would do such things as described by those who knew her well, there was nothing she would *not* do, including contract for her husband's slaying.

Mary Ann Lau, the administrative assistant to the executive director of one of Huntsville's largest hospitals and a former friend of Betty's, told a by-then familiar tale. She had met Betty through Alcoholics Anonymous, they liked each other, they began going to meetings together and then seeing each other socially: having meals together, shopping together, and eventually exchanging confidences.

Her friendship with Betty, Lau testified, began to dissolve in the late fall of 1989; some two and a half years, incidentally, before Nancy Nelson would meet Betty and go through an almost identical experience. The reason their friendship fell apart, Lau said, was because Betty began using her as an alibi to conduct her liaisons. "I felt like we were moving in opposite directions," Lau said, "and I couldn't live like that."

In response to Fry's prodding, Lau said Betty consistently treated Jack in an extremely condescending manner, sharply criticizing him in front of others because of such trivial issues as his lack of interest in his apparel and his proclivity to shed his shoes at every opportunity. More brutal, she said, was Betty's delight in ridiculing Jack's health problems. It was not uncommon for her to explicitly describe to others, in Jack's presence, the results of his bowel operation, crudely referring to his ostomy container as his "shitbag."

Showing an even darker side, Betty often confided about a recurring dream in which Jack died or was fatally injured. "She said she wished it would really happen," Lau testified.

Did you ever talk to her about the possibility of just divorcing Jack? Fry asked.

"Yes," Lau replied, "but Betty would never consider it. She said she would never live without 'her things.'"

When the defense's turn came to cross-examine Lau, Drake, anxious to paint a somewhat brighter picture of Betty, or at least lessen the impact of the negative statements about his client, questioned the witness closely about Betty's relationship with her grandchildren. "She took very good care of them, didn't she?" he asked.

"Yes," Lau conceded, "she did." Lau, however, apparently had a superficial view of Betty's relations with the grandchildren.

"And," Drake added, "about the shitbag. That's what it is, isn't it?"

Lau nodded. "Yes," she answered softly.

Riffling through a stack of papers in his hand, Drake produced a document which he said was a copy of Lau's original statement to investigators. Why was there nothing in there, he asked, reflecting what she had just testified to regarding Betty's alleged comments about Jack's death? Why had she not told that to police when they interviewed her instead of waiting until she was in court to reveal it?

Lau appeared flustered, explaining that on the day she was questioned she had been somewhat preoccupied. "That was the day my husband left me," she said.

Drake took issue with that explanation. "You saved the good part for the newspaper people, did you not?" he asked bitingly.

It was too much even for Younger, who again warned Drake to be careful in his accusations.

While the defense could not consider the results of Lau's cross-examination a victory, it had not been a clear-cut defeat either. However, the same could not be said for Nancy Nelson.

Looking frightened and uncomfortable, aware that she was going to have to betray things that had been told to her in confidence, Nelson began by explaining how she had met Betty and how their friendship had grown over the months. Unlike Lau, however, who could testify only to Betty's personality traits, Nelson could offer additional evidence that related directly to the charges against her former friend, evidence that further substantiated White's testimony.

She had been with Betty on the weekend of May 16–17 when both were attending the AA convention at Guntersville State Park, Nelson testified. She had, in fact, been Betty's roommate during the event. She and Betty, Nelson related, had been at a dinner meeting in the lodge's main dining room and planned to attend one more late evening gathering before calling it a day. That last meeting was to be attended by a relatively small group and it was to take place around the swimming pool, beginning at about ten that night. They had just seated themselves when Betty rose, excused herself, and left.

"Do you know where she went?" Fry asked.

"To answer a telephone call," Nelson replied.

"Did she ever return?"

"No," Nelson answered, saying the next time she saw Betty was about an hour later, at roughly eleven o'clock, when she returned to the room she and Betty were sharing. When she walked in, Betty was on the phone.

"Do you know who she was talking to?" Fry asked.

Nelson nodded. "Her sister, Peggy," she said.

Fry paused for dramatic effect. "Do you know what they were talking about?" he asked.

"Her sister was having marital problems," Nelson answered nervously, "and had called to talk to [Betty]."

Fry proceeded cautiously. Having established that Betty had talked to Peggy that night, the same time that White had testified there were several calls involving the three of them—himself, Peggy, and Betty—the prosecutor was anxious to bring White directly into the loop.

Was that the call she left the poolside meeting to answer? Fry asked.

"No," Nelson replied, explaining that Betty had told her the first call had been from a mutual acquaintance who had telephoned to say that she would not be able to attend the convention that weekend.

At that point Fry dropped the subject, fearful that if he continued, his questions would simply initiate a storm of objections from the defense. The implication, however, was that the call had *not* been from another AA member, but from White, who had been frustrated in his attempt to pick up his expense money because he could not get past the security guard at the park gate. What he did, White claimed, was call the lodge and have Betty paged. When she answered his summons, she then made arrangements to get the library book, *The Sleeping Beauty and the Firebird*, which contained two one-hundred dollars, hand-carried to him by a security guard, as the guard had confirmed earlier.

Instead of revisiting this issue, Fry turned his questions to Nelson to the series of events immediately before and after Jack's murder: how Nelson had met Betty for dinner on the night Jack was killed, and how Betty had arrived in uncharacteristically casual dress, wearing "wrinkled clothes" and a pair of "flowery tennis shoes."

The morning after Jack's murder, as soon as she learned of the incident, Nelson said, she went to the Cagles' house to comfort Betty and stayed with her throughout the day and into the night.

That day, while she had no suspicion that Betty may have been involved in Jack's death, Nelson said one unusual event occurred. When she first arrived at the Cagles, Betty was almost hysterical, and she remained that way throughout the day, until she left to give a statement to investigators.

"I remember when she came back from the police station, she was just calm . . . she was okay," Nelson said. After that, once Betty had calmed down, she began talking about her extramarital affairs, Nelson began, then paused, seemingly reluctant to go on.

"I just wish there was some other way to say this," Nelson stammered after Fry reminded her that she was a witness in a murder trial and was obligated to answer his questions, "but Betty had shared with me [the knowledge] that she had an affair with a black man, and that she had other affairs . . . but that she told me that those were over . . . that she was through with the affairs, all that type of thing, that what she had in her life was enough."

Seizing the opportunity, Fry asked if Betty had mentioned anyone else she knew having affairs.

"Yeah," Nelson replied hesitantly, "she said, 'We have all had affairs,' and she said that her sister was having an affair with a carpenter."

Aware that he had dropped a bombshell, Fry hurriedly wound up his questioning and sat back, waiting to see what the defense would do with the new information.

Hooper, throwing back his shoulders and setting his jaw, wasted little time on preliminaries, pointing out that Nelson had not mentioned the item about Peggy's alleged affair in her earlier statement to Investigator Bud Parker. "So you decide to come before us today and surprise everybody, right?"

"I came forward to tell the truth," Nelson said resolutely.

"Yes, ma'am," Hooper spat. "And when you were talking about Betty talking to you in confidence and having affairs, I guess she could have lied to you. She didn't have to tell you anything, right?"

Barely giving her a chance to confirm, Hooper pressed on. "But it was a two-way street. You were telling her about your affairs, too, weren't you? Isn't that right?"

Fry jumped up. "I object, your honor. What she was telling Mrs. Wilson is irrelevant."

"Oh, yeah, Judge," Hooper interjected before Younger could rule. "He wants only half the conversation." Turning to Nelson, without waiting for a response from the judge, Hooper continued. "You were telling her about yours, weren't you? Can you answer that one?"

"Yes," Nelson replied almost inaudibly.

"Sure you were," Hooper yelled, "because you've had a long, checkered history yourself, haven't you?"

Again Fry protested. "Irrelevant and immaterial," he objected.

"Sustained," Younger replied quickly, apparently unwilling to be steamrolled a second time by an aggressive defense attorney.

Momentarily stymied, Hooper turned to Nelson's account of how she had called Betty on the afternoon of the murder to suggest that they have dinner that evening before the speaker meeting at the AA Fellowship Hall, questioning her closely about the time she made the calls and how many times she had talked to Betty in the days immediately before Jack's murder.

"Do you have a good memory?" he asked accusingly. "Do you think you do?"

"Yeah, I think I do," Nelson answered.

"Since you went on this program, have you had some lapses where you have gone back to drinking again?" Hooper asked, trying to plant the seed that her testimony might be unreliable because it may have been affected by alcohol.

"No!" Nelson replied firmly.

Unwilling to let the subject go, Hooper began questioning her about a telephone call he said she made to Betty the night before the murder, a call Nelson denied making.

"Are you sure about that?" Hooper persisted. "You are positive about that? Just as sure as you are about her telling you about her sister's affair, right?"

"No," Nelson shot back. "I'm not as positive about [the phone call] as I am about [Betty's claim that Peggy was having an affair with a carpenter]."

Hooper thrust a sheaf of papers at her. "Those are your phone records. Can you identify your phone records, lady?"

"I don't know what this is," Nelson said in confusion. "What is this?"

Hooper pointed to a line on one of the pages. "Do you know your phone number?" he demanded. "Is that the number right here?"

When Nelson admitted that it was, Hooper pointed to another line, explaining that the record showed a thirty-minute call from her house to Betty's on the eve of the murder.

"You have a heck of a memory, don't you?" he said. "You don't recall that, do you?"

"No," Nelson replied, "I really don't."

Turning a page, Hooper asked her if she had called Betty at Peggy's house in Vincent on May 20, the day White said he met Betty and Peggy to accept the pistol.

When Nelson said she did not remember it, Hooper waved the sheaf of papers. "Well, let's look at your phone bill one more time, Mrs. Memory," he said sarcastically, pointing to a line that showed a call from Nelson's number to Peggy's house in Vincent. "And you don't even have any memory of that, do you?"

"Not really," Nelson replied.

"I didn't think so," Hooper commented, switching to Nelson's testimony about what Betty was wearing the night of the murder.

"Apparently you didn't like the way Mrs. Wilson came dressed to the AA meeting Friday night, is that right? You didn't like the clothes she had on?"

"No," Nelson said defensively, "it's not that I didn't like them—"

"Yeah . . ." Hooper interjected.

"—but it was unusual for Betty to be dressed like that."

"I guess the AA group you are in, you have got to make a fashion statement every time you show up, is that correct?"

"No, we don't," Nelson replied, flustered.

"So you had to lower yourself to go to McDonald's to eat. Is that what was upsetting you?"

"No, that didn't upset me," Nelson said.

Turning his attention to the AA convention at Guntersville on May 16, Hooper began questioning Nelson about the time the poolside meeting started and whether she was certain that Betty did not return to the meeting after excusing herself to take a phone call.

"And when you say she didn't come back, you can vouch for that. I mean, you just have a good recall. You know every person there and what meeting they are in, right?"

"I do not remember Betty coming back," Nelson replied stoically.

Hooper raised his eyebrows. "You just don't remember?"

"Right," Nelson said.

"And we know that you just don't remember a lot of things, right?"

Before Nelson could reply, Fry was on his feet again, objecting to the relevancy of the question.

Younger, looking weary, agreed with the district attorney. As if the starch had been taken out of his attack, Hooper asked a few more questions about her phone calls and returned to the defense table. Slipping into his chair next to Betty, he locked eyes with her and shrugged. I did my best, his glance seemed to say.

Whether his best was good enough was up to the jury. Although he had managed to confuse Nelson, causing her to stumble and answer hesitantly, and had even caught her in several mistakes about her memory of telephone calls, his pugnaciousness was mainly a smoke screen that he hoped would hide the core of Nelson's testimony: that for the first and what would prove to be the only time in the trial, a witness other than White had given direct evidence that indicated a sexual relationship existed between Peggy and White, which was one of the more vital elements in the prosecution's case. If Fry's witnesses could convince jurors that Peggy was indeed having an affair with "the carpenter," it would not be difficult for them to make the link between White and Betty.

Turning to his investigator, Bobby Smith, Fry allowed himself a tight smile. Although his witness—Nelson—had taken a severe battering, her testimony remained solid. Also, he felt certain, Hooper had not endeared himself to jurors with his belligerence. If he and Drake kept it up, he thought, they might alienate everyone on the panel.

TWENTY

DRAKE AND HOOPER DID, INDEED, KEEP it up. With each successive witness, as testimony zeroed in more definitively on Betty, the two attorneys became increasingly hostile, trying to turn cross-examination into personal attacks on hapless and often confused people, especially women, who had no idea that it was all part of the defense strategy, strategy that probably was being dictated by Betty herself.

For the most part, Fry was forced to sit helplessly as Drake and Hooper bullied their way through one cross-examination after another. His feelings, as he watched the exercise progress, were mixed. While he felt empathy for those under attack, he was secretly buoyed by the defense approach. It might fly up North, he thought, listening to the defense attorneys' stream of sarcasm and innuendo, their thinly-veiled threats commonly delivered at high volume, but it wasn't going to go over very well with a Southern jury. Southerners, especially Southern men—of whom there twelve on the fourteen-person panel—did not like to see women pushed around and unnecessarily harassed. Drake and Hooper's method, Fry was certain, would come back to haunt them. At least he hoped it would.

Sighing in frustration at his own powerlessness to do

anything but keep plunging ahead, Fry studied his notes, glancing over the list of potential witnesses. His eye stopped at Bobby Cummings's name and he paused, quickly calculating the benefits of calling the stockbroker.

Cummings had been a friend to both Jack and Betty, Fry knew, and had been privy to many of their secrets. During his pretrial conference with Cummings, Fry had been impressed by the man's sincerity, his powers of recall, and his wealth of information about the Wilsons. The prosecutor had been particularly intrigued by one particular anecdote the stockbroker had related to him.

According to Cummings, he had gone to the Wilsons' house one evening for no special reason other than to say hello. Betty was making coffee, he said, and Jack, looking pale and ill, was sitting at the kitchen table. The ophthalmologist's first words to him, the stockbroker reported, were, "I'm going to have to hire you as a taster."

Cummings grinned, sure that Jack was leading up to another of his jokes. Realizing some response was required before Jack would continue, Cummings played the straight man: "Why's that?" he had asked.

Before Jack could reply, Betty chirped: "This idiot ate some cake I had out for a rat."

That statement puzzled Cummings. Glancing at the couple, he noted that both were smiling and looking at him expectantly, obviously waiting for his reaction. "What's going on?" he asked.

Betty smilingly explained that she had been troubled by a rodent in the kitchen and had decided to try to get rid of the varmint by heavily lacing a piece of cake with rat poison. She had then left the cake out on the table where she was certain the rat would find it. Instead of the rat, Jack had eaten the cake and gotten quite ill.

"I put a note on it," Betty had said, "warning Jack not to eat it because it was poisoned."

"I never saw any note," Jack insisted.

Cummings wasn't sure what to say. In his experience, people who are interested in poisoning rats put the lethal object on the floor where the rodent can have easy access to it, not on a pedestal table sitting in the middle of the room. But since neither Jack nor Betty seemed to be upset by the incident, Cummings figured it was not his place to comment. So he laughed halfheartedly and changed the subject. In fact, he told Fry, he had forgotten the incident entirely until after Jack was murdered.

The prosecutor found the story fascinating, and it fit with what others had told him. In the weeks before the murder, Fry had heard, Jack's schedule took a strange turn. He seldom ate at the family dinner table, either bringing in food from a fast-food restaurant or dropping by the house of his friend, Dr. Sam Huston Hay, and joining his family at their table. There were nights, too, when he slept away from his house, curling up on the floor of his office with a blanket and a pillow. Although he was close to his employees, he never explained this behavior to them. And since they were accustomed to his eccentricities, they did not ask.

Although Cummings's cake story would dovetail nicely with these other reports, Fry balanced whether it was worth the time and trouble. To get his points across, he would have to call a number of witnesses and fight an aggressive defense team at every turn. In the end he decided that he would not try to present it to the jury. For one thing, the cake incident had occurred considerably before Jack was killed, at least two years, and he knew the defense would object on the grounds of remoteness. They probably would win that argument, the prosecutor reckoned. For another, it was not legally explicit enough. Cummings did not *know* the cake was poisoned, and neither did he *know* that was what had made Jack ill. Jack could simply have been suffering from a bout of intestinal flu, which may have hit him harder than it would most people because of the delicate state of his bowels. And Betty, who had a mischievous sense of humor herself, could have been joking about the whole thing. She might simply have been taking advantage of Jack's illness to pull a practical joke of her own by making him *think* he had eaten poisoned food. Besides, when Dr. Embry performed the autopsy on Jack, one of the things he did routinely was order a series of tests to determine of there were traces of poison in Jack's body. The tests were negative, which indicated either that Jack had *not* systematically ingested a common chemical, or if he had been poisoned, it was with an exotic substance that would not show up in the normal tests. It was really a moot point anyway, Fry concluded, because even if Jack *had* been poisoned, poison was not what had killed him. He had obviously died from a beating with a metal bat and two stab wounds in his abdomen.

Somewhat reluctantly, Fry skipped over Cummings's name. He could always come back to him later if it seemed necessary, he thought. Instead the prosecutor opted to call a woman who had much more significant testimony to offer concerning Betty's possible connection to Jack's murder, someone who could relate that Betty actually asked for help in murdering Jack. Turning to the bailiff, Fry asked him to fetch Brenda Cerha.

When Cerha walked through the courtroom door, looking straight ahead and ignoring Betty as much as possible, Fry was struck again by the aptness of her nickname, Elvira, if simply for physical appearance alone. Wearing a dark dress, with her midnight, shoulder-length hair falling as straight as a builder's plumb, her skin as pale as if she had been dipped in talcum, Cerha did in reality bear a striking resemblance to the TV character.

As Cerha took the oath and settled herself in the witness chair, Fry breathed a sigh of relief. Even at that stage, it was not certain that she would be permitted to testify. But the fact that he had been allowed by Judge

Younger to get this far was encouraging to the prosecutor.

Less than a week before the trial began, Drake had filed a motion asking Younger to bar Cerha's appearance on grounds that events he expected her to testify to had occurred too long ago—in legal terms were too remote —to be of significance in the current trial.

Younger still had not ruled on the motion. But before permitting the jury to hear what Cerha had to say, the judge had decided to hear her words for himself. Asking the jury to retire to their room behind the courtroom proper, Younger ordered Fry to proceed.

In quick order Fry determined that Cerha had known Betty for a decade, that they had become friends after they were thrown together as a result of the relationship between their husbands. Jack and Vlad Cerha, an anesthesiologist, were best friends. By 1983, she said, she and Betty were best friends as well.

That situation took a drastic turn in March 1986 when Cerha's husband committed suicide. As soon as Betty heard the news, she rushed to Cerha's house to comfort her friend.

It was about mid-morning, Cerha said, and the two of them were sitting at the table in her kitchen. "We were discussing my husband's death and the fact that I was a widow, and how I was feeling at that time."

"Now," Fry said, phrasing his question carefully, "did Mrs. Wilson at that time say something to you that startled or annoyed you?"

"Yes!" Cerha said emphatically. "She said, 'Brenda, did you kill Vlad?'"

She was shocked and hurt by the question, Cerha explained. But instead of changing the subject, Betty continued in the same vein. "She looked me straight in the eye and said, 'Are you sure? You can tell *me*.'"

Cerha said she stared back at her and repeated her denial. "I said, 'No, Betty, I did not. You know the circumstances of my husband's death: he was suicidal. Plus, I loved the man. I had no reason to want him dead.' "

But Betty refused to accept that answer. "She kept saying, 'Are you sure? You can tell me.' And I kept saying no."

By that time, Cerha said, she was in tears and had little interest in talking about it any longer. But Betty was *still* not ready to let it go. "Finally she said to me, 'Well, I want to kill Jack. Will you help me, and do you know how we can do it?' "

That question was more upsetting than the first. "I just looked at her incredulously," Cerha asserted, "and I said, 'Betty, if you're unhappy, why don't you divorce him?' And she said, 'I can't because I would lose everything. I would lose my house and my style of living.' "

Fry asked her if Betty had said anything else.

"She told me that she was envious of me and my lifestyle, that I was a widow, that I had received all my husband's estate, and that I could do anything I wanted to."

"Is that the lifestyle she wanted?" Fry asked.

"Yes," Cerha said.

After that one time, Cerha said, Betty never again mentioned her desire to kill Jack. But soon afterward, she added, their friendship began to deteriorate, and eventually Betty quit speaking to her. "I just know that she wouldn't have anything to do with me for some reason, and I didn't know why," Cerha said.

When Cerha finished, Drake renewed his request to Younger to prohibit her from repeating her testimony before the jury. "First of all," he argued, "it's extremely prejudicial. Second, it is not in any way related to the crime with which the defendant is charged. And third, it is too remote in time to the events surrounding the death of Dr. Jack Wilson."

Younger shook his head. "I'm going to overrule your

objection," he said, signaling a deputy to bring the jury back.

When the jurors reseated themselves three minutes later, Fry led Cerha through a repeat of the testimony she had delivered outside their presence. With only a few additional statements in response to Fry's attempts to elaborate upon the background of the situation, Cerha's testimony was essentially the same, except she added the information that Vlad had committed suicide in her presence while they were in bed together.

As soon as Fry finished, Drake bounded to his feet and began firing questions at her. What time of day did this alleged conversation with Betty occur? What did she do after that? How long did she stay at your house? Did she eat lunch with you? And then: "After she left, I'm sure you called the police, didn't you?"

Cerha looked surprised. "No," she replied, "I did not."

In response to additional questions, she denied calling the district attorney as well, or even Jack, to warn him about his wife's state of mind.

"You didn't report it to anybody, did you?" Drake asked sharply.

"No, I did not," she repeated. Instead, she testified, she and Betty continued to be friends for another three years.

"And you didn't any more think at the time that she meant that than she was saying she was going to go to the moon, did you?" Drake asked.

"No," Cerha replied, "because she was my best friend."

"Not only was she your best friend," Drake shot back, "but she was a drunk, wasn't she?"

Cerha appeared momentarily taken aback. "Yes," she said.

Not only was Betty an alcoholic, Drake said, but Cerha

herself was having problems with substance abuse. "You were a drug addict, weren't you?"

Despite Fry's objection, Drake persisted, repeating the question.

Cerha nodded. "I had a drug problem," she replied, adding that she indulged in painkillers prescribed as a treatment for migraine headaches. "And my husband wrote prescriptions for me so that he could take drugs," she added.

Over the next few minutes, Drake drew admissions from Cerha that her husband had been addicted to cocaine although she herself denied using the narcotic.

When she said that, Drake looked at her skeptically. "Now when you were admitted to Crestwood Hospital in July 1987, they gave you a urinalysis, didn't they?" he asked, adding that the test showed traces of barbiturates and phenothiazine in her system. "Isn't it true that people use barbiturates to come down off a cocaine high?" he asked.

"No," Cerha replied. In any case, she explained, the drugs she thought he was referring to were Vistaril, which is used to help control nausea, and Fiorinal, which is used to help relieve headache pain.

Drake, however, continued to hammer at her about phenothiazine, which he said was a family of drugs whose main derivative was Thorazine, a drug commonly used in psychiatric treatment.

"Have you ever taken Thorazine?" he asked.

"No," she replied firmly.

Although he stopped short of accusing her of being a psychotic, Drake flourished her hospital record, pointing to a section that quoted Betty as telling authorities that Cerha abused her daughter, Ashley.

" 'Betty indicates that Brenda treats her kids very poorly, treats Ashley like a dog,' " Drake read. " 'She indicates that she yells and screams at the kids on a number of occasions, and that on occasion she has lost control while spanking Ashley. Ashley confirms this report,' " he continued, " 'and indicates that Brenda would lock her in her room before she would spank her.' "

"Those are Betty's words," Cerha replied indignantly. She was not present when Ashley purportedly made her statement, and her daughter never told her that was what she had said.

Drake pounced. "The record indicates that on June sixteenth, 1987, you told your counselors [at the hospital] that you were indeed an addict. There is no question about that, is there?"

"No," said Cerha.

"And did you tell the people at Crestwood that Betty had told your daughter that you were going to jail because of your drug involvement?" he asked.

"That's why I was upset with her," Cerha replied.

"And you were furious at Betty about that, weren't you?" Drake asked quickly, hoping he could get her to say yes and thus expose to the jury a possible motive for saying that Betty had tried to enlist her help in having Jack killed.

However, Cerha did not cooperate. "At that time," she replied, carefully enunciating the words.

Drake refused to give up. Foiled in the attempt to show she might be seeking revenge against Betty, he turned instead to an implication that Cerha was having severe psychological problems.

"Do you still suffer from depressive neurosis?" he asked. "Are you still in treatment?"

"No," she said without elaboration.

Ever resourceful, Drake pursued another angle.

"Where was your husband when he shot himself?" he asked.

"In the bed," Cerha said.

"Are you still sleeping on that mattress today?"

Cerha looked shocked. "No!" she responded.

"Didn't you turn it over and continue sleeping on it for several years?" Drake persisted.

Cerha clenched her jaw. "No!" she repeated.

A few minutes later, on redirect, Fry returned to the issue Drake had raised about the possibility of Cerha's motive for testifying against Betty.

"Mr. Drake didn't ask you," Fry began, hinting for the jury's benefit that the defense attorney had not been altogether forthright in the information he included in his questions, "but I want to ask you when you were in the hospital, what were you furious at the defendant about?"

Appearing relieved at being given the opportunity to explain herself, Cerha said that while she was in the hospital, she discovered that Betty had been taking her youngest child, who was then about three, to AA meetings with her and badmouthing her in front of Betty's fellow members. Also, she added, Betty had been telling her daughter, Ashley, that she, Cerha, was a drug addict and was going to jail. "I felt like these were things that I should tell my child, that she should hear from me first."

TWENTY-ONE

HANGING ON A WALL IN FRY'S OFFICE IS A successor to the old blackboard: a white, plastic rectangle on which the prosecutor can make notes with erasable felt-tip markers. Scrawled on this board at the time of Betty's trial were a half-dozen names that Betty had given to investigators soon after Jack's murder, names of men with whom she admitted having affairs of considerable duration. Near the top of the list was the name Erroll Fitzpatrick, which was familiar to Fry because it had been in the news, linked to Betty's.

On June 23, 1992, the *Huntsville News* had published a story under the headline CITY OFFICIAL TIED TO WILSON CASE RESIGNS. The story, written by staff writer Greg Heyman, said that Fitzpatrick had quit as the city's risk management officer after Betty gave his name to police. After Fitzpatrick quit, he moved to California, and returned to Alabama only after he was subpoenaed by Fry.

When he was called as a witness in Betty's trial on Friday, February 26, the fourth day of the trial, Fitzpatrick testified that he had met Betty through AA. They began as friends, he said, but the relationship then turned into a physical one. The affair began late in 1990 or early in 1991, he said, and continued on an on again/ off again basis until a couple of weeks before Jack's murder. Sometimes, he testified, they met in motels in Birmingham to have sex, but the most common venue was his Huntsville apartment. Once, he admitted, they made love in Betty's bed at the Wilson house.

Drake rushed to the lectern as soon as Fry had worked through his short list of noncontroversial questions. "Are you as offended as I am," he thundered, "that the prosecutor brought you here to show that you are black?"

Before Fitzpatrick could answer, Fry leaped to his feet to object. He was sustained by Judge Younger, who undoubtedly was not anxious to have what he considered an uncomplicated, straightforward murder trial turn into a racial issue.

Although it was impossible to gauge Fitzpatrick's impact on the jury, Drake had a point. The region has changed in many ways in the previous thirty years, but Tuscaloosa is still very much the Old South, a place where whites are still uncomfortable with racially mixed sexual relationships. But for the defense to contend that the only reason Fitzpatrick was subpoenaed to appear was because he was black may simply have been another facet of the defense's strategy to destroy by implication.

In truth, Fitzpatrick's testimony, in terms of pure content, offered little of obvious value to the prosecution's case. Under cross-examination he said that Betty had never even spoken ill of Jack in his presence. But there was one subtle point that Fry hoped the jury had noted: Fitzpatrick's revelation that Betty had taken him into her own bed in the house that she shared with her husband. It was one thing to have affairs in motels and distant apartments, but quite another to bring a lover into your own home. That was poignant proof, the prosecutor felt, of the contempt that Betty felt for Jack. Fry's next witness would build upon that point.

Up to then, all of the female "character" witnesses

called by Fry had been contemporaries of Betty's, either friends of hers, or Jack's employees, or both. But Shirley Green broke the pattern.

A frightened, frazzled-looking woman in her mid-thirties, Green explained that she had been a maid at the Wilsons' for four years, servicing their house three times a week. During that period, she said, she had the opportunity to see a side to Betty that she mostly kept hidden from her friends.

According to Green, Fitzpatrick was not the only one of Betty's lovers that she brought into the house. There was another man who stopped by with regularity, a man Betty seemed so infatuated with that she once took Green to his apartment and ordered her to clean it. "He didn't even have any cleaning supplies, so Betty went to the store to get some," Green said indignantly.

At home, Green testified, things were anything but peaceful between Jack and Betty, with the ophthalmologist serving as a constant source of irritation to his wife. "No matter what he did, it wasn't right."

One thing Betty was particularly critical of, Green testified, was Jack's ostomy bag. It stank, Betty complained, and sometimes it made the entire house smell.

One day when she came to work, she said, Betty told her that she did not have to make her bed because she had already done it herself. Earlier that morning, she told Green angrily, Jack had tried to make love to her, but his ostomy bag had broken in the process, soiling the bed and forcing her to replace the sheets. As a result, Green quoted Betty as saying, she told him never to touch her again.

On cross-examination Hooper focused not on what Green had said, but her alleged motives in saying it. Much as Drake had done when he questioned Mary Ann Lau, Hooper accused Green of delivering sensational testimony solely to attract media attention. "You just want to sell your story to books and movies, don't you?" he yelled.

"Noooo," Green stammered.

Green's appearance marked a turning point in the trial. Although he had subpoenaed half again as many witnesses as the forty he had called so far, Fry felt he had made his case successfully and there was no reason to lengthen the proceeding with repetitive testimony. When the maid, visibly upset at the accusations that had been hurled at her by the obstreperous Hooper, left the stand, Fry decided to wind up his presentation by calling the two principal investigators: Harry Renfroe and Mickey Brantley.

A large, mustachioed detective, pithy to the point that he made Younger seem effusive, Renfroe succinctly explained how Betty had at first seemed puzzled when the investigator told her that a man named James Dennison White was a suspect in her husband's murder. Finally, he said, it dawned on her who he was talking about.

"Oh, you mean Mr. Carpenter," he quoted her as saying.

When he expressed puzzlement, Betty told him that was how she thought of White, as Peggy's carpenter friend.

Betty denied ever meeting White, Renfroe said, or paying him to kill her husband. She had, in fact, told him that she had never paid him for *anything*.

By the same token, the investigator added, Peggy, in a separate interview, told him that she knew White only casually and that she simply had been trying to help a person she felt was down on his luck and needed all the assistance he could get. When he asked her if she were having an affair with White, Peggy had flatly said that she was not. When he asked if there had been *any* sexual contact between them, Peggy had just as emphatically said no.

What happened then? Fry asked.

Renfroe appeared to be suppressing a grin. "At that point," he commented wryly, "she said she didn't want to talk to me anymore and she didn't."

Brantley, who was only marginally more garrulous than his colleague, detailed for the jury's benefit the story of the investigation, beginning with his arrival at the Wilson house at 10:23 on that Friday night, through the trip to Shelby County to question White, and into the ordeal of the series of interrogation sessions that resulted in the multiple, sometimes confusing, often contradictory statements that he made. It was only after he learned about Janine Russell's comments, Brantley added candidly, that he began to believe that Jack had been murdered by an outsider.

"My first thought," he said, "was that one of the children may have been involved." In those first few days, he confirmed, Betty was not a suspect. When she rose to the top of his list, his suspicions about the children dissolved.

What really began pulling the case together for him, he said, were the telephone records. They substantiated the things White had told him and made sense of the series of events that White had disjointedly described. When White said he called Peggy from a convenience store outside Guntersville State Park because the security guard would not let him through the gate, Brantley was able to find a telephone company record confirming a call from the grocery to the Lowe house. When he said he called Peggy and Betty from a supermarket across the street from Jack's office on the day before the murder, the record showed a call from a pay phone outside a Winn-Dixie to Peggy's house.

One after another, Brantley said, the telephone records coincided with White's statements, leaving him convinced that White was telling the truth in his own garbled fashion.

Not surprisingly, the defense disagreed.

Making his first appearance at cross-examination since his grueling questioning of White, the dapper Bobby Lee Cook launched an equally blistering attack on Brantley. Although his manner and tone were not as strident as Drake's and Hooper's, his intent was the same: demolish the witness and shatter the case against Betty.

Polite where his colleagues had been rude, soft-spoken where they had been boisterous, and pacifying where they had relied on ridicule, Cook nevertheless proved he could be just as sharp-tongued and ruthless.

After painstakingly leading Brantley through each of White's statements, pointing out, as he had in his cross-examination of White, the contradictions and discrepancies, he waved the bundle of papers in the air dramatically. "Were you the guiding hand in signing a deal with this crazy, cold-blooded murderer?" he asked shrilly.

When Brantley confirmed that he was, Cook commented for the jury's benefit: "He will be eligible for parole in seven years and be back on the street."

If Cook's style could be summed up in one word, it would be "theatrical." A master of movement and voice inflection, Cook could turn a simple hand gesture into a symbol of the utmost contempt, or, in a single word, convey enormous and total disbelief. With his client's life at stake, and the man who did the most to put her in such a precarious position outside of White himself on the stand, Cook did not restrain himself.

Without actually accusing Brantley of negligence, he tore into the detective's investigatory techniques, claiming he failed to carry through on such basics as checking White's background or trying to determine the veracity of his claim that it was indeed Betty he had dealt with in planning Jack's murder.

"Did you ever ask James White for a description of Betty Wilson?" Cook asked.

"No, sir," Brantley replied.

"Did you ever show him a picture of her and ask him to identify her?"

"I don't recall," the detective replied.

Did he ever try to obtain White's military or hospital records, which showed that White was unstable? Did he ever try to follow through on White's claim that he had sex with Peggy, by trying to determine if she had any identifying marks on her body? Did he know anything about a note Jack Wilson may have written just before he was killed?

No, Brantley answered to each question.

"Well," Cook said, feigning surprise, "if it could be shown that Jack Wilson wrote a note after the time that White said he had killed him, what would you think of that?"

Brantley blinked in surprise. "It would be disastrous," he conceded.

And, Cook added, what if it could be shown that White actually checked into the Ramada Inn twelve hours later than he said he did? Or what if the defense could prove that White actually was in the motel bar at the time he claimed to be waiting in the Wilson house for Betty to come home so she could drive him away from the scene?

Brantley shrugged, unsure if Cook was asking questions or making statements.

When he saw that a response was not going to be forthcoming, Cook imperiously dismissed the investigator with a wave, a gesture that seemed to tell the jury, "Wait until you see what *we* have!"

Glancing at his watch, Fry noted it was 5:44, as good a time as any to quit. Rising, he addressed Judge Younger. "The state rests, your honor," he said without elaboration.

Younger nodded, hardly surprised. Come back tomorrow at eight-thirty, he ordered, thereby breaking an unwritten but what many judges seem to feel is an inviolable prohibition regarding Saturday court sessions.

It was not, however, a decision the judge made impulsively. For the previous two days, a rumor had been circulating among courtroom personnel that the judge, who had already demonstrated his preference to work long days, was ready to go through the weekend, or as much of it as he could, to get the trial finished as soon as possible. The jury had been polled on the issue, it was later learned, and they agreed with Younger. Sequestered as they were, they had indicated an unwillingness to be away from their families and their jobs any longer than absolutely necessary.

For Fry the decision to rest brought a feeling of temporary relief; his major role was accomplished. Even though his case was entirely circumstantial, it had been the most capable he could put together under the circumstances. From now until the time came for closing arguments, there was little he could do except defend what he had already championed. His most optimistic expectation was that the defense would have no major revelations, no surprise witnesses waiting in the wings who could devastate his delicately balanced presentation.

There *was* one witness Fry was worried about: David Williamson, the man who Cook had melodramatically paraded into the courtroom during White's testimony. Although he had tried to interview Williamson as soon as he discovered he was going to be a witness, his attempt was frustrated by the defense. For Fry, Williamson was a huge unknown, someone who had the potential of ripping his carefully prepared case to shreds. Fry barely knew who Williamson *was* and had no more than a troubling suspicion as to what he was prepared to testify about. Nevertheless, the prosecutor figured if the defense went to such lengths to try to keep his identity a secret, the man was worth investigating. The problem was getting to him.

As soon as Williamson had left the courtroom during White's testimony, Fry sent Brantley after him to attempt to set up an interview. But when Brantley had tried to approach Williamson, Charlie Hooper jumped between them and refused to let the investigator talk to the potential witness. Afraid that Williamson was going to leave town and not reappear until it was time to testify, thus frustrating his effort to question him beforehand, Fry secured a subpoena to prevent him from departing Tuscaloosa. Angered by this move, Hooper ran to Judge Younger and demanded that Williamson be allowed to leave.

"All I want to do is talk to him," Fry argued. "If he'll talk to me, then he can go."

"He wants to go home *now*," Hooper yelled.

"Fuck him," Fry replied, feeling his blood pressure rise. "Either he can talk to me now or he can go home when I go home."

Younger vacillated, refusing to come down on either side of the argument. Finally, Peggy's lawyer, David Cromwell Johnson, approached Fry.

"Why are you being such an asshole about this?" Johnson asked.

Fry smiled. "I'm just that kind of guy," he replied.

The next day, Johnson again approached Fry, saying that Williamson would agree to talk to him briefly but only if one of the defense team members was present.

In the end Fry was able to question Williamson for about ten minutes, but the man had been remarkably close-mouthed and hostile toward the prosecutor. Fry had instinctively disliked him, sensing there was something strange in the way the man's eyes, magnified behind thick glasses, darted back and forth when he talked.

Fry shrugged inwardly. There was nothing he could do

about Williamson, he told himself, nothing except wait and see what developed and worry about it then.

He called a quick conference among members of the prosecution "team"—ADA Kristi Adcock, Investigator Bobby Smith, and Huntsville detective Brantley. Rather than celebrating the attainment of a milestone, they went immediately to work trying to puzzle out who the defense would call as witnesses and how Fry would handle the cross-examination.

Neither was it a time of celebration for Betty's lawyers. In the morning they would begin trying to tear down the prosecution's house of cards. At the same time, there was no overriding feeling of anxiety, no feeling of impending doom. They had seen the best the prosecution had to offer, they felt, and they were not terrifically impressed. From their point of view, the entire case against Betty relied on White's credibility. And they reckoned that Cook had done a pretty good job of demolishing that during his intense cross-examination. The most impressive of the other witnesses, people like Mary Ann Lau, Nancy Nelson, and Brenda Cerha, had made some fairly destructive statements about Betty, but they had not been able to relate her character traits to the *crime* of Jack's murder, something that would be necessary before the jury could find her guilty beyond reasonable doubt.

As for the others, Fry's "place" witnesses, the defense team had its own plans to counter what they had said, plans that would begin unfolding for the prosecutor and jury in less than fifteen hours.

TWENTY-TWO

THE DEFENSE'S LEAD-OFF WITNESS WAS A tall, dark-haired man with a bushy mustache named Jerry Wayne McDaniel, a phlegmatic former chief investigator for the Madison County District Attorney's Office who left public service in 1989 to open his own private detective agency.

McDaniel, who came equipped with a shopping bag full of photographs and videos designed to show that police botched the investigation from the beginning, testified that he had been hired by Betty, acting through Charlie Hooper, on May 26, the same day that White was arrested and charged with Jack's murder, which was an indication that Betty knew from the beginning that the trail was going to lead to her.

Most of the information that McDaniel would be called to testify about dealt with issues centering around Jack and Betty's house, either with material actually found in the house or nearby. Although he was prohibited from entering the residence for thirty days because police technicians were still working inside, he said, once he got in, he found a surplus of items that Brantley and his crew had either overlooked or ignored.

For instance, he began in a slow, deep voice, there was a photograph on the mirror in Jack's bathroom and several stick-'em notes apparently meant as reminders, although he never said what was written on the note papers or what the photograph depicted. In addition, he said, there was a prescription pad sitting on the counter nearby, presumably blank, and in a book next to Jack's bed he found an application for a life insurance policy in the amount of $1 million with Betty's name scribbled in as beneficiary.

But most importantly, McDaniel said ponderously, was a small notepad that he found lying on a chair in Jack's bedroom. Written on the top sheet was a note reminding Jack to do several things. At the top of the note were the numbers 1715 and what appeared to be a date, 22 May. This apparently was the note that Cook had referred to in his cross-examination of Brantley, the missive that purported to show that Jack was still alive after White said he had killed him. The defense argued that the numbers represented a time on the twenty-four-hour clock, which is commonly used in Europe and, in this country, almost exclusively by the military. Translated, that would be five-fifteen P.M.

According to Sheila Irby, that was fifteen minutes *after* she saw White afoot on Boulder Circle heading *away* from the Wilson house. Also, it was roughly the same time Irby said she almost collided with Betty's car, which, under the prosecution scenario, held White, who was crouched on the floor in the backseat, hidden under a pink garment bag.

The time was crucial because there were other verifiable events that occurred before and after that. At 4:55 P.M. Betty left a boutique a short drive away from her home. At 5:25 she ran into another AA member in a parking lot several miles away and the two exchanged greetings. If the defense could prove that Jack was alive at five-fifteen, the prosecution's entire case would be in danger. The problem was, Betty's team could not prove it.

Although the defense later called a handwriting expert to testify that the scrawl on the note was indeed in Jack Wilson's hand, there was no way to certify that the numbers represented a time. By then it had been more than twenty-five years since Jack had been in the military, and there was no compelling reason why he would be thinking in military time, or even why he would be timing reminders at all. In addition, even if the numbers *did* represent the time, the figures were grammatically incorrect. To have been written correctly, the series of numbers should have read 17:15, with a colon between the seven and the one separating the hours from the minutes. But if the figures did not represent a time, what did they depict? No satisfactory explanation was ever offered. Although the defense continued to insist that the numbers meant five-fifteen, Fry argued just as persuasively that they could have signified almost anything.

Having dropped the note bombshell, McDaniel dug into his bag and produced four videotapes, which the defense claimed further damaged the prosecution's case.

The first film showed the path that ran behind the Wilson house to the next major street down the hill. It apparently was intended to throw doubt on the prosecution's contention that the plastic bag containing clothing allegedly belonging to White had remained hidden for as long as investigators claimed. Cook insinuated that the bag was planted.

Two of the other videos depicted traffic flow patterns and apparently were meant to prove that Betty could not have adhered to the state's alleged timetable even if she had wanted to, because of school crossings and heavily used intersections.

The fourth and most puzzling video consisted entirely of film of the opening and closing of the Wilson garage door, the front door, and the door from the garage into the house, as well as a panoramic view of nearby Gover-

nor's Drive from Jack's bedroom. Exactly what this film
was meant to prove was never made clear.

To bolster its assertion that Jack was alive when the
prosecution said he was dead, the defense presented a
woman named Pam Hyde, who was a patient of Jack's
and whose husband, a dental service technician, occasionally worked with the ophthalmologist.

Hooper presented an audio tape which he said came
from Hyde's answering machine. Jack's voice was on the
tape directing Hyde's husband to bring an item to his
office the following week.

Under Hooper's guidance, Hyde said she had checked
the machine at five o'clock that Friday afternoon and
there were no messages on it. She went outside to mow
the lawn and came back about forty minutes later to find
the message light blinking. When she pushed the play
button, she heard Wilson's voice.

However, Fry raised enough points on cross-examination to throw the reliability of the recording into question.

The message, Fry pointed out, contained no time or
date to prove it had been left on May 22 or sometime
long before. Hyde was no help for the defense since she
was unable to say with certainty that the message was a
fresh one.

"How old is that tape?" Fry asked.

"I don't know," Hyde replied.

"Could it have been in the machine for a week?" he
queried.

"It could have been," Hyde conceded.

"A month?"

"Yes."

"Six months?"

"I couldn't say," Hyde replied.

Fry, who also could rely on dramatics when necessary,
paused and studied the witness. "How long have you had
that machine?" he asked innocently.

"I couldn't say," Hyde replied, agitated.

Again Fry paused for effect, then added, in his best good ol' boy style: "I don't understand. The message said for your husband to bring that item to Dr. Wilson's office the following week." He stopped for a heartbeat. "But his office was going to be closed all that week because he was supposed to be on vacation in Santa Fe."

It was a comment, not a question, and Hyde simply shrugged.

At mid-morning, after Younger's customary brief recess, Bobby Lee Cook rose and strode to the lectern, a move that triggered a collective intake of breath among the spectators. Even though it was a Saturday, the line outside the courtroom had begun forming before seven o'clock in anticipation of verbal fireworks at the beginning of the defense presentation. Every seat was filled and an additional fifty people stood outside, hoping to get in. Cook's move to the center of the room signaled an event of major import because he was the star of Betty's legal team. When reporters and spectators who had been following the trial closely saw Cook shift into position, one word was whispered around the room: "Williamson."

The defense's "surprise" witness, David Williamson, was a short, blocky man of forty, an unobtrusive-looking fellow with a crew cut and a short, neatly trimmed, reddish-brown beard. He wore a dark sports coat, white shirt, dark tie, and thick lenses set in modified aviator frames. He lived in the tiny northern Alabama town of Arab, he said, but he was not there much since he spent much of his time on the road running his own business, trying to provide for his wife and seven children. His business, he added, was selling memorabilia of Alabama college athletic teams, mainly photos depicting great moments in Auburn University and University of Alabama sports history.

He had been in Huntsville the previous May 22 and

had checked into the Ramada Inn. Late that afternoon, he said, he had been in the motel lobby, hovering over a display of sports pictures he was offering for sale, when a man entered through the door that led to the swimming pool/patio area and started walking in his direction.

The man, Williamson testified, clad in jeans and a plaid shirt, which was open enough to show a white tee-shirt underneath, looked wild-eyed and angry. "He kept staring at me," Williamson said, "and then he walked over to me and he said, 'What the hell are you doing here?'"

Williamson, exhibiting a natural sense of theatrics, paused. "Three times he said that: 'What the hell are you doing here?' Then he said, 'I want to make that bitch pay for what she's done to me. I want to show her what lonely's all about.'" After he said that, Williamson added, he turned and walked away.

Frightened by the man's demeanor, certain he had stared into the eyes of a wild man who might do *anything*, Williamson hurried to the motel desk to report the encounter. But, he said, the desk was abandoned. Deciding to take matters into his own hands, he ran into the parking lot, retrieved a pistol from his truck, stuck it in his belt, and went back inside the motel. A few minutes later, at roughly five o'clock, Williamson went into the motel restaurant, which adjoins the lobby, and saw the man sitting at the bar. When the man turned in his direction, he looked right through him, Williamson said, apparently having forgotten the incident in the lobby a few minutes earlier.

A week or so later, Williamson said, he was watching the local news on television when a film clip flashed on the screen showing the man he had seen in the motel. It was then that he learned the man's name was James White and he had been charged with murdering a Huntsville eye doctor.

From the defense's point of view, Williamson's story

was even more important than the note purportedly written by Jack at five-fifteen. While there were ambiguities about the note—whether 1715 represented a time or had some other significance—there was little doubt that Williamson believed he had an encounter with James White at the Ramada Inn at about five o'clock on the afternoon of the murder. If Williamson was correct—and to believe that he was, the jury would have to disbelieve Sheila Irby —White's story fell apart because he said he was still waiting for Betty to come home at that time.

The broad implications of these two defense contentions were awesome. If Jack was alive as late as five-fifteen, and White was sitting in a motel bar at roughly that time, when was Jack killed, and who killed him? And if was not White, why did White confess to the crime?

The defense could not have cared less about the answers to those questions. All Cook et al were concerned with was clearing Betty of the charges that she paid White to murder her husband. If her lawyers could convince the jury that the murderer could not have been White, then Betty could not have hired him. That, therefore, would add to the probability that Betty may have been right in the first place, that Jack was killed by a burglar. As far as the defense was concerned, it was not their responsibility to track down the actual murderer; that was a job for the police. It was not their fault, Betty's lawyers were saying, that the Huntsville P.D. botched the investigation.

But to get to that point in the reasoning, Betty's team had to convince the jury of the veracity of the note, and/ or the recorded message, and/or Williamson's story. Convinced that he had pretty well discredited the significance of the note and the taped message, Fry leaped on Williamson like a tick on a dog.

Showing he, too, could be brutal if he were so inclined, the prosecutor began machine-gunning questions at Williamson, who was sitting like a statue in the witness chair, staring at the back wall.

"Are you the David Williamson who's also known as Jimmy D. Williamson? Have you ever been convicted of a crime of moral turpitude? Have you ever been convicted of writing bad checks?" Williamson had never been convicted of any crime, but he had once been accused of writing bad checks. Fry hoped to bait Williamson into admitting the existence of that accusation.

The defense objected to each of the prosecutor's questions, and Judge Younger sustained. But Fry had made his point. It wasn't necessary for Williamson to answer for Fry to plant the idea in the jurors' minds that there was something suspicious and faintly disreputable about the witness.

"You refused to talk to me the other day, didn't you?" Fry barked, adding that Hooper had almost bowled him over to keep him away from the prize witness.

"Mickey Brantley almost arrested me out there in the hall!" Hooper interjected, screaming his interruption across the courtroom.

Fry glanced at the defense lawyer and smiled inwardly, happy that he had struck a sore spot. When he had sent Brantley to try to set up an interview with Williamson, and Hooper had refused to let the investigator talk to him, Brantley had threatened to arrest the lawyer for interfering with an investigation. However, the investigator quickly reconsidered his impulse and backed off, deciding to let the situation play itself out before making possible trouble for himself and the prosecutor.

Turning back to Williamson, Fry continued almost as if he had not heard Hooper. "You refused to talk to Investigator Brantley, didn't you?" he asked. "Finally, Mr. Sandlin prevailed and you talked to me for five minutes, didn't you?"

The prosecutor was not seeking answers to these questions. They were statements for the jurors' benefit rather than his own edification. Questions he *did* expect answers to, however, dealt with Williamson's behavior. Assuming that his story was true, Fry wanted to take issue with what Williamson did.

"You say this man was foaming at the mouth, his eyes were blazing, yet you didn't call motel security?" he asked.

"No," Williamson replied. "I went to the desk to tell someone and there was no one there."

Fry raised his eyebrows. "You mean there was no one at the motel desk between four and five o'clock on a Friday afternoon?" he asked disbelievingly.

"That's right," Williamson answered.

Fry shook his head. "You went to the truck to get your gun because you were afraid for your life?"

"That's right," Williamson said.

"Yet you never reported it to anyone at the Ramada Inn or called the police?"

"That's right."

Fry's tone changed. "Tell me something," he said congenially. "How did you happen to get together with Charlie Hooper?"

Williamson's eyes darted to the defense table. "Someone called me and told me to call Mr. Hooper because he wanted to buy some photos."

"Is that right," Fry commented dryly, smiling at the burst of laughter from the spectators.

"That's right," Williamson said solemnly.

"Well, tell me this," Fry continued. "Did he buy a picture from you?"

"No," Williamson replied hotly, adding, "Mr. Hooper hasn't paid me one dime to be here today. I didn't want to be here."

"What a coincidence," Fry said scornfully. "You get a call to go to Charlie Hooper's office because he might want to buy some pictures, and it turns out that you're the *only* man who can identify James White as being in the motel. Isn't that strange?"

"Yes," Williamson mumbled.

Satisfied that he had made his point, Fry walked to his chair and sat down.

Studying his notes, the prosecutor determined that he was not unhappy with the way the morning had gone so far. The issue that Cook had been bragging about the day before, the note that allegedly proved that Jack was still alive at five-fifteen, had not lived up to its advance billing. Also, he felt that the threat posed by Williamson —a witness whose testimony the defense was counting on heavily—had been defused. As it turned out, this assessment was remarkably accurate. One juror said later that the group put little credence in the note, the tape recorded message, *or* in Williamson's testimony.

What Fry did not know was that the defense had not given up its attempt to break White's story and had one more major witness waiting to testify about events that not only might prove Betty's accuser a liar, but, they hoped, would endanger the entire prosecution case by offering what they considered a plausible motive for White to concoct a web of lies. The defense planned to counterattack by presenting a complicated conspiracy theory.

TWENTY-THREE

BY THEN THE STRATEGY THE DEFENSE INtended to follow in presenting its case was becoming clearer. Unlike the prosecution, which began with its most dramatic witness and then worked backward to fill in the gaps, Betty's lawyers were beginning with minor witnesses and building toward a climax. The note had hardly been conclusive proof of Jack Wilson's health beyond the time of his alleged demise. To believe Williamson, jurors would have to disregard not only White's testimony, but Sheila Irby's as well. And the tape recording had been even weaker. Therefore, in an effort which some saw as increasingly desperate, the defense stepped up its tempo, deciding to make one last effort to demolish White's version of events.

Again Bobby Lee Cook strode to the lectern, setting the courtroom abuzz. The spectators had learned to read the signs: when Cook took an active role, something important was about to occur. The witness Cook summoned in the defense's latest effort to topple the prosecution's case was a portly, baggy-eyed man in his early fifties named John Self, the night auditor at the Huntsville Ramada Inn.

For the jury's benefit, Self explained that his shift ran from eleven at night to seven the following morning, and his duties, in addition to keeping the books up to date, included helping out on the desk by registering guests.

"Did you check James White in on May twenty-first?" Cook asked.

When Self replied that he had, Cook then asked the crucial question. "*When* did he check in?"

"It was after I came on duty, which was after eleven P.M.," Self replied.

Cook paused to let the response sink in. What Self was saying was that he believed that White had checked in almost twelve hours later than White—and the computerized record—indicated he had. If that were true, then White could not have made the long distance calls to Peggy's house earlier that evening from Room 222 because the calls would have been made some six hours before he was assigned to the room and given a key.

"You *do* remember James White, don't you?" Cook asked, anxious to ascertain that Self did not have him confused with some other guest.

"Oh, yes," Self replied, explaining how White had wanted to pay in cash and how motel policy required that he show some type of pictured identification. "We chatted for a little bit," Self added, "and he said he was looking for work."

That, however, was only the preliminary to what the defense had in mind by calling John Self. In addition to trying to show that White lied about his timetable, Betty's lawyers wanted to plant in jurors' minds the possibility that evidence backing up White's story had been falsified, and were eager to try to prove *why*.

To do that, Cook asked Self a series of detailed questions about what happened when Hilda Smith, an investigator for Peggy's legal team, went to the motel to double-check the details of White's story. When Smith questioned him about the prosecution's timetable, especially the phone calls, Self said he sent her to see the motel manager, Gary Houck.

Since Self was unable to testify about what allegedly happened in the meeting between Smith and Houck, Cook had to finish with Self before he called Smith. And before he could do that, he had to turn Self over to Fry for cross-examination.

Sensing what was about to happen, Fry began questioning Self about his work habits.

Although his name was on the work schedule from eleven P.M. to seven A.M., Self admitted that he actually worked considerably longer hours. Since he lived in a room at the motel and had few outside interests, he frequently stayed on the job long after his shift formally ended. In fact, he told Fry, during the previous year he had worked 108 straight days without a day off, most of them extending beyond his scheduled shift. Commonly, Self said, when his normal shift ended, he joined the morning crew at the desk and assisted them in checking guests in or out and helped them take care of the normal early-day duties. Not infrequently he stayed around until after the noon hour so he could relieve the regular clerks when they went to lunch.

Waving the computer-generated log that showed White checked in at 12:47 P.M., not A.M., Fry asked Self if he could not have been mistaken when he told the defense investigator that White's check-in time was closer to midnight than noon.

Self studied the paper. In an unhappy turn for Betty, Self admitted he must have been wrong in his statements to the defense. "This tape is correct," he said, deferring to the computer record. "I guess I was just off by twelve hours."

Unwilling to let the issue die, Cook went back to the lectern, intending to question Self further, when he peered into the spectator section and spotted the Ramada manager, Gary Houck. Insinuating there was something suspicious about Houck's presence in the courtroom since he had finished his formal testimony two days earlier, Cook leveled his index finger and bellowed, "I would like to recall that man!"

When Houck was on the stand a second time, Cook tried to intimate that it was peculiar for Houck still to be in Tuscaloosa instead of returning to Huntsville once he had given his testimony.

Didn't I see you in a restaurant here the other night? Cook asked. And weren't you having dinner with Jack Wilson's sister?

Houck reddened. "Yes," he said. "She's a friend."

Cook nodded portentously. "Do you remember," he began, seemingly changing the subject, "meeting with Hilda Smith and that she made certain inquiries of you?"

He remembered her, Houck said, adding that she had asked for documentation substantiating points in White's version of events about when he was staying at the motel on May 21–22.

Was anyone else present at the meeting with Smith? Cook asked, hoping that his answer would ring a warning bell with jurors. Cook knew what Houck was going to say, and he had built up to the question carefully, timing it for its dramatic impact.

As Cook had expected, Houck looked flustered. "Yes," he replied, adding that Jack Wilson's first wife, Julia, was there.

Cook turned slightly to the jury and raised a bushy eyebrow. What he said, without uttering a word, was, Ahhhh, what have we here? Julia Wilson, Jack's first wife and presumably Betty's enemy, suddenly appearing in a position where she could do major harm to his client.

Realizing that he was in a situation that sounded worse than it was, Houck squirmed. Julia Wilson, he added, was the motel's manager for sales and catering.

Again Cook's eyebrows shot up. Do you expect this jury to believe, his expression said, that Julia Wilson just *happened* to be working in the motel where the main witness against Betty said he spent the night before the murder? Do you expect the jury to believe, Cook all but shouted, that this is a simple coincidence?

It was unnecessary for him to actually vocalize these statements. The veteran Cook, a highly skilled master at courtroom pantomime, said it all with a couple of shrugs and a few surreptitious glances toward the jury. What he wanted the jury to believe—and it was a point he would elaborate upon later—was that there *was* something suspicious about Julia's presence.

Julia Wilson, however, had a different explanation. Asked after the trial about the coincidence of her working at the one motel in Huntsville in which White stayed while on his murder mission, Wilson rolled her dark eyes. "I can just hear Betty now," she said softly. "Betty knew exactly where I worked, and I can hear her as clear as day telling White, 'Why don't you stay at the Ramada Inn,' figuring if it was ever discovered, it would make trouble for me in the long run."

In reality, both Cook and Julia Wilson may have been chasing shadows. It would take a great leap of imagination for jurors to accept either side's explanation without a large grain of salt. In all likelihood it probably *was* a coincidence that White chose the Ramada Inn, a choice dictated perhaps by nothing more than its convenience to Jack's office and the Wilsons' house.

"Did you call her in [for the meeting with Smith]?" Cook asked Houck, still pursuing his point.

"I believe she was already in my office," Houck replied.

"What was she doing there?" Cook asked, pretending outrage. "She's in catering?"

Houck flushed. "She's also one of my employees," he replied testily.

It was not exactly the way he intended to introduce the theory, but Cook was laying the groundwork for the defense suggestion that there was something questionable

about the hotel records contradicting Self's memory and
Julia Wilson's involvement.

The theory, which Cook would not touch upon again
until closing arguments, revolved around White's choice
of motels. It was more than coincidence, the defense
hinted, that White went to the Ramada Inn where Julia
Wilson worked. And Julia was interested in seeing Betty
convicted for Jack's murder because her children would
benefit financially. According to the defense, Self had
been correct when he said White checked in at about
midnight and the motel's records were wrong by twelve
hours. For the defense's suggestion to work, the check-in
time would have to have been falsified, and computerized records from the telephone company, which showed
the times calls were made from Room 222 to Peggy's
number would have to have been changed. Plus a whole
series of witnesses would have had to have lied on the
stand. Whether the jury could absorb and accept all that
was another question. But it is a lawyerly homily that the
more outrageous a claim, the more likely it is to be believed.

Cook was anxious to leave the question hanging, give
the jury something to ponder over the weekend. The
more time they had to think about it, he reckoned, the
better it would be for the defense. After calling Hilda
Smith and guiding her through a series of questions
about meeting with Houck and Julia Wilson, Cook asked
Judge Younger if they could quit for the day.

Younger glanced at the clock. It was only noon, and he
would have liked to work until late afternoon as usual,
Saturday or not. But he had little choice other than to
accede to the defense request because Cook had no
other witnesses waiting to be called that day.

The defense team was not only anxious to give the jury
as much time as possible to mull over the issue Cook had
raised, but they needed to make some last minute adjust-
ments in their strategy. Although they had subpoenaed

150 witnesses and had called only ten, the consensus among team members was that they should wrap up their case quickly. Feeling they had come a long way toward tearing down the prosecution's contentions, the defense team thought it would be better to leave well enough alone and not confuse the jury any further. But there was one big question remaining, one issue they felt they needed the remainder of the weekend to resolve: would Betty or Peggy or both be summoned to the stand?

At an all-day meeting on Sunday, Betty's four lawyers, Betty, Peggy, and her two lawyers wrestled with the question. Both Betty and Peggy said they would be willing to testify if their lawyers thought it would help.

It was a delicate situation, especially as far as Betty was concerned. Prosecution witnesses had painted her as a calculating, cruel person, a harridan who repeatedly cuckolded her husband and cared little about who knew it. *If* Betty was called as a witness, her lawyers could, through a carefully constructed series of questions, bring out her better qualities. On the other hand, that also would expose her to Fry's cross-examination, and the prosecutor would be free to delve more deeply into situations that other witnesses had simply alluded to. He could, for example, question her in painful detail about a whole string of affairs, none of which had been publicly mentioned so far in the trial.

But one thing the prosecution had *not* done, Betty's lawyers felt, was build a convincing case against her as a murderess. And in the long run, that was all that counted. She could have the worst reputation in town as long as she was not legally branded a killer. If they called her as a witness, they asked themselves, would they simply be exposing her to a devastating and embarrassing examination by Fry for no reason. If the prosecution had not proved its case against her beyond a reasonable doubt—and they leaned strongly toward the belief that Fry had not—there was no need to call her.

One team member who dissented from this view was Marc Sandlin, the former prosecutor turned defense attorney. He had never been involved in a case, he maintained, in which his client did *not* take the stand. It was important for the defendant to testify, he felt, if only to show jurors that they were passing judgment on a real human being. Jurors, he believed, could hear all the testimony they could stand *about* Betty, but that meant little until they had a chance to actually listen to her describe events in her own words. Even if Fry were to tear her apart, Sandlin argued, it was vital for the panel members to judge her for themselves.

The lawyers turned to Betty. How did she feel about it?

Betty shrugged. "I'll do whatever you think I should," she said. "I'll go along with your decision."

They put their heads together again. It was important, they agreed, that the jurors hear from *someone* directly involved in the case. If Betty was too vulnerable, they asked themselves, how about Peggy, whose personal reputation was spotless? In many ways, she could be just as effective. Because of the close relationship that existed between the sisters, and because Peggy was actually *the* connection with White, Peggy could testify just as effectively about events connected to the murder as Betty, plus she was not saddled with Betty's personal baggage. The downside was what it might do to Peggy. *She* was not on trial, and her lawyer, Johnson, might feel that it would be exposing her to unnecessary danger. Anything she said at Betty's trial presumably could be used against her later, when and if she was tried. If Fry could break her down, it might not only hurt Betty, it might prove detrimental to her own case.

"It's fine with me," Peggy replied when presented with the options. "If it's okay with my lawyer, I'll be willing to take the stand."

Betty's team conferred with Johnson, and the decision

was made: Monday would be family day for the defense. Peggy's husband, Wayne, would be the first witness, followed by Betty's youngest son, Trey, then Peggy. They would leave the option of calling Betty open until after Peggy testified. If they felt it was necessary they could always call her then. But if Peggy proved credible and Fry did not wound her too badly on cross-examination they could put their case to bed.

TWENTY-FOUR

SENSING THAT THE TRIAL WAS NEARING its end, the number of would-be spectators, afraid the show was going to close before they could see it, increased dramatically after the weekend recess. Despite overcast skies, a forecast of showers, and temperatures in the forties, those anxious to get inside began lining up on the courthouse steps even before the doors to the building opened at six. Reporters showing up at seven for the session scheduled to start at eight-thirty found themselves hopelessly stuck at the end of a long queue. Taking up more than two dozen spaces at the head of the line—enough to fill roughly one-fourth of the available courtroom seats—were members of two high school classes, who had been transported to the building in the predawn darkness in a pair of yellow buses. Left standing in the hallway for the morning session of what promised to be one of the most dramatic and crucial days of the trial were newsmen from the Associated Press and the *New York Times,* plus a handful of representatives from local TV and radio stations.

Even under those conditions, Judge Younger refused to modify his edict and guarantee media access to his courtroom. His attitude hardly surprised those who had been watching him in action on a daily basis. From the beginning, Younger had proved himself in the eyes of many observers to be a diminutive despot with little but contempt for everyone within his perceived jurisdiction, which included not only the media, but the lawyers trying the case as well. Sometimes, it seemed, he even went out of his way to make it clear that *he* was in charge and that anyone who crossed him would do so at his own peril. Early in the trial, for example, when Cook's cross-examination of White had been going on for almost ninety minutes, Cook found himself at a point where he had exhausted one avenue and was ready to begin on another complicated tack, one that would take up considerable time once he got involved. Glancing up at the clock, Cook noted that it was six minutes before noon. Turning to Younger, Cook explained his situation and suggested that the judge might like to call the lunch break five minutes early. Younger peeked over the bench and shot Cook a cold stare. "We'll go until noon," he said icily, forcing Cook to backpedal and stall for time to kill the remaining five minutes.

Those who managed to get seats in the courtroom that morning were far from disappointed in the spectacle. Wayne Lowe, looking spiffy in a new suit and a whiter-than-white starched shirt, was called first. Appearing every inch the aging innocent—a naive, country-boy music teacher caught up in a situation that was beyond the scope of his imagination—he proved to be soft-spoken, polite, and deferential, calmly confirming that his twenty-year marriage to Peggy was as solidly rooted as the well-known statue of the foundry worker that towers over nearby Birmingham.

When he was called to the stand, a sort of electrical current swept through the courtroom. Spectators, some of whom had been standing in line since dawn to get inside, hoped for some titillating testimony, some explanation of how it felt to be married to a woman who allegedly helped engineer her brother-in-law's murder and was accused of having flirted, at least at one time, with the idea of having *him* murdered.

But if that was what spectators were expecting, they were deeply disappointed. Wayne Lowe's testimony proved lackluster, pedestrian, and benign. He was on and off the stand in a matter of minutes, and neither the defense lawyers nor Fry questioned him about White's testimony that he had sex with his wife. Exactly why the defense called him was not clear, since his contact with Betty was only superficial and he had barely exchanged more than a few sentences with James White.

Fry barely acknowledged Lowe's presence, apparently figuring he had nothing to gain by aggressively attacking him since his wife was not on trial, and anything he might have to say about Betty was inconsequential.

Following Lowe as a defense witness—and potentially a much more revealing one—was Trey Taylor, the youngest of Betty's three sons. A tall, thin youth with a prematurely receding hairline and horn-rimmed spectacles, Trey looked and sounded uncomfortable about being called to the stand. After being released rather quickly by Betty's lawyers, Trey turned and stared defiantly at Fry.

Under the prosecutor's questioning, Trey denied that there was anything suspect about his decision to leave early on his trip to Florida the morning Jack was killed. It was simply a spur of the moment action that seemed like a good idea at the time, he said truculently. He had cleared it with Jack and anyone who suggested that it might have stemmed from advance knowledge of an impending attack on his stepfather was mistaken. He also denied a claim by an earlier witness, Jo Ann Chiri, that made him appear vengeful toward Jack.

According to Chiri, she had been collecting donations from the office staff for a birthday gift for Jack when she got to Trey. When she asked him what he would like to contribute, Chiri said, the youth raised the middle finger of his right hand, made a sweeping upward gesture and said, "You can give him this for me."

That never happened, the youth testified.

Wayne Lowe and Trey Taylor, however, were the warm-up acts for the star of the day. Their testimony had taken some two hours, so it was about 10:45 when Peggy appeared in answer to the bailiff's summons. Clad demurely in a black long-sleeved dress with broad white cuffs and a white Peter Pan collar, Peggy looked pale and vulnerable as she marched to the witness stand, flashing a quick, cheerless smile at Betty as she passed her chair. Despite her fragile appearance, her voice was strong and clear as she began answering Cook's artfully phrased and delicately put questions.

Under Cook's gentle guidance, Peggy explained that she and her first husband, Ken Godfrey, had been married for nine years and had two children before they divorced and Peggy married Wayne Lowe.

Wayne, she said, adopted the two children she had by Godfrey, and together they had one other child, a daughter named Stephanie, then fifteen.

"Wayne and I have always had a very loving relationship," she said, speaking so softly that spectators in the rear of the room had to lean forward to catch her words. "We have sent two children to college and we have worked hard. But," she added, "our family is our life; [the children, and their only grandchild] are the center of our universe."

"And what is the relationship that you and Wayne have had with the community?" Cook asked.

"Well," Peggy replied easily, "as long as Wayne and I have been married, we have been in church work."

Cook's obvious aim was to underscore how different Peggy's life was from that of the man accusing her and her sister of conspiring to murder Jack Wilson, and to prove to the jury the absolute ludicrousness of White's claim that Peggy took him into her bed. But to make sure the jurors had not been asleep during the opening statements and that they understood her situation, Cook spelled it out.

"You are also indicted for the offense of murder, aren't you?" he asked.

"Yes, I am," Peggy replied, dipping her gaze.

"In the same type of indictment as your sister?" Cook persisted.

"Yes, sir," Peggy whispered.

With the background laid, Cook deftly made the transition to a more sensitive subject: the murder itself. Instead of continuing with a chronological illumination of her life, leading to how and when she met White, Cook skipped dramatically ahead to the day after Jack's slaying, eliciting from Peggy the information that she had learned of the incident through a telephone call from Betty early on Saturday morning, May 23.

"And what did you do upon learning of his death?" Cook prompted, his tone indicating he would prefer a long response to a brief one.

Peggy obliged, tearfully detailing how she had been shocked by the news and not altogether certain that she had understood what her sister had told her.

"I went into the kitchen and I asked Wayne to come in the kitchen and sit down for a minute," she said. "And we sat down at the table and I told him that Betty had called and that she was very erratic and that she was crying, but that I had understood her to say that something had happened to Jack; that I thought she said that Jack was dead.

"Wayne and Linda Vascocu," she sobbed, pausing to wipe her eyes, "helped me put a few things in a bag, and I left and drove to Huntsville."

Once she got to the city, she continued, she became caught up in a series of events that left her puzzled, frustrated, wounded, and angry.

Painting a much different picture of her encounters

with investigators Brantley and Renfroe than had been presented so far, Peggy detailed how she, after watching as Betty was taken away for questioning within minutes of the memorial service for Jack, was herself summoned for the first of what would prove to be several interrogation sessions.

That night she was at the home of her sister and brother-in-law, Gedell and Dean Cagle, she said, when there was a knock at the door. It was about nine o'clock. Answering it, she was confronted by two police officers who asked her to go with them, presumably to the same place where officers had taken Betty earlier. "They told me that they wanted to take me down to the police station for some elimination fingerprints."

First, she said, they took her to a room where she was fingerprinted. After that, she thought, they were going to return her to the Cagles'. When they got to the elevator, one of the officers told her that she also was to be questioned.

They went to a second building, she said, where she was taken into an empty office and told to wait. Eventually, a man who she later learned was Investigator Harry Renfroe, came in and sat at the desk across from her. " 'Mrs. Lowe,' " she quoted him as saying, " 'tell me about James Dennison White.' "

At first, Peggy said earnestly, she did not know who Renfroe was talking about because she had never heard White's middle name. "And I said, 'James *Dennison* . . .' but before I could even get it out, he said, 'Oh, come on, Mrs. Lowe, you know, the man you hired to kill Jack.' "

In the retelling, Peggy's eyes widened and she looked uncomfortable, as if she were again sitting in the sterile office in the Huntsville Police Department.

"And I said," she continued dramatically, " 'Mr. White is a carpenter.' And he said, 'You are a terrible actress.' And he said, 'James'—he called him James—

'James is in the next room and your sister is in another room, and we have put them both together and they told us—they have confessed—that they killed Jack, and they have both fingered you.' "

"And what did you say?" Cook interjected softly.

"I said, 'That's impossible . . .' And I said, 'Well, I would like for you to bring him in here and say that to my face,' " she recounted spunkily. "And he said, 'You are going to get your wish in a minute. We are going to bring you, and we are going to bring Betty, and we are going to put all three of you in here and you are going to get a chance with Mr. White . . .' "

She soon learned, she recounted bitterly, that it was a bluff, that White had not yet arrived in Huntsville from Vincent.

At the time, however, Renfroe told her they were going to give her a polygraph test that would prove she was lying. "And I said, 'Okay.' And he said, 'When we hook you up to that lie detector test in a minute that needle is going to go all the way off the end of the screen.' And I just kind of nodded my head. I said, 'Okay.' And he said, 'Every bone in little Jackie's body is broken, and it's your fault.' And I said, 'His name is not Jackie.' "

Renfroe kept her at the police station that night until almost midnight, she said. Finally, Betty was brought into the room where she was being questioned, and the two of them were told they could go home. But before they left, she said, Renfroe cautioned them not to relate what they had been talking about. " 'I don't want you girls to say a word about what went on here tonight,' " she quoted him as saying. " 'Nobody knows what was said here tonight except the three of us.' "

A few minutes later, Peggy said, she and Betty were back at the Cagles' preparing to retire. Betty had changed into a pair of pajamas and they were just about to climb into bed when there was another knock at the door. It was Renfroe, the investigator whose office she had left not long before.

"He said he wanted to see us again," Peggy recounted. "So we went into the den, and he said, 'You girls come with me. I want to see if we can do something.'"

They climbed into a police car, Peggy said, and drove with Renfroe to the parking lot of a convenience store. Renfroe turned to her and said, "'Damn, Peggy, it looks like you're going to get your wish . . . They are bringing James White in, and with a little luck we can intercept the car and you will get to see him face-to-face.'"

They sat there for about twenty minutes, Peggy recounted, before Renfroe made another comment. "'Well,'" she quoted him as saying, "'it looks like it's not going to work out.' And he took us back home."

When Peggy related how Renfroe had cautioned them not to say anything about what they had discussed in the police station, several jurors nodded understandingly. Later that night, over dinner, some of the panel members discussed the implications of that simple statement. Although Judge Younger had warned them not to talk about the case among themselves until they were ready to begin deliberations, they had decided to commit a minor infraction of his order. Since they were sequestered and were prohibited contact with anyone outside the group, they quickly learned there was little they *could* discuss except the event in which they were all participating. Except for the trial, they had almost nothing in common. Rather than passing their meals in silence, they fell into a common understanding that some discussion of the day's activities, while not technically proper, was infinitely more practical.

Earlier, one of the jurors said later, the group had been mightily impressed by Cagle's testimony. They had considered it particularly significant when the twins' brother-in-law recounted the women's peculiar behavior on the morning that White's arrest was announced in the *Huntsville Times*. But what Peggy had said put her brother-in-law's testimony in a different light. The twins had acted strangely, jurors were now certain, because Cagle's "news" had not been news at all to them; they had known since the previous night that White had been arrested in connection with Jack's death and that they were being accused.

But that was only one facet of the impact of Peggy's testimony. At that point in the direct examination, Cook was barely getting warmed up. He had a long road to travel with Peggy, and the journey was just beginning.

TWENTY-FIVE

THE PREVIOUS SATURDAY, SQUEEZED BE-
tween David Williamson and John Self, the defense had
called an accountant named Ross Melvin, who had testified about a conversation with Betty soon after Jack's
murder. Melvin, who had handled Jack's financial matters, said that Betty and a man named Gene Montgomery had come to his office, and Betty had asked his
advice on what to do, financially speaking, in the wake of
Jack's murder. Although he was imprecise about the day
the meeting took place, he said it was within a day or so
after the memorial service for Jack and before Betty was
charged. During that meeting, Melvin said, he had suggested to Betty that she set up a separate bank account
for the estate from which she could pay the couple's
outstanding bills. He also recommended that she open
her own personal account separate from the joint account that she and Jack had. Plus, he added, he had
advised her to begin thinking about selling Jack's medical practice.

The defense had wanted the jury to hear Melvin to
counter an impression left by the prosecution that Betty
had been acting avariciously when she opened a separate
bank account soon after the slaying, as if she were overly
anxious to get her hands on Jack's money. Melvin had at

least partially countered that implication, but his testimony opened another door the defense now had to slam shut: Who was Gene Montgomery and what was he doing with Betty? The prosecution also had pointed out that when Betty was arrested on Thursday, May 28, less than a week after Jack's death, she had been picked up at Montgomery's apartment. And when she was taken away in handcuffs, she had been wearing Montgomery's pajama bottoms and one of his monogrammed dress shirts.

Since Betty's affinity for men other than her husband was a major underlying theme in the prosecution's case, the defense team wanted to try to erase the notion that Betty had a whole *army* of lovers. They couldn't do anything about Erroll Fitzpatrick, but they didn't want the jury to make any assumptions about Montgomery. To accomplish that, they used Peggy to suggest that the Montgomery connection had been totally innocent.

Montgomery, Peggy explained, was someone who Betty "knew socially" and was someone she felt she could trust. Not wishing to return to the house where Jack was murdered, Betty and Peggy had been staying with the Cagles since the night of the killing. By the middle of the next week, however, they were beginning to feel cramped, so the twins went to stay with Montgomery. They had spent the night there on Wednesday, May 22, the day after the encounter with investigators. The next morning, Thursday, they had been using Montgomery's facilities to wash their clothes when Brantley and Renfroe arrived to arrest them. That, Peggy said, was the reason Betty had been wearing Montgomery's clothing.

On the way to Montgomery's earlier in the day, they had passed a van emblazoned with the call letters of a local TV station, Peggy said, and they were certain the reporter was looking for them. That was why they did not answer the door when they heard a knock; they were sure it was the news crew. When there was another knock a few minutes later, Montgomery peered through his drapes. " 'This is not the TV station,' " Peggy quoted him as saying. " 'This man has handcuffs on.' "

While Montgomery went to open the door, Peggy ran to the telephone and tried to call Betty's lawyer, Charlie Hooper. He was not there, Peggy related, but she talked to one of his colleagues, who told them that they would have to go with the investigators. At that time, she said, Renfroe and Brantley "just kind of pushed the door back and came in."

Renfroe, she said, walked over to Betty and grabbed her arm. Slipping his hand under the band on her watch, the policeman "tore it off her arm and slung it on the floor." He said, she quoted, " 'You are not going to need that where you are going.' "

Reluctantly, she added, the investigators allowed her to put on a pair of gym shoes before they took her and Betty away in handcuffs, but "they wouldn't even let Betty put on clothes."

The next day, she continued, after spending the night in jail, she and Betty were chained together with White and taken into court for a preliminary hearing.

"You were chained with Mr. White?" Cook interjected dramatically, feigning disbelief.

"Yes, sir," Peggy said, nodding vigorously.

"I told Betty," she continued, "that's Mr. White. And she said, 'Is that the man who killed Jack?' And I said, 'Yes.' "

Using that passage to reintroduce White, Cook skillfully segued into a new series of questions designed to elicit Peggy's version of her relationship with the handyman. Not surprisingly, Peggy's version was radically different from White's.

Although her description of the *way* in which they met —that White had been doing some carpentry work for a teacher in an adjoining room at the school—was identical to White's, the tale then took a completely different path.

While White had claimed that Peggy had been friendly from the first, receptive to his attempts to find a shoulder to cry on, Peggy claimed that she had been cool and distant and had tried to keep the relationship on a purely professional basis.

Cook interrupted her. Leaning over the lectern with a stern expression on his face, he said portentously, "Let me ask you a question at this point. Have you ever, *ever in your life,* had any sexual relationship with or intimacy with James Dennison White?"

Peggy stared the defense attorney in the eye. "Absolutely not!" she said emphatically.

"Have you ever at any time in your whole life, since you have known James White, from August of 1991 until the time he was placed in jail, kissed him, or has he kissed you, or anything which would even remotely indicate that had happened," Cook asked.

"No, sir! No, sir!" she said flatly, adding that it would have been virtually impossible for her to have been involved in a relationship such as White described even if she had wanted to, because her husband's classroom was just down the hall from hers and they ate lunch together every day during the period that White was working at their school, along with Stephanie.

Cook nodded in satisfaction, urging her to continue.

White, she said, resuming her narrative, told her he didn't expect to be paid for his work at the school because his children were students there. But since, White said, his wife had run off with one of his friends and he was a bachelor again, he was hungry for a home-cooked meal.

"At that time I was real busy," Peggy said coyly, "and I remember saying, 'Yeah, my husband would like a home-cooked meal, too.'"

"I would, too." Cook smiled.

"We just weren't getting very many of them then," Peggy responded, smiling tightly in return. In any case, she added, she and the other teacher discussed the situation. "But neither one of us wanted to invite him home to eat it, but what we could do was bring it to the school."

In the end, Peggy said, the other teacher gave him some money and her principal promised her that White would be paid for the work he had done in her room. He never got the promised meal.

After that period of work, which took less than a week in August of 1991, she said, she had no further contact with White until December, when he again showed up at the school to build some choir risers for her husband's music room.

Although she saw him once or twice around the school, she had no personal contact with him until after Christmas, when White's son, who was a student at the school, delivered a note to her from White. It was a request for work, she said.

"I showed Wayne the note and we determined then that we would call him and try to help him," she said.

Eventually, sometime in February, she believed, White came to her house and he and Wayne worked out a schedule for him to do some carpentry. Another month went by, she added, before he actually did the work.

Late one afternoon toward the end of March, she testified, White showed up at her house with his daughter and asked if he could come inside to measure an area in which he was supposed to work. Before he left, he pulled Peggy aside and told her he was in deep trouble financially and asked her if she could give him an advance toward the work he had promised to do. She wrote him a check for $150. She also arranged, she said, for White to pour a concrete driveway for Wayne's mother in Birmingham, for which he was paid $960 in cash. The defense hoped this would explain where White got the money that the prosecution witness said he used toward his loans and child support.

"Why were you and Wayne doing that for Mr. White?" Cook prompted.

"We were trying to help him," Peggy replied. "He seemed like he was just a pitiful little man, and he seemed to be making an honest effort."

It was not long after that, she said, that a new side of White's personality surfaced. He began calling her on the telephone, she said, and telling her how despondent he was over his situation. "He was telling me that several times over the past few months he had tried to commit suicide," Peggy said. Quoting him, she said, " 'My wife has left me. She has taken my babies. I have lost my friend. They have deceived me. They were having an affair right under my nose. I have lost my friend. I have lost my wife. I have lost my children,' " he said, referring to the fact that his children had decided to go live with their mother rather than with him.

On top of that, she added, White told her that he was not able to make enough money to keep up with his child support or pay his bills.

When she asked him if he had tried to talk to anyone about his circumstances, White told her that he had been to see his pastor, who was also his former brother-in-law, a man to whom he had earlier lent some money. " 'I asked him to pay back the money,' " Peggy quoted White as telling her, " 'and he said that he couldn't or he wouldn't.' And he said, 'You know what I'm going through; you know my wife has left me.' And he said his pastor just laughed at him and said, 'You are lucky. If my old lady left me, I would be glad.' "

He also told her, Peggy continued, about how he had discovered when he was a child that he was a bastard, and about how he had to drop out of school and go to work when he was very young. "He was very angry, very hurt," Peggy said. "He was just a pitiful, pitiful man."

By April, she said, White's emotional condition was deteriorating and his telephone calls were becoming more frequent. But it was not until May, she said, that the situation reached a crisis.

"He contacted me and he said that this was the day he was going to [commit suicide] and that he just wanted to tell me good-bye because I had been the only person who had been kind to him and had tried to help him without asking anything in return from him. He was telling me that he was afraid that he was going to start drinking, that he had had a serious drinking problem in the past and that he was afraid that with his life caving in the way it was . . . he was afraid he was going to start drinking."

It was at that point, she added, that she made the mental connection between White's situation and a similar situation that Betty had gone through before she joined Alcoholics Anonymous.

"I told him that I was hearing him say the kinds of things that I had heard my sister say. I began to tell him that she was an alcoholic—a recovering alcoholic—that she had been sober at that time for over five years, and that she had found help. For the past five years," Peggy said she told White, "her sister's sobriety had saved her life."

A month or so earlier, she backtracked, she had suggested to White that he might want to leave Vincent and move to Huntsville, where he would have a better chance of finding work. To help him get started, she was sure that Betty would hire him to help her redecorate her kitchen, and that would help him solve the immediate problem of finding work in a strange city. She told him, she said, to contact Betty and Jack. "I told him they had plenty of money and they had a lot of work they wanted done."

After telling White that, she testified, she contacted Betty and told her that she had given her name to a man

who was looking for work. "I told her I didn't know at
the time if he were [sic] an alcoholic, but I just told her I
knew he had had some drinking problems in his past,
and that he was really, really emotionally drained. And I
said to her, 'Betty, I'm hearing him say the same things
to me that I heard you say, and I want to know if I
suggest to him that he come to your house and work, if
you would be willing to help him?' And she said, 'You
know I would.' "

Soon after that, she continued, there was the annual
AA meeting at Guntersville State Park for alcoholics and
their families. Betty had invited her to attend, Peggy
said, but she did not think she would be able to go.

"On Saturday morning," she said, "it must have been
the sixteenth [of May], Mr. White called. And this was
the particular day that he told me that nobody was there
to stop him [from committing suicide]. And that's when
he told me that he wanted to tell me 'bye."

After she talked to White, she called Betty. "I told her
about the conversation and asked her if I could persuade
him to go [to the AA meeting], if she would help him."
She repeated that she would. So Peggy talked to White
again and told him that her sister would help him if he
would drive to Guntersville and meet her at the convention.

"He said," she quoted him, " 'I don't even have
enough gas money to get to Guntersville.' And I said,
'Well, Mr. White, if you could just come up with enough
change or something to get gas money, then I know
Betty would help you. She would help you stay somewhere, stay there or somewhere for the weekend to go to
the [AA] meeting.' "

Acting as intermediary between Betty and White,
Peggy said she called Betty back and tried to make arrangements for the two to meet. But Betty told her that
she might be hard to find at the meeting, so she told

Peggy that she would put some money in her car for White.

"Did she say where she would put it?" Cook asked.

Peggy nodded. "I think she said she would put it in a book or something. Leave it on the front seat of her car."

When she told White this, she said, he asked her how *much* money Betty was going to leave.

"And I said, 'Well, I don't know. I didn't discuss that with her, but Betty is generous and she likes to help people, and I know that whatever she puts there will be sufficient for you."

The next time she heard from him, she said, was several hours later when he called her from a convenience store near the state park, complaining that he had not been able to get through the gate to pick up the money from Betty's car. "He was real panicky," she added.

She told him to keep trying to reach Betty, and she assumed he had made contact because she did not hear any more until the next day when Betty called. She, Wayne, and Stephanie had just returned from church, she said, when the phone rang and Betty was on the other end. " 'Tell me that so-and-so's number,' " she quoted Betty. "And I said, 'What so-and-so are you talking about?' She said, 'Mr. White. I left money in my car for him and he had me paged and I got the money to him, and to my knowledge he didn't have the courtesy to stay for the meeting, or if he did, he never identified himself to me.' " Betty also was angry at White, Peggy added, because he had never shown up earlier to begin the work he was supposed to do in her kitchen.

When she talked to White later, he told her that he did not go to the meeting because he felt out of place.

The next contact she had with White, she said, was on Tuesday, May 19, three days after the Guntersville incident. Still feeling sorry for him, she said she had told him that she and Wayne were cleaning out their basement and he was welcome to the material that they were getting rid of. If he couldn't use it, she said, he might be able to take it to a flea market and sell it. Tuesday was the day that she and Stephanie stopped to fill a prescription for Stephanie. When they got home late that afternoon, White was at the house loading the material from the basement. While he was still there, Stephanie took the medication and suffered a severe reaction. After calling their doctor, Peggy rushed away with Stephanie to take her to the hospital for emergency treatment. When they returned about midnight, White was long gone.

The next day, Wednesday, May 20, she stayed home with Stephanie, and Betty drove down from Huntsville to visit her ill niece. That evening, Stephanie asked her to get her a movie and some ice cream, so she and Betty got into Betty's BMW and drove to Vincent to pick up the items.

According to White, Cook interrupted, that was the evening that she and Betty met him at Logan Martin Dam to give him the pistol that he was supposed to use to kill Jack. "Is that the truth?" he asked.

"It is absolutely false!" Peggy insisted.

"Did Betty bring a gun with her?" Cook asked. "Did she bring this pistol that was registered in her name and say, 'We've got to go out and meet James White and give it to him?' "

"No, sir!" Peggy responded.

How about the next day, Cook asked. Did she hear from White then?

Yes, Peggy replied, he called her early that morning and asked her to call him back because he was at a pay phone and he could not afford to pay for the call. When she rang the number back, she said, White told her that he was in Huntsville and he was ready to start the work at Betty's house. She told him she didn't think Betty wanted him to work for her anymore, but she put Betty on the phone so she could tell him that herself. "And I think at that point I handed Betty the phone and she pretty much told him she was not interested in him doing her work."

Soon afterward, she said, Betty left to return to Huntsville because she wanted to attend the Tim Morgan fundraiser that night.

The next day, the day Jack was killed, Peggy said she again stayed home with Stephanie. The two drove to Vincent to return the movies they had rented on Wednesday night, went shopping in Talladega, and stopped at the grocery store on the way home. "My Sunday school class was coming for breakfast on Saturday morning and we were real busy getting the food and things like that," she said.

When she paused, Cook spoke up. "Mr. White," he said gently, "in some of his statements, says that you wanted him to kill your husband. Is that true or is that false?"

"That's false," Peggy replied quickly.

"In some of his statements he refers to setting up a boating accident. When is the first time that you or your husband ever owned a boat?"

"Just a few days before Jack was killed," Peggy said.

In response to additional questions, Peggy also denied giving White $2500 as a down payment on Jack's murder.

"Have you at any time ever had any reason, any desire, or any design, or even intent of harming or hurting your husband or Jack Wilson?" Cook asked.

"Absolutely not."

"Have you ever entered into any type of agreement, either expressly or implied, with James White to commit murder upon Jack Wilson or to do him any harm whatsoever?"

"No, sir," she answered.

Cook nodded slowly, smiling beatifically, like a piano teacher whose prize pupil had just worked through a flawless recital. "Mr. Fry will ask you questions," he said softly. "Answer them as best that you can."

TWENTY-SIX

COOK'S INTENTION HAD BEEN TO KEEP
Peggy on the stand for approximately as long as White
had testified during his direct examination. When he finished, she had been answering questions for an hour and
forty-five minutes. White's direct examination had taken
two hours. It was about as close to equal time as the
defense could get. But they probably could double that if
Betty testified as well. The big difference, though, between the time Peggy and White spent on the stand was
in cross-examination. While Cook had pounded at White
for more than four hours, Fry's cross-examination of
Peggy was amazingly brief.

As he rose slowly to his feet to begin his grilling, Fry
considered his options. He could rant and rave, as Drake
and Hooper had with his witnesses. Or he could rip
Peggy with sarcasm and ridicule, as Cook had done with
White. Or he could follow his own style and firmly point
out what he considered the illogic of some of the things
she had said. He was not interested in attacking Peggy
personally. It was Betty who was on trial, he wanted to
emphasize, not her twin sister.

Studying Peggy, who was staring back at him defiantly,
her jaw firmly set and her chin high, he decided that he
would probe only into the areas that dealt directly with

Peggy's credibility in an attempt to show that it was White, not Peggy, who had given a more realistic description of the relationship that existed between them. At the same time, he realized that he might have to treat her roughly in the process. The trick was in avoiding the excesses that seemed to be the hallmark of the defense's case up to that point. He began inoffensively enough, asking her if White's description of how they had met had been more or less accurate.

She agreed that it had been.

And had White been correct when he said that he had done some work at her house?

Yes, she conceded reluctantly.

And the telephone relationship? Fry asked. That had been initiated by White as he had said, had it not?

"Yes," she confirmed.

"Okay," Fry nodded. "And y'all had many conversations, didn't you?"

"We sure did," she replied.

"In fact," he added, "didn't you tell Officer Harry Renfroe at one time that you might have talked to [White] thousands of times?"

"Well," Peggy said hesitantly, "thousands of times is a figure of speech."

"You and James White talked to each other quite a bit in April and May of last year, didn't you?" he asked.

Peggy nodded, agreeing that they had. Then she added: "But you are going by my phone records, and not every time Mr. White called my house did he talk to me."

Fry nodded at the reasonableness of her comment. "He talked to other people, too, then?" he asked.

"Sure," she agreed.

"And you talked to him sometimes for hours at a time?"

"Sometimes I did, yes," she admitted.

Satisfied that he had made his point, the prosecutor

turned to the next major claim White had made, which
Peggy had denied under questioning by Cook: that she
had sex with White on the Friday before Jack's murder.
Knowing she would deny it again if he asked her directly,
Fry decided to back into the question, leaving it to the
jurors to work out for themselves whose version to believe.

Had she indeed remained home from school that day,
Fry asked Peggy, and had she been there alone?

She said she had taken the day off because she had a
dental appointment. Stephanie had gone to school and
Wayne was teaching, so, yes, she was alone.

On the next night, Saturday, had she talked to White?
"When he says he called you from Guntersville at ten-
seventeen on that Saturday night, that's the truth, isn't
it?"

"Yes," Peggy replied.

Fry bobbed his head. "Now it's a fact, is it not, to go
from Vincent from where you live, the fastest way is to
go across the Logan Martin Dam?"

"That's the fastest way," she conceded, agreeing that
was the route she and Betty took on Wednesday evening
when White said he met them, and Peggy dropped
Betty's pistol on the seat of his truck. Again Fry did not
ask her directly if she had met with White, as White had
said, because Cook already had asked her that. What Fry
wanted the jury to note was that she and Betty were
exactly where White had said they were.

Progressing to Thursday, the day before Jack's murder, Fry asked Peggy if it was not true that she had called
White at a pay phone in Huntsville and talked to him for
almost ten minutes.

"He asked me if I would call him back at that number
and I did," Peggy responded, once more confirming what
White had said.

"Now," Fry said, plodding ahead, "you say you didn't
talk to James White anymore after that, is that right?"

Peggy began her reply by saying that she had talked to White when he was in Guntersville when Fry interrupted her. He was talking about Thursday, he said, the day before Jack was killed, not the previous Saturday.

Peggy paused. "I don't remember," she said.

Fry toughened his approach. "I thought you answered Mr. Cook's question that after you talked to him that Thursday morning on the telephone, you didn't talk to him anymore," he commented.

"The telephone calls are just kind of . . ." Peggy began, becoming flustered. "I mean, they just sort of run together." Trying to turn the tables on the prosecutor, she asked him sharply, "Do you know who you talked to yesterday?"

"I sure do," Fry shot back.

"That wasn't a year ago," Peggy replied feistily.

"Well, Mrs. Lowe," Fry said firmly, "you have had a pretty good memory on everything else here this morning—"

"I have tried," she interjected.

"—but you don't remember the phone calls. You remember the one from the phone booth that morning, but you don't remember getting two that night before nine o'clock?"

"From where?" she asked.

Fry knew he was belaboring the phone call angle at the risk of having jurors lose interest. At the same time, he felt the phone records were probably the most crucial items in the defense presentation. They were incontrovertible proof that there was a surfeit of contact among White, Peggy, and Betty, that the records of the calls were the heart of what made White's story credible.

"From Mr. White," Fry replied patiently.

"From where from Mr. White?" Peggy asked, stalling.

"From Huntsville."

"No," Peggy said flatly, finally replying directly to the prosecutor's original question about whether she re-

membered talking to White in Huntsville on the night
before Jack was killed.

"Well," Fry persisted, anxious to clarify the issue forever, "did anyone else at your house talk to Mr. White
that night?"

"If they did, they didn't tell me," Peggy replied.

"They probably would have, wouldn't they?" Fry
asked, becoming frustrated with her evasiveness.
"Wouldn't you expect them to tell you if they talked to
Mr. White?"

"Not necessarily," Peggy replied, still dodging the
question. "Mr. White called our house a lot."

The prosecutor was getting weary of the cat-and-
mouse game. Would she, he asked, like to offer an explanation for the records that showed there were two phone
calls from the Ramada Inn to her house that night?

She, too, may have been tired of the contest. "I did not
talk to Mr. White Thursday night," she said emphatically.

Despite the trouble he was having getting her to answer directly, Fry was pleased with the way the cross-
examination was going. Although her responses were reluctant and vague, she had conceded every point that he
had tried to make in drawing the parallels between what
White had said and what she would admit to. While she
denied the details of White's testimony, her answers indicated that his statement was plausible. Before winding
up, Fry also wanted to try to demonstrate that the trans-
fer of two hundred dollars from Betty to White was unlikely to have occurred under the circumstances that
Peggy had described. But since he was not able to come
right out and call her a liar, Fry had to try to get Peggy to
admit that her version was improbable.

Reminding her that it was her contention that Betty
had agreed to give money to a man she had never met by
leaving cash for him inside a book in her car, which was

parked in a lot at a state park, Fry asked Peggy if she did not think that was rather odd.

Peggy shook her head. "Betty didn't want to be confined to try to meet him someplace."

"Then why didn't she just leave it at the desk?" Fry asked. "Wouldn't it have been pretty simple to put money in an envelope and put 'Mr. White' on it, give it to the clerk and say, 'This gentleman is going to be by. Please give him this for me'?"

"Well, inevitably that's what happened," Peggy replied.

Fry stared at her. "Inevitably it *didn't* happen, did it?" he said, his voice rising. "There is no evidence of any money being put in an envelope at the desk. Wouldn't it have been pretty simple to make sure that Mr. White attended the meeting, to have made a reservation for him at the lodge? She could have done that, right?"

"She could have, I guess," Peggy replied.

"Okay," Fry said, "let me ask you this, Mrs. Lowe: We have a guy here that you and your sister want to help. He is basically a drunk, is that right?"

Peggy took exception to that, claiming she did not know if White was drinking.

Fry rephrased his question. "So he suggested to you that he had a drinking problem, is that fair to say?"

"Sometime in his past," Peggy responded, unwilling to give ground.

Fry ignored her reply. "Doesn't it seem a little odd to you that someone who has been in Alcoholics Anonymous for five or six years, who knows a lot about drunks, would give a drunk or someone with a problem like that cash money?"

"That's exactly why she would have done it," Peggy replied.

Fry looked incredulous. "So he could go out and buy beer?"

"No!" Peggy said firmly. "So he could get help at the meeting."

Fry stared at her for several seconds. I'm beating my head against the wall, he told himself. It was like arguing about the invincibility of the Crimson Tide with an Auburn fan. I think the jury understands what I'm trying to say, he thought; the best thing I can do is get the hell out. "No more questions," he said.

The defense team called a quick huddle. This was the time, if there was to be one, to call Betty to the stand. They agreed that Peggy's testimony had been exceptionally effective. They felt she had succeeded in giving a reasonable explanation for every major point in the prosecution's case. Additionally, they believed that Fry had made little or no headway in attacking Peggy's credibility. Besides, they asked themselves, what reasonable juror could look at White and at Peggy and have any doubts about who was telling the truth?

Just to be sure, they conferred with a quasisecret member of the team who was viewing the proceeding from an entirely different perspective. The man, whose name was never revealed, was a forensic psychologist who had been hired by Betty to play the role of simulated juror. His job was to sit anonymously in the courtroom every day and judge how the trial was progressing from the viewpoint of the jurors. He tried to ignore what he knew about the case and evaluate the evidence—as well as the performance of the lawyers—from a neutral position. His impression of Peggy was that she was *extremely* impressive. She's made your point, he told them.

That confirmed what they had already decided among themselves. As they say in the South, it was time to piss on the fire and call in the dogs. At 2:22 P.M. on Monday, March 1, six days after the trial started, the defense announced that its presentation was complete; Betty would not take the stand. They had called only a dozen witnesses, but they thought that was enough. When Judge Younger ordered a recess until the next day to give Fry a few extra hours to decide what, if anything, he planned to present in the way of rebuttal, the defense team was confident that Betty would soon be a free woman.

Remarkably, considering they had all sat through the same trial, Fry was equally confident of victory. That afternoon, after closeting himself with his single assistant, his lone investigator, and Brantley, he decided he would call only one rebuttal witness: Brantley. There were a couple of relatively minor points that Cook had raised during his cross-examination that the prosecutor wanted to straighten out for the jurors, and then he, too, would be ready to turn the case over to the jury.

TWENTY-SEVEN

THE LINE BEGAN FORMING OUTSIDE THE courtroom at five-thirty the next morning; by seven there were already enough people jamming the hallways to fill every available seat. Would-be spectators, bleary-eyed and smelling of Right Guard and Old Spice, clutched bags with Hardee's and McDonald's imprints, stuffed just full enough to provide an energy shot to get them through the tedium of standing for two and a half hours in the hopes of getting the chance to walk through the metal detector. The reward was the privilege of sitting on a hard wooden bench for three and a half hours until lunchtime, then rushing back into line to start the process anew. But this, they knew, would be the last day, the final opportunity to witness a high drama in which a woman's life was at stake.

Beginning the day before, the spectators had become testy. The demand for seats was so great that some were resorting to various stratagems to get in. Groups were sending one person to the courthouse to stand in line, then joining the queue at the last minute, adding four or five or six persons to an already swollen column. Those farther back in the echelon were angered by this practice, taking the position that anyone who wanted to get in had to do their own waiting.

On the last day, spectators set up their own barricades, a sort of vigilante vigilance. Anyone who was not already in line beyond that particular place was not allowed to pass, not even if they claimed that someone farther up was saving a spot for them. Successful line-breakers were reported to the hard-pressed deputies, who summarily ejected them.

Adding to the confusion that reigned in the narrow hallway were the television crews, floodlights blazing, who operated from a small, specially designated area against one wall, and a constant stream of "legally connected" observers who *were* given dispensation by Younger to jump the queue. These included courthouse employees, relatives of lawyers participating in the trial, family members of Jack and Betty, those who had already testified, Peggy's lawyers and investigators, and, seemingly, any lawyer within a day's drive.

Prominent among those who got special permission to enter was an Episcopal minister from Huntsville, the Reverend Mike Cleckler, who had counseled Betty when she was being held in the Madison County Jail. He had been selected as Betty's spiritual advisor because he was one of the few, if not the only, minister in the city with a law degree.

Soon after she was arrested, Betty complained that she did not want to share the normal jailhouse clerics with the other prisoners and was entitled to a clergyman of her own choice. Sheriff Joe Patterson denied her request, telling her that the only nonregulation visitors she would be allowed outside of anyone normally assigned to the jail were her lawyers. So she went shopping for a minister who also was an attorney. Cleckler fit the bill. He subsequently proved to be an excellent choice because he was known locally as a staunch liberal who could also serve as Betty's antiestablishment crier. He had not been Betty's advisor for long before he went to the local media with grievances alleging that Betty was being forced to use the same shower stall as a woman prisoner who had been diagnosed with AIDS, and that she had been forced to sit in the dark for an extended period after the bulb in her cell's overhead fixture burned out.

Once the spectators had settled down and Judge Younger took his seat behind the bench, barely visible from the rear of the courtroom, Fry called his only rebuttal witness, Investigator Mickey Brantley.

Compared to his earlier appearance, when he had been questioned extensively by Cook, Brantley went through the courtroom like a rocket. Fry had called him mainly to explain why the prosecution had not produced any evidence to show that White had been in Betty's car, as he claimed, for the trip to and from the Wilson house. Something like that is difficult to hide from modern crime technicians, who now have in their arsenal sophisticated new tests that perform with an amazing degree of exactitude. Devices and chemicals can now be used to uncover fingerprints and stains that formerly would have remained hidden; new microscopes can pinpoint minute particles of debris and tie them to suspects; and isolated threads of fiber almost too small for the naked eye to detect can be traced to specific items, which can further be traced to specific individuals. Sophisticated fiber evidence, in fact, was what tightened the noose around Wayne Williams and helped lead to his conviction as Atlanta's "child murderer," a case in which Cook, a Georgian, was well-versed. Given the scope of these new tools, it would not be unreasonable to expect that if White had been telling the truth about being twice in Betty's car, he would have left *something* behind for investigators to find: a hair, a fingerprint, a spot of dirt or grease, even a fiber from his jeans or his flannel shirt. But nothing was found. Cook claimed it was because White had never been in the car. Brantley said it was because technicians never got a chance to examine the car thoroughly.

Investigators had looked at the vehicle cursorily soon after the murder, but had released it to Betty almost immediately when she said she needed it to transport family members who would be arriving for Jack's memorial service. The day *after* the memorial service, Betty called him, Brantley said, and claimed she remembered that the car's trunk may have been ajar on the night of the murder, possibly indicating that someone—maybe Jack's murderer—had broken into it. When investigators went to get the vehicle for a detailed exam, they were notified that the car, on orders from Betty, had been cleaned inside and out, allegedly in preparation for the memorial service. Both the interior of the vehicle and the trunk had been thoroughly vacuumed, he said.

After Brantley's testimony, events slipped back into a rigidly preordained formula. All that remained was for the lawyers to make their summations, the judge to issue his instructions to the jury, and the jury to come up with its verdict.

The ritual invariably observed in U.S. courts is for the prosecutor to get the first and last word. Fry would begin the closing arguments, followed by Drake and Cook. Then the prosecutor would again take the stage. In their opening statements, the lawyers had given jurors an outline of the case and told them what they expected to prove during the trial. Closing arguments were the opposite side of the coin. During that procedure, the lawyers would explain what they thought they *had* proved, and point out the holes in the other side's case. As with the opening statements, they did not have to adhere strictly to fact, but were allowed to express opinions and suggest conclusions. Closing arguments, in effect, are sales pitches from the opposing camps.

As on the opening day of the trial, the participants were dressed more formally than they had been during

the long days of testimony. Appearing for the first time
en masse were members of both families. On the left side
of the courtroom, behind the prosecutor's table, were
Julia Wilson, Jack's first wife, and their three sons, Steve,
Perry, and Scott. Across the aisle, behind the defense
table, were Betty's mother and her second older sister,
Martha, both of whom had sat in the same spot every day
of the proceeding, and her three sons, Trey, Dink, and
Bo.

Nell Woods, Betty's mother, an attractive octogenarian with short gray hair and round, horn-rimmed glasses,
had sat stoically throughout the trial, smiling her support
at Betty whenever her daughter turned to glance in her
direction. Her second daughter, Martha, who accompanied her mother every day, also wore her brown hair
short and favored the same style of spectacles. Neither
woman showed a particular resemblance to either Betty
or Peggy, especially Betty, who had undergone extensive
plastic surgery over the years when she was married to
Jack.

By the same token, Betty's sons resembled their
mother only vaguely. Trey, because of his receding hairline, looked to be the oldest rather than the youngest,
while Dink, the oldest, looked to be the youngest, possibly because of his long, Elvis-style sideburns.

Betty sat quietly surrounded by her lawyers, resplendent in a turquoise jacket, a black turtleneck sweater,
and a black, high-collared blouse. Her hair color and
style, thanks to her imported attendant, had changed almost on a daily basis during the trial, from brunette to
deep red to dark with auburn streaks. For the final day,
her modified pageboy had returned to natural: brunette
with a puff of gray over her right brow. Although she
turned to wave and smile tightly at her family, she looked
grim and anxious.

In contrast, her attorneys seemed relaxed and confident, laughing and joking among themselves. The ten-

sion, always evident among lawyers before a trial, had disappeared because they all realized that the ceremony was complete; that they had done whatever could be done and the outcome was now up to the jury.

Absent from the courtroom was Peggy, who was quartered in a nearby motel, along with Wayne and their daughter, Stephanie, trying to pick up what they could from local news broadcasts.

Fry, wearing an undertaker-black suit with white shirt and dark tie, kicked off the final ceremony by rising slowly and taking a position in front of the jury box.

The first part of his summation was a carefully organized presentation he had been working on for weeks, since well before the trial ever began. It included material that he had available from the beginning, mainly personal observations about Betty and her lifestyle that he wanted to repeat to the jury. The second half of his final argument, which would follow Drake's and Cook's presentations, would include more topical detail, items that he had picked out during the trial, or information that countered what Drake and Cook might say.

"I'm asking you for justice," he began, speaking in a quiet, conversational tone, striving to reach out to jurors as individuals rather than as some amorphous body. "She," he said, turning to point at Betty, who stared blankly back at him, "had everything anyone could want. She had a Mercedes *and* a BMW. She had a maid who took her furs, all four of them, to the cleaners. But more was never enough. She wanted it *all,*" he said, his voice rising, "and she wanted it *now.* She wanted to wrap herself in it, to roll in it." And, he added, she did not want to wait until Jack died a natural death to enjoy those benefits.

"She lied to her husband about where she was," he continued. "She brought other men into her husband's house. Her whole life was a lie."

Fry likened Betty to a terrorist who was planning an

assassination. She "disassociated herself" from him, the
prosecutor argued, and she quit calling him by his name,
referring to him instead as "the old shitbag" and other
derogatory appellations, "because then it's easier to kill
him."

Switching abruptly to White, Fry painted him as one of
life's losers, "a guy whose dream is always bigger than his
search." The prosecutor slowly shook his head. "In the
fall of 1991, James Dennison White was not only down
and out," he said, "he was vulnerable. His family had left
him. He hurt physically, mentally, and morally." Fry
paused, his tone lightening slightly. "Besides," he said,
"he is not the brightest guy in the world."

It was at this point, the prosecutor contended, one of
the low points in White's existence, that some hope came
into his life. "Enter the schoolteacher!" Fry exclaimed.
The *only* thing connecting White, Betty, and Jack, he
argued, was Peggy Lowe.

"On the other hand," Fry continued, returning briefly
to the subject of Jack Wilson, "here was a man who was
good to his patients, a man who died because of someone else's greed and lust."

Assuming the speech pattern of a fundamentalist
preacher arguing in favor of biblical revelation, Fry
painstakingly laid out the points he wanted the jury to
remember:

"James White said he met Peggy Lowe when school
started. That's true. He said he made phone calls to
Peggy. That's true. He said they talked for hours at a
time. And that's true. He said he worked at her house,
and he did."

Swiveling to face one of the jurors, an elderly woman,
Fry asked in a reasonable tone of voice, "Would Peggy
Lowe recommend someone who was not dependable to
go to her sister's mansion to work?"

Leaving the question unanswered, he continued tick-
ing off the elements he wanted to emphasize.

"James White said he had sex with Peggy Lowe on May fifteenth. Well, what happened that day? She called her sister early that morning. Then she didn't go to school. But her daughter was at school and her husband was at school. Those are facts."

Crossing quickly to the clerk's desk, where items entered into evidence were kept, Fry retrieved the library book that Betty allegedly used to secrete expense money for White. "May sixteenth is the day that ends with a book of fairy tales," he said, waving the slim volume over his head. "Betty Wilson gives this book to a man at the gate and tells the guard to tell him, 'I want the book back *but have a good time.*' Why," he asked, "would anyone give hundreds of dollars to a drunk? *We* know," he added, dropping into a conspiratorial tone, "what he is going to do with that money."

Again he turned and pointed at Betty. *"This woman,"* he spat, "says she never talked to James White. But telephone records show two calls from her number to James White's number. Who called? Why?

"And then," he added, "there's the 'handoff,' " referring to the alleged meeting on the Logan Martin Dam in which White said Peggy and Betty met him, and Peggy gave him Betty's pistol. How, Fry posed the question, if White had been making up his whole story, would he have known that on the day he said he met the twins that Betty indeed was visiting her sister. Plus, he added, the pistol that was recovered from White was undeniably Betty's. "That's uncontested. It's hers. There's no question about it." As for the defense claim that White took it when he was burgling the Wilson house, "Why," Fry asked, "would he take *her* gun? Why didn't he take Trey's gun? Why did he hide it?"

Moving quickly through the other factors in his argument, Fry pointed out that it had been proved that White was at K mart, as he said he had been; that he was registered at the Ramada Inn; that he had twice called the Lowe residence from the motel. "Peggy Lowe says she didn't talk to him? Wayne Lowe says he didn't talk to him. Who did he talk to?" he asked rhetorically.

Leaning closer to the jurors, Fry mentally shut out everyone else in the courtroom, speaking to them as if they were sitting around a dining room table. "You have to connect *her* with the product," he said earnestly. "You can do that by establishing her proximity to the crime itself. And Sheila Irby does that for you. It doesn't take a Sherlock Holmes to solve this case," he said softly. "It doesn't take a Columbo. You can *smell* what's going on here. You can *feel* it. As sorry as he is, James White told you a lot of truth."

Knowing he would be back in front of the jury before they began deliberating, knowing he would have one more chance to rebut whatever argument the defense attorneys would make, Fry left his argument there. He hoped he had given the panel enough to consider.

TWENTY-EIGHT

FRY HAD TAKEN FORTY-SEVEN MINUTES to give jurors his basic outline. Jack Drake, whose turn it was next, would take sixty-two minutes, and Bobby Lee Cook an additional forty-three minutes. Then Fry would return and speak for another twenty-eight minutes—altogether three hours of argument and conjecture, not including thirty-five minutes that would be consumed by Judge Younger in his final instructions to the panel. By lunchtime it would all be over except for the deliberations.

So far, the lawyers were acting according to type. Fry, the good ol' boy, had used persuasion and reason to make his case. Drake, who had been strident and confrontational during the trial, would continue in that vein in his summation, referring to White as "a smelly man," "a cheap, two-bit thief," "a dope dealer," "a monster," and a "psychotic and obsessive liar." Turning to face Fry, since White was not in the courtroom, Drake asked, "Can you imagine Peggy Lowe exchanging a few kisses with *that* man?"

The scenario laid out by Drake was complex, requiring jurors to give excessive credit to White's reasoning ability. For reasons he did not expound upon, Drake contended that White had set out to destroy Betty Wilson, "stalking" her as she made her round of stores to complete her pre-vacation shopping, breaking into her home and killing her husband, then trying to frame her for the crime. He spied upon her when she bought a pair of shoes, Drake said, otherwise he would not have been able to describe her footwear in such detail. By the same token, he must have shadowed her so he could be accurate later in describing her movements. "I think he followed her partway through the mall on Thursday and again on Friday," Drake postulated. "Why did he do this?" he asked rhetorically. "Who knows? He's a monster. Maybe he was going to kill *her*."

White was a disreputable sort who kept "a large quantity" of marijuana in his trailer, a man who lied so obsessively that he would tell an untruth even in the face of documentation that proved otherwise, Drake asserted. Even worse, he was a man who would stoop at nothing to hurt others. "He's going to put two innocent people in the electric chair," the defense attorney screamed.

Drake may have had more success reaching the jurors if he had restricted his attacks to White. Instead, to give credence to his theory, he brought others into the alleged conspiracy to persecute Betty.

Drake alleged that someone had to have helped White after the fact. "[White] is capable of writing to someone and telling them to get some jeans and a shirt and put them in a bag and then telling them to go bury it under a rock," Drake said. In a slam at allegedly incompetent investigatory tactics, Drake also reminded the jury about the lack of evidence the clothing yielded. "Can you beat a man to death with a baseball bat and not get blood on yourself? I don't think so," Drake averred, hinting that the prosecution was wrong when it claimed the clothing was White's.

Nancy Nelson, he charged, was a snob who got some of the information she testified to from the newspapers. "In Tuscaloosa County," he said self-righteously, "we don't put people in the electric chair for wearing wrinkled clothes." And Sheila Irby, Drake insisted, was nothing but "a dingbat."

Attacking Nelson and Irby was perhaps Drake's greatest mistake. An undercurrent throughout the trial had been the strength of Southern women. While others might ridicule them for an avowed tendency to dye their hair blond, speak slowly and softly, pepper their language with terms like "my goodness" and "gracious me" as well as the ubiquitous "y'all," or laugh about how they bat their eyes, are predisposed to acting helpless, profess to possess an amazing incapacity to understand anything more complicated than a credit card or the face of a Rolex watch, those are illusions. Beneath the carefully cultivated facade that they begin learning in infancy, Southern women are incredibly capable, determined, and strong-willed. And no one recognizes this more than the Southern man. The age of feminism has not yet dawned in many parts of Dixie, and Drake either did not understand this or seriously miscalculated. When he attacked Nelson and Irby, on top of his earlier assaults on them and other female witnesses, Drake was risking alienating the majority of the jurors he was trying so desperately to reach.

Seemingly oblivious to his faux pas, Drake steamrolled ahead in his defense of Betty and made another miscalculation in attempting to convert male jurors to the notion that Betty's admitted infidelity was both understandable and permissible.

"Mrs. Wilson admitted these affairs to police before she was arrested," Drake intoned, as if that made them acceptable. "I think Jack Wilson knew about her affairs," he added. "I think they had an agreement," a thought guaranteed to raise a Southern man's hackles.

The idea that she would actually have him killed because she wanted his money was absurd, Drake contended. "She could have come out well-fixed if she had divorced him." She would have gotten a large share of their cash assets, he said, as well as at least one car, half the house, and alimony for the rest of her life. "If she had wanted to," he said, "she could have gotten four million dollars and put it in [a bank in] the Cayman Islands and *no* lawyer would have gotten it back." Besides, he added, Jack was making $1 million a year, at least part of which would have gone to her. "Why kill him?" he asked.

"Betty Wilson doesn't have to *prove* anything," Drake said. "The *prosecution* has to prove beyond a reasonable doubt that she hired James White to kill her husband. If you find Betty Wilson innocent," Drake asserted wrongly, "they will tear up this agreement and put James White in the electric chair."

More articulate and less shrill than his colleague, Cook continued hammering at the alleged inadequacies of the state's case, reminding jurors how Brantley had failed to ask White to identify Betty, how there was no evidence that he was in the Chick-Fil-A restaurant, that he was seen at Parkway City Mall, or that he had any connection at all with Betty. "No one ever saw Betty Wilson and this man together in their whole lives," he pointed out.

Cook also defended the theory alleging that the evidence from the Ramada Inn was faked. "John Self has given a written statement about when James White checked in," Cook said, urging jurors to discount the recantation Self made when faced with computerized evidence to the contrary. "Mr. Self says Mr. Houck got him to change his mind. And where is Mr. Houck?" he asked, turning to examine the spectators. "He's not here," he said when he did not see him, as he knew he would not. "He ran out of the courtroom and he hasn't been back."

It was, Cook added, Julia Wilson who had prepared the telephone records, and it was her children that would benefit from Jack's estate.

"It's nothing but circumstantial evidence," he said, referring to the state's case. "It was flawed from the beginning. It was a rush to judgment."

The real culprit, he said, was not Betty Wilson but James White, a man that by Cook's count admitted to lying fifty-eight times. To convict Betty, the defense attorney contended, the jury would have to believe everything that White had said, not just selective portions of his testimony. If they did not believe everything White said, Cook continued, the jurors were obligated to acquit Betty.

"The worst possible thing that has occurred in this case is the contingent plea agreement," Cook argued. "It offends a sense of decency and literally compels a psychotic to stick to his story however wrong it may be. It can corrupt the judicial process and poison the well of justice. If I were the district attorney," he concluded, "I'd tear it up and prosecute James White for capital murder." If the jury wanted to punish White, Cook added, it would have to acquit Betty.

His argument was in part disingenuous. Betty's possible conviction was not an either/or situation. White's guilty plea was a fait accompli, and acquitting Betty would not assure his trial, conviction, and execution unless it was proved that he lied on the stand. And neither was it, as Cook further claimed, a guaranteed ticket that White could redeem for freedom in less than a decade.

Fry, who had been relatively restrained in his initial trip to the lectern, grew emotional when he rose to refute what Cook and Drake had said.

"There's no need for me to untangle the whole web that has been woven here," he said, indicating he did not have to account for every inconsistency that seemed to pop up.

Fry asked them to consider the note that Wilson allegedly dated after the time he was believed to have been killed. "It doesn't make sense that a man is going to make a note to show he's still alive." And the fact that Betty's bank account did not reveal any large withdrawal in the period immediately before White said she paid him $2500 was equally meaningless. "To Betty Wilson, that was pocket change."

As for showing up at the AA meeting in uncharacteristically casual clothing, that was an accident. "I suggest she never intended to go to AA," Fry argued. "She was going home to find her husband dead, but instead she found James White still there. To put time between then and when she could go home again, she went to AA."

The other piece of evidence the defense claimed showed Jack was still alive after White had said he killed him—the recording on Pam Hyde's answering machine —was equally spurious, Fry said. "Why was Jack's voice the only thing on that tape?" he asked. "And why did Mrs. Hyde keep it for thirty days without erasing it or before giving it to anyone?"

Turning to one of his favorite subjects, Fry mentioned David Williamson, then dismissed him with a few words. "This is the *only* man who purports to see James White in a crowded motel," he said. "And this man just happens to be trying to sell photos to one of the defense attorneys." He paused, then added loudly: "It stinks! It stinks to high heaven!"

Lowering his voice to a conversational pitch, Fry questioned Betty's motive. "Why would she want to kill her husband? The reason is six million, three hundred thousand dollars. If he were killed, she'd never have to ask 'Old Shitbag' for another dime. *There,*" he added dramatically, "is your reason."

While he was talking he had unobtrusively picked up the metal bat that had been used to batter Jack to death. "Let's just kill old Jack," he said, swinging the bat against the wooden lectern, probably harder than he planned, causing a horrific thunk. The sudden noise caught one of the elderly jurors by surprise, startling him and making him spring upright in his chair. Seeing this, Fry momentarily panicked. He knew the man wore a pacemaker and he feared for a moment that he might have caused him to have a heart attack. When the man settled down again, Fry breathed easier. "Let's just kill the old shitbag," he said in a quieter voice. "He's no good sexually. He was a nobody. He was a nothing."

The case went to the jury at 12:28 on Tuesday, March 2, and both sides expected a quick verdict. Fry was convinced he had made a strong case and the jury would quickly see the logic of his argument. By the same token, the defense team felt it had ripped away all the alleged ties between Betty and James White, which would leave the jurors no choice but to vote for acquittal.

"If I was on the jury," Marc Sandlin whispered to Betty when the jury retired, "we'd have a not guilty verdict in two hours."

As it turned out, the verdict did not come until the next afternoon. After a quick lunch of sandwiches and soda, and some ten and a half hours of deliberation, the jury foreman sent word to Judge Younger that the group had reached a decision.

At 1:46 P.M. eleven of the panel members marched grimly into the courtroom and took their seats, then turned nervously to the door to the jury room waiting for the twelfth panelist. He sauntered in some three minutes later, appearing somewhat puzzled about why everyone in the courtroom was staring at him.

With all the jurors present, the group foreman handed a slip of paper to a bailiff, who relayed it to Younger. The judge glanced at the note, then announced the verdict in a soft monotone: "Guilty of capital murder."

A loud murmur rippled through the spectators, who were heavily anti-Betty. From her seat on the bench immediately behind her daughter, Betty's eighty-four-year-old mother broke into tears, lowering her head to her chest and sobbing heavily. Her daughter, Martha, sitting beside her, whimpered and doubled over, stuffing a tissue into her mouth. Betty herself took the news without emotion, as did her sons, who stared fixedly ahead.

Laying the piece of paper on his desk, Younger leaned forward and looked down at Betty, motioning her to come forward. Betty threw her shoulders back and, accompanied by a morose Charles Hooper, marched resolutely to the foot of the bench, where she stood at rigid attention.

"Is there any reason for you to disagree with this sentence?" Younger asked.

Betty, perhaps in shock, shook her head slightly and mouthed the word no. What she was thinking was impossible to tell because throughout the trial she had insisted upon her innocence and for her to answer Younger's question in the negative seemed at odds with her claims.

Deciding not to explore the incongruity himself, Younger nodded, then waved Betty and Hooper back to their seats. To give both sides time to recover from the jolt of the verdict and to prepare their next moves, Younger ordered a recess. Normally the trial would have shifted immediately into the next stage, called the punishment phase, during which lawyers would repeat the witness-calling process. At the conclusion, the same jury would be asked to vote again, on whether Betty should be sentenced to die in the electric chair or be ordered to prison for the rest of her life without possibility of parole. There was, however, one option that was rarely used. With the consent of both the prosecution and defense, Younger could forego the punishment phase, thereby sidestepping the possibility of a death sentence, and mandate a life term. After a quick huddle involving Fry and members of the defense team, Younger announced that was his decision.

"We waive our right to participation by the jury," Fry announced after Younger rapped the court back into session, formally sanctioning Younger's decree. "We recommend mercy," he added. "We recommend life without possibility of parole."

Drake jumped to his feet, adding that the defense agreed with Fry.

Again Younger summoned Betty to the foot of the bench. Had she discussed this resolution with her lawyers? Younger wanted to know.

"Yes," she replied softly.

"Do you concur?" he asked her.

"Yes," she whispered.

Younger nodded gravely. In a somber voice he said he would accept the prosecution's recommendation and sentence her to life in prison.

Betty accepted the judgment without flinching. But Hooper, who was standing at her side, took the words worse than she. When the guilty verdict was announced, the blood had drained from Hooper's face and his knees seemed to sag. Although he had regained some of his composure during the recess, he still looked pale and ill. Fry, who was watching the defense attorney intently, worried that Hooper might collapse. Summoning a reserve of strength, Hooper squared his shoulders, spun on his heel and walked steadily if not sprightly back to the defense table.

After the trial, jurors revealed that the decision to convict Betty had been a logical and relatively congenial one. Unlike some deliberations, in which jurors belligerently defend their points of view and sometimes come close to blows, Betty's jury was uncommonly harmonious.

The group spent Tuesday afternoon sifting through the documents that had been entered as evidence in the case, particularly the telephone records. When they looked at the documents carefully outside the emotional environment of the courtroom, the jurors individually decided that the computer trail was undeniably significant, that there were too many verifiable calls made to the numbers of the main players, Betty, Peggy, and White, to be easily explained away.

On Wednesday morning, after sleeping on their findings, the panel took its first vote. Ten members were in favor of conviction, one was for acquittal, and one was undecided. Calmly they reviewed the issues. The main points in the prosecution's favor were:

- White said he had become friendly with Peggy, a fact that was substantiated by testimony.
- Betty *was* in Talladega/Vincent and *was* absent, along with Peggy, from the Lowe house at the time White said he met the two of them at the Logan Martin Dam to acquire Betty's pistol.
- White's contention that Peggy was having marital problems of her own was confirmed by at least one independent witness, Betty's friend, Nancy Nelson.
- White's presence in Huntsville was confirmed by several witnesses: computer records confirmed he checked into the Ramada Inn when he claimed he did; he bought what he said when he said at a discount store; he was seen on the street in front of the Wilson house when he said he was there.
- Reputable witnesses or records kept by individual stores confirmed that Betty was where White said she was on the eve of her husband's murder, notably that she was within fifty feet of the fast-food restaurant where White claimed she met him to pass along expense money.
- Testimony from bank officials confirmed that White was monetarily flush soon after he testified he received $2500 from Betty as an advance payment for murdering Jack.
- The prosecution successfully established motive: Jack's $6.3 million estate.
- A succession of prosecution witnesses, particularly

the unimpeachable minister's wife, Brenda McDowell, confirmed Betty's demonstrated contempt for her husband.

But most important of all were the telephone records, which seemed to substantiate White's claims of conversations with the twins. Even though the records could not prove that it was White talking to Betty and Peggy, calls *were* made from White's motel room, from White's trailer, and from pay phones in White's vicinity to Betty's and Peggy's homes, and from Betty's and Peggy's homes to locations where White was at the time, either in his trailer, at a pay phone outside a grocery across the street from Jack's office, or a convenience store near Guntersville State Park.

On the other hand, the defense had its points as well. They were:

· No witnesses ever placed Betty and White physically together.
· No witnesses ever confirmed that Peggy showed any affection for White.
· There was no handwritten evidence connecting Betty to White, such as a map, a check, or instructions.

Although the prosecution was largely successful in corroborating White's testimony about the *time* he said certain events occurred, such as when he said he arrived and left the Wilson house, there were minor contradictions.

· There was no eyewitness testimony to substantiate that Betty picked White up, took him to her house, and dropped him off afterward at a busy intersection near his truck.
· The prosecution was unable to prove that the pistol

found under the wooden porch near White's trailer, and which was subsequently shown to be registered to Betty, was actually given to White, as opposed to White stealing it from the Wilson house, as the defense claimed.

· No physical evidence was ever presented to substantiate White's claim that he was ever inside Betty's car.

· It was never proved that the knife found in the bag under a rock in Betty's yard was the one used to stab Jack. If that was not the knife, where was the one that inflicted the lethal wounds? No other knife was ever produced. This issue was further complicated by White's claim that he never stabbed the doctor. The result was confusion, which bolstered the defense's case more than the prosecution's. When it was learned that White had denied stabbing Jack, a rumor swept through Huntsville that Betty may have returned home, found Jack still alive, and stabbed him herself. This was never alluded to in the trial. A more believable explanation is that White is sufficiently cunning to deny stabbing the doctor because that would incriminate him to a degree beyond what he admitted to in his statement.

· There was ample evidence that the investigation was sloppily handled. Particularly troubling was the fact that investigators never attempted to get White to actually identify Betty. Also disturbing was the inability of technicians to find any physical evidence showing White was ever inside Betty's BMW.

Of lesser importance were four questions that were never answered: Was Jack writing a time when he scribbled the numbers 1715 on the note found in his room? When did Jack record the message found on Pam Hyde's answering machine? Did Officer Jim Donnegan, the first policeman on the scene, actually see a bloody palm print next to Jack's body, since no other investigator noted it? And, who did David Williamson see at the Ramada Inn late that Friday afternoon? Disposing of that issue first, the jurors decided that Williamson had been a relatively unreliable witness and their credence in his statements did not outweigh the physical evidence the state had presented.

After lunch on Wednesday, after a simple review of the evidence and a calm discussion of the points that had been raised, the jury foreman asked for a second vote. That time the group was unanimous: all twelve cast ballots for Betty's conviction.

Going into deliberations, the defense lawyers had been confident of a rapid acquittal. Then, when the jury did not return as quickly as they expected, they grew more concerned. Although the popular wisdom is that a slow verdict is encouraging for the defense, the four attorneys did not feel that was true in Betty's case. "Somehow," Sandlin said afterward, "as the hours dragged on, we began to feel that they were looking for a way to convict her."

Fry, although he had been expecting a quick verdict, was not discouraged by the long deliberation. During his closing arguments, he had studied the jurors carefully, and he was sure he was getting through. "There were three of them," he said later, "who I felt would have stayed with me forever." The worst that could have happened, he felt, was for the jurors to be unable to agree, thereby causing the proceeding to end in a mistrial. "What made the difference," he said, "was that I could conceive of losing, while the defense could not."

TWENTY-NINE

BETTY WAS CONVICTED ON MARCH 3, BUT it would be another six months before her twin would get her day in court. Peggy and her contingent of lawyers began arguing her innocence on September 13 in Montgomery, the state capital, before Circuit Judge William Page, a 60-year-old former Alabama Insurance Commissioner with nineteen years' experience on the bench. As colleague Thomas Younger had done earlier, Page had selected a neutral site for the trial, to avoid the possibility that potential jurors might be contaminated by the massive publicity given the case in Huntsville. And with the new judge and the new venue came an entirely new cast of participants.

Betty's prosecutor, Jimmy Fry, was replaced by Assistant Attorney General Don Valeska, the A.G. office's chief trial lawyer. Although Fry, who already knew the case inside and out, was asked to prosecute Peggy as well, he bowed out because of the need to attend to matters in his own district. And Betty's army of defenders—Sandlin, Cook, Drake, et. al.—were succeeded by a team led by David Cromwell Johnson of Birmingham and Herman "Buck" Watson of Huntsville.

Valeska, a rail-thin, hyperactive 49-year-old who seemed constitutionally incapable of remaining motionless for more than sixty seconds at a stretch, was the temperamental opposite of Fry, who appeared as energetic—and ultimately as dangerous—as an alligator dozing in the sun. In some ways, Valeska's job would be more difficult than Fry's; in others, easier. Working in Fry's favor during Betty's trial was the personal history of the defendant, who was generally regarded by many of those who knew her as a foul-mouthed libertine with a marked penchant for liberally spending her late husband's money even while demeaning him to anyone who would listen. Peggy, on the other hand, was viewed by her friends and neighbors as a model of propriety: the soloist in the Baptist church choir, the beloved teacher of young and impressionable children, the soft-spoken Christian woman who gave shelter to the needy and money to the down-and-out. Before her trial was over, she would earn the sobriquet of "Saint Peggy."

While physical evidence against Betty was skimpy it was nonetheless lavish compared to what existed against Peggy. Although there were witnesses who would testify that Peggy *knew* White—she, in fact, had already readily admitted that much herself—there were none who could claim that the relationship went beyond Peggy's avowed empathy for the unfortunate.

However, there were three things going for Valeska as Peggy's trial day dawned: White would repeat his damning testimony of how Peggy had taken him into her bed to clinch the agreement he had with Betty to kill Jack; Peggy was locked into her testimony because she had spoken under oath during Betty's trial, and, most significant of all, *Betty had been convicted.* Not only had the evidence presented by Fry been sufficient for a jury to determine Betty's guilt, but it would be difficult to convince another jury that Betty had not operated without Peggy's help because Peggy was the link with White. Peggy's defenders, on the other hand, would be taking the side of the righteous. Rather than defending their client against a barrage of attacks on her character and morals, they would be trying to clear her name from blemishes put there by the disreputable White, who, they would aver, anyone with an ounce of sense could see was a thoroughly disagreeable fellow.

Peggy's defense team members also lacked the stridency of Hooper and Drake. The 51-year-old Johnson, who was regarded as the more aggressive member, was docile compared to Betty's shrill defenders. Watson, a 60-year-old former prosecutor with a hound-dog mien and a self-deprecating sense of humor, was as laid-back as Fry and polite to the point of obsequiousness.

And, while Valeska had an advantage in having Peggy's story carved in stone, the defense had the same advantage vis-à-vis White. The admitted murderer could not take the stand during Peggy's trial and change or elaborate upon what he had said earlier.

Additionally, there was one new wrinkle in Peggy's trial that was not present during Betty's and which seemed to favor the prosecution. Just weeks before Peggy's trial was scheduled to begin, a second grand jury indicted her on two counts of conspiring to commit capital murder, once with Betty and again with White. As a result of the grand jury action, she would be tried simultaneously for capital murder and conspiracy.

At a hearing held less than a week before the trial was set to begin, Peggy's lawyers attacked that tactic. The attorney general's office, however, argued that the inclusion of the conspiracy charges insured that Peggy would be called to account on all possible grounds. By trying her simultaneously for murder and conspiracy, the jury had the option of levying the death penalty by convicting her of the former, or mandating a prison sentence only by convicting her of the latter.

Judge Page sanctioned the prosecution plan, but warned Valeska that he would have to tell jurors before they began deliberations which charge he wanted them to consider.

While the crowd that jammed the hallways of the Tuscaloosa courthouse during Betty's trial was predominantly anti-Betty, the opposite was true during Peggy's trial. When would-be spectators began lining the corridors of the Montgomery courthouse, many were carrying placards or sporting buttons announcing their support for the accused schoolteacher. Calling themselves "Peggy's Posse," they poured into Montgomery from Vincent, the town where Peggy taught and where she was a star soloist in the choir at the First Baptist Church, which was directed by her husband, Wayne. Proclaiming dual beliefs in God and in Peggy, members of the "Posse" began each day with a prayer session before lining up for admission into the courtroom. Also present each day to show their support were Peggy's three children, Angie, 26, and Blake, 23, by her first marriage, and Stephanie, 15.

Wayne, smiling quietly and confidently, hovered shyly in the background, never betraying the fact that White claimed that he also had been a potential target until he was supplanted by Jack Wilson.

Clad tastefully in a dark skirt and white jacket with dark piping, accented by a string of pearls, quarter-sized faux-pearl earrings, and a small gold pin depicting an angel, Peggy sat calmly as Valeska launched his attack. The prosecutor told the jury, which was composed of five black men plus four black and three white women, that Peggy Lowe was a master manipulator who "played James White like a fiddle" in an effort to convince him to kill the husband of her twin sister, who Valeska described as one of the "rottenest" people they would "ever care to hear about." Peggy Lowe, he argued, maneuvered White into a relationship that culminated in a sexual tryst in her own bed while her husband was at

work and her daughter was in school. To prove how she
had accomplished this, the prosecutor said, he would
produce telephone records which showed an extraordinary number of calls between White's trailer and the
Lowe house. Additionally, White himself would testify
about his affiliation with Peggy.

The dean of Peggy's defense team, the gray-haired and
patrician-looking Watson, surprised those familiar with
the case when he told jurors in his opening statement
that White, who admitted battering Jack with a baseball
bat, may not have been the single attacker that everyone
presumed him to be. In an apparent attempt to dilute the
prosecution's contention that White acted alone, Watson
threw out the possibility that various others may have
played a part in the killing.

Also, in an attempt to sow more confusion, Watson
brought up Julia Wilson's employment at the Ramada
Inn, the motel where White spent the night before the
murder. In Betty's trial, it was the motel telephone
records detailing calls from White's room to Betty's and
Peggy's houses that helped convince jurors that Betty
had hired the handyman to kill her ophthalmologist husband. Those records, Watson averred, were "questionable."

After setting the scene with virtually the same witnesses Fry had called during Betty's trial—including
pathologist Joseph Embry, and Ramada Inn manager
Gary Houck—Valeska called his star witness, James
White. Looking small and harmless in his prison jumpsuit and shiny handcuffs, White appeared almost cheerful when he took the stand. Shortly before, Judge Page
had to send a deputy to the cell behind the courtroom
where White was being held until he could be summoned
to order White to restrict his exuberance. To pass the
time in the lonely cell White had broken into song,
choosing a selection of hymns that he recalled from his
own church-going days. Gradually, his voice had grown

so loud that it was disrupting the testimony of other witnesses.

Under Valeska's questioning, White repeated almost verbatim the testimony he had delivered during Betty's trial: How Peggy had recruited him to kill Jack; how he had gone to Huntsville to do the job; how he had been frustrated in his first attempt to commit the murder and had to spend the night in a Huntsville motel; how he had talked by telephone to both Betty and Peggy on the eve of the killing; how Betty had driven him to her home, left him there, and then returned to pick him up and drive him to his truck, leaving a battered, bleeding and dying Jack lying on the floor of an upstairs hallway.

Later, when Johnson was cross-examining White, the defense attorney accomplished what Bobby Lee Cook had been unable to do in his fierce and lengthy attack during Betty's trial: he got the state's main witness confused. When pressing him on the *time* when he said he was picked up by Betty at the Wilson house and driven back to his truck which he had left parked at a strip center, White exhibited an uncertainty he had not shown during his earlier testimony. While first claiming that he had "no idea" when Betty had returned to the house, White then estimated it was between 6 and 6:30 P.M. If jurors accepted that statement as gospel rather than a desperate attempt by a man of limited intellectual ability being questioned by a determined and aggressive defense attorney, it would demolish the state's carefully constructed schedule of events. During Betty's trial, White had said she returned about 5 P.M., which was consistent with the time Sheila Irby said she saw him in the neighborhood. It also fit nicely with testimony about Betty's whereabouts that afternoon and evening.

What damage White's newly revealed indecision did to Valeska's case was questionable since Irby later also repeated her testimony about spotting White walking down the street near the Wilson home at about 5 P.M.

Other witnesses from Betty's trial also told the same stories that they had disclosed during the Tuscaloosa proceeding.

In two major areas—each with significance to one side —testimony at Peggy's trial differed from Betty's. During the Tuscaloosa trial, a former friend of Betty's, Nancy Nelson, told jurors how she had returned to the Guntersville Lodge room she had been sharing with Betty during a convention weekend to find Betty on the telephone. According to Nelson, when Betty hung up after a prolonged conversation she explained that she had been talking to her sister, who was having marital problems and was "having an affair with a carpenter."

While that testimony had little if any effect on Betty's case it could be extremely damaging to Peggy, who claimed that her relationship with White had never been anything but platonic. To help avert the harm Nelson's testimony could wreak on Peggy's claims, her lawyers asked Judge Page to prohibit Nelson from repeating that story on grounds that it was "hearsay." To Valeska's frustration, the judge agreed. Although Nelson was allowed to reiterate much of her earlier testimony, she was prohibited from touching on what Betty had told her about her sister's alleged sexual affair.

On the other hand, to Valeska's satisfaction and the defense's disappointment, Judge Page, unlike Judge Younger in Betty's trial, allowed the prosecution to call Janine Russell, a friend of White's who was prepared to testify about *her* view of the Peggy/White relationship. Although the defense objected, the judge allowed Russell to appear after Valeska argued that her testimony would help prove that Peggy was part of a conspiracy to murder Jack Wilson. Unlike her sister, Betty had not been charged with conspiracy.

Under Valeska's prodding, Russell said that White had come to her home before the murder with a wad of cash in his pocket. Flashing the roll, he bragged that it was a downpayment on a killing he had agreed to commit in Huntsville. In addition, Russell said, dropping her bombshell, White had told her that he was having an affair with Peggy.

On Wednesday, September 21, the day after the defense began presenting its witnesses, Johnson surprised the prosecution by calling a woman who they hoped would punch another large hole in White's story. Trying to accomplish what Betty's lawyer had sought to do with the testimony of David Williamson, i.e., discredit White, Peggy's lawyers summoned Debby Brannon, who owned a convenience store in the tiny community of Bon Aire. She testified that White and *another man* were in her shop at 9 A.M. on May 15, 1992, roughly the same time White had claimed to be in Peggy's bed several miles away. She remembered White, she said, because he and his companion, who she described as "a short man with long, stringy hair," offered to repair a leaking pipe in the store's parking lot. When she told him that she had already made arrangements to have the rupture fixed, White tried to undercut the bid of the other repairman. He told her, she said, that he needed the money because he was taking a work crew to Huntsville to work on the home of Dr. Jack Wilson and he needed some operating revenue.

How could Brannon be so certain that the conversation had taken place on May 15 rather than some other day? Johnson asked.

That was easy, she replied. It was her wedding anniversary.

Taking the stand in Peggy's behalf, as he had in Betty's trial, was her husband, Wayne, a balding, pudgy middle-aged man who spoke softly but without hesitation. Repeating what he said at Betty's trial, Wayne told the jury that he and Peggy simply had been trying to help White, who was burdened by a number of personal problems. For example, Wayne testified, Peggy once gave White

$150 so he could have his utilities turned back on after they had been shut off for non-payment. He and Peggy had discussed White's problems, he said, and they decided that it would benefit White if they could introduce him to Betty, who, as a recovering alcoholic, might be able to help him through his troubles with drink and drugs.

When Wayne rose to leave the witness stand after a brief, unsuccessful cross-examination, Peggy smiled broadly at him and mouthed, "I love you." A few minutes later, during a recess, the two embraced and kissed in the courtroom.

While Fry had called a series of witnesses during the Tuscaloosa trial to attack Betty's character, Peggy's defense team called an equally long list of witnesses, all of whom testified to Peggy's good moral character and her willingness to help those in need. Two young women told jurors that Peggy and Wayne had made room for them in their house when they were going through difficult periods in their lives and desperately needed a place to stay. Barbara Hedrick testified that the Lowes converted their dining room into a bedroom for her and that they shared their home with her for more than a year until she could get back on her feet. Another woman, Lisa Turner, said the Lowes offered her shelter for several months in 1989 when she ran into financial difficulties.

Peggy's three children, two by her first marriage and one by Wayne, also testified about growing up in a house filled with love, warmth, and religion.

As she had in Betty's trial, Peggy also took the stand. Predictably, she denied ever having sex with White or doing anything to make him believe that she was romantically interested in him. On his part, she added, White never indicated to her that he liked her more than a friend or that he treated her any differently than he had her husband.

Before winding up their presentation, however, the

defense had one final witness to call: A pathologist from Atlanta named Kris Sperry. In contrast to Dr. Joseph Embry, the Alabama pathologist who had performed the autopsy on Jack, Sperry testified that Jack may not have been battered with a baseball bat as Embry had concluded, but with a piece of heavy metal much smaller in diameter, such as a tire iron, crowbar, or fireplace poker. Sperry said he also doubted that the beating had taken place in the relatively small second-floor area where Wilson's body was found because there were not enough blood spatters on the wall to be consistent with the type of beating Jack endured. However, he did not suggest an alternative site or speculate about how Jack's body got to the head of the stairs where it was found by Betty when she returned from an AA meeting.

The case went to the jury shortly after 5 P.M. on Wednesday, September 22, nine days after the proceeding began. The group deliberated only two hours and eleven minutes before returning with its verdict: Not guilty.

"Thank you, Jesus!" a spectator called from the back of the room before a scowl from Judge Page cut off the applause and further comment. In the hallway outside, however, Peggy's supporters, members of her growing "Posse," knelt in prayer and sang hymns. Inside the courtroom, as soon as Judge Page dismissed the jury, Peggy, Wayne and the children fell to their knees and prayed softly.

Asked by reporters afterwards what had been the deciding factor in concluding that Peggy was innocent, jurors agreed that they had found White unbelievable. Although they took several votes before getting a unanimous decision, one juror said, each ballot was heavily in favor of acquitting Peggy.

On the way out of the courthouse, surrounded by jubilant members of her family, including her octogenarian mother, and her supporters, a tearful and fatigued Peggy faced the television cameras and said she had a message for her sister. "Betty, I love you," she declared, adding: "We're coming to get you."

EPILOGUE

ON SEPTEMBER 10, JUST THREE DAYS BE-
fore Peggy's trial began, Betty's lawyers filed her appeal
with the five-member Court of Criminal Appeals. Sandlin and Drake, the document's primary authors, settled
on three major issues as the basis for the plea: jury selection, alleged withholding of evidence by the prosecution,
and the question of whether White's testimony constituted corroboration under the state statutes.

Alabama law specifies that an accomplice's testimony
that leads to the conviction of another person must
"tend to connect the defendant with the commission of
the offense." According to the appeal, White's testimony
did not fulfill that function. Although the confessed murderer's statements about the delivery of the library book
and his descriptions of Betty's shoes, for example, supported his personal credibility, they did not necessarily
connect Betty to the murder.

Not surprisingly, Fry disagreed. White's testimony did
not have to *prove* that Betty was involved in the murder,
he contended. The operative word in the statute, he
added, was *connect*, which is not the same as *convict*.
Fry's interpretation of the law is that White's testimony
did not have to be absolutely true; the only requirement
from the prosecutor's viewpoint was that the jury con-

sider White's testimony as a "connector" *linking* Betty to the murder.

Betty's lawyers also claimed that blacks were systematically excluded from the pool of prospective jurors despite defense objections, and that the defense was hampered because Betty's lawyers had not been told in advance—as required by law—about the substance of Sheila Irby's testimony, specifically that she was ready to testify that she had seen a man she subsequently identified as White near the Wilson home late on the afternoon of the murder. Betty's lawyers claimed that Irby should not have been allowed to testify about this because she was never able to pick White's picture out of a photo array. Cook said during the trial that the Supreme Court has ruled that a person could not testify to identity unless the identification was positive, which it was not in Irby's case. However, Fry countered that the high court decision applied only to persons who are actually on trial. Since White himself was not on trial, the prosecutor contended, Irby's identification of him did not have to be positive.

There was no indication when the appeal would be settled but it is apt to be years in the future. Sandlin said he expected the Court of Criminal Appeals to announce its decision sometime between early 1994 and mid-1996, but that is only the first step. If that court, which works almost exclusively with the trial record and very rarely asks for lawyers to appear and argue their points in person, upholds the conviction, the next move would be to ask the nine-member state supreme court for a review. If the conviction is affirmed at that level, Betty could then turn to the federal courts.

It had been the defense's contention throughout Betty's trial that the plea-bargain agreement between White and Brooks, which later was accepted by Brooks's successor, Tim Morgan, was self-serving and rewarded White for framing Betty. Her lawyers claimed Morgan should have ripped up the agreement and tried White for murder. Drake, in fact, claimed during his closing arguments that if the jury would acquit Betty the state would tear up the agreement and "put White in the electric chair," an assertion that was at best disingenuous, at worst deliberately misleading.

Fry, however, argued that it was not as simple as Drake would have had the jurors believe. The Brooks/White agreement was legally binding, he pointed out, and could only be voided if White had lied about a material point, or if he had refused to testify against the twins, neither of which he did.

Interestingly, after Peggy's acquittal, Drake wrote Morgan claiming that the fact that the jury had found Peggy not guilty proved that White had not been telling the truth. Drake then urged the district attorney to set aside the guilty verdict against Betty because White's testimony had played a large role in her conviction.

Morgan ignored the request, telling the *Huntsville Times:* "I can't make the call whether White is lying or not."

At the same time Drake wrote Morgan he also wrote Fry asking him, in light of Peggy's acquittal, to join the defense in petitioning the appeals court to toss out Betty's conviction.

The normally mild-mannered Fry responded hotly, telling the Huntsville newspaper that he had tried Betty, not Peggy. Betty had been convicted on evidence presented against *her,* he said angrily, not on anything that happened in Peggy's trial. "It will take me about as long as it took Mr. Drake's secretary to lick the stamp she put on his letter to say 'No!' " Fry added.

Two days after Peggy's acquittal and the day after receiving Drake's letter, Morgan reaffirmed that he planned to honor his predecessor's agreement with

White, claiming the verdict would have no effect "at all" on the arrangement.

No matter what the final ruling of the courts will be on Betty's appeal, one thing is certain: the process has been *very* expensive for her. Her bill for legal services between the time she was arrested and the end of her trial was estimated at more than $400,000. By the time the appeal was filed, it probably approached $500,000. In contrast, the cost to the state was figured at $20,000, although that did not include any fees to the prosecutor or investigator since they are salaried.

On the opposite end of the scale, Peggy got her defense team for free, or almost so. Johnson and Watson said they would not charge for their services but Peggy gave them $10,000 she borrowed from Wayne's mother.

What helped run Betty's bill so high was her extravagance. She had four veteran lawyers at her command in the courtroom, including Bobby Lee Cook, who is reputed to be one of the best defenders in the country. She also had ten others working for her, most of them lawyers, who labored in the background doing research and helping devise strategy. During the trial, the group of non-courtroom lawyers met three times a day in the Tuscaloosa office of another attorney to evaluate the ever-changing situation.

Where she expects to get the money to pay these enormous expenses is not quite certain. Although she transferred $85,000 from a joint checking account she had with Jack to a personal account of her own soon after the murder, that probably will not go very far toward paying her legal bills. Shortly after withdrawing the money a judge ordered all of her funds frozen pending settlement of the estate. However, she also was believed to have removed from the house early on a number of items which could be sold for ready cash, such as furs. In addition, she had several pieces of property in her own name as well as two luxury automobiles.

The larger problem will be how Betty will pay for the appeal. Once she was convicted of murdering her husband she apparently was cut off, by state law, from any inheritance. However, her lawyers are still trying to convince the courts that she is entitled to half of her husband's estate simply because of the state's community property law, regardless of the inheritance statutes. That amount could total more than $3 million. If she were to win that argument and get half of Jack's estate, and if her conviction were to be overturned somewhere along the line, she could one day end up free *and* rich, which would fulfill half of her alleged ambition to be a wealthy, respected widow.

A victory in the courts, however, would be easy for Betty compared to an attempt to win respect among Huntsvillians. Her husband, Jack, was a tremendously popular person. Betty, on the other hand, never enjoyed the same celebrity. Balance that with the perception that she planned her husband's murder and the result is that she, at least in the days immediately following the trial, was not likely to win any popularity contests among her neighbors.

On the day after she was convicted, a double handful of anonymous handwritten notes appeared on the door to Jack's office saying things like "Justice prevailed!" and "H'ray!"

Several weeks after the trial, Betty gave a brief interview to a Huntsville television reporter in which she said that she was adapting to prison life but looked forward to being freed by an appellate court. She passes the time in the Julia Tutwiler women's prison in Wetumpka by working in the prison library and laundry. She also has volunteered to teach other inmates nursing or history but there apparently has been little demand for those services. Her mother visits her twice a month.

After her acquittal, Peggy said she planned to return to teaching in the Vincent elementary school where her principal had reserved a third class for her pending the disposition of the charges. However, because of threats of disruptions at the school by protesters who disagreed with the jury verdict, she later said she would continue in her administrative job with the school system instead of returning to the classroom, at least in the immediate future.

Charlie Hooper, who was perhaps Betty's strongest supporter on or off the legal team, left the law firm he was with and opened his own practice in Huntsville.

James White has begun serving his life sentence, but will be eligible for parole before the turn of the century. By then, he will be 49 years old.

AFTERWORD

PEGGY'S ACQUITTAL CREATED A CURIOUS situation. The woman who prosecutors claim was behind the plot to have Jack Wilson murdered is free while her twin sister Betty, the beneficiary of Peggy's alleged planning, will die in prison, barring, of course, a reversal by an appeals court somewhere along the line.

While the Betty/Peggy case undoubtedly will give legal scholars something to debate for years to come, the lesson to be learned, from a layman's point of view, is that the country's trial-by-jury system is highly capricious. One jury had little trouble deciding that Betty was *guilty*. Another jury, viewing almost the same evidence, had even less trouble deciding that her sister was *not guilty*.

One key to understanding this puzzle may be in the ways the two juries approached their tasks. From what panel members in Betty's trial told reporters afterward, they made a conscientious effort to analyze the evidence that had been presented by Fry, examining the physical data, especially the record of telephone calls, weighing the testimony of the witnesses and comparing that with the story told by White, the confessed murderer. The first jury apparently placed tertiary importance on the confessed murderer's tale, using his words only to corroborate other known facts in the case. The second jury, on the other hand, from what members of that panel told reporters, relied almost entirely on White's veracity, which they determined to be totally lacking. The first jury mulled the possibilities for some ten hours before reaching a verdict. The second jury returned its acquittal in barely over two hours, which apparently included time for dinner as well.

Still, a determination of why Betty was convicted and Peggy was acquitted goes deeper than that. In the words of the witnesses at Betty's trial, the Huntsville twin came across as a less than likable person, a factor which may have influenced her jury as well. Of the prosecution witnesses who testified about her character, only a handful had much to say about her redeeming qualities, and one of them was one of her former lovers. Others qualified their compliments, carefully balancing them with admissions that she also had glaring faults. A few had nothing good to say about her whatsoever. Her lawyers called only two witnesses to testify about her merits: one was Peggy; the other was her son, Trey.

Peggy, on the other hand—"Saint Peggy" in the words of one acerbic spectator—was praised to no end. She came across as unblemished as Betty appeared flawed. Faced with the testimony of a half-dozen upstanding citizens who lauded her character, as opposed to only one, White, who claimed to know her darker side, the jury, in a sense understandably, came down on the side of those who praised her virtues. One of her most ardent fans undoubtedly was juror Ruth Gilliland, who was quoted in the *Huntsville Times* as saying: "She was an innocent woman fixing to get into trouble and we [the jurors] got her out."

Another factor to be considered was Fry's efficacy as a prosecutor. The quintessential Southern lawyer, Fry is a slow-talking, slow-moving good ol' boy with an innate ability to press the right buttons for a Southern jury. Behind that image of lethargy lurks a razor-sharp mind and a carefully hidden proclivity to go for the jugular. He can slice a defendant to shreds and leave him bleeding and dismembered on the courtroom floor before the shocked victim is aware of what has happened.

Peggy's prosecutors, in contrast, had problems from the beginning. After Fry declined to prosecute her, the attorney general's office began a search to find someone willing to take on a decidedly tough and thankless task. When other potential prosecutors looked at the facts of the case, they rightfully came to the conclusion that Fry had had much more to work with than they could hope for, given the available evidence. As a result, the A.G. was unable to find a district attorney willing to take the case. In the end he had to assign the responsibility to a member of his staff, a career prosecutor and no slouch as a lawyer in his own right. But he was no Fry, and he had a lot of problems to contend with, not the least of which was the inability to find anyone except James White who would say anything even remotely damaging about the woman he was trying to send to the electric chair.

And then there were the defense lawyers. Fry's job was undoubtedly made easier by the fact that two out of four of Betty's courtroom defenders came across as genuinely disagreeable people. Jack Drake not only tended to screech, he seemed to try to actually mislead the jury about White's plea agreement. Charlie Hooper was piercing as well, but, as opposed to Drake, he exuded the air of a man with a personal interest at stake, a man who could not sit idly by while others said terrible things about a person for whom he had a strong affinity. Perhaps the jurors sensed this as well. Peggy's lawyers, however, were a well-balanced crew: the intense David Cromwell Johnson, who managed to be fervent without being strident, paired well with the Fry-like Buck Watson.

It boiled down to this: In Betty's trial, the prosecution went in with all the cards; in Peggy's case, the advantage was to the defense from the very beginning. All of which has little to do with the twins' actual guilt or innocence. Probably, unless there is an unlikely confession by someone more credible than James White, no one will ever know for sure what led up to Jack's murder. The case now moves out of the realm of public speculation and becomes a legal issue for the appeals courts.

There are, however, several things I would like to point out before the debate ends. I find, for example, a lot to admire in Fry's arguments. Based on the testimony of a string of witnesses and physical evidence in the form of the records of the phone calls, jurors came to the conclusion that Betty had indeed committed the crime outlined in the indictment against her. And that's good enough for me, especially when considering that White's testimony apparently was not the major factor that resulted in the verdict. Rather, his testimony simply gave support to what other witnesses had said. I sense that the jury concluded that White is not bright enough to have made up the story he related from the witness stand.

Speaking of fantasy, I find totally inconceivable the argument that White did this whole thing to frame Betty, or that Jack's former wife could have participated in a plot to make Betty the victim. That leaves Betty as the instigator.

The question of Peggy's involvement is more complicated. If Betty's guilt becomes a given, which it must in light of the Tuscaloosa jury's decision, how does that affect Peggy's status as far as Jack's murder goes? Not in the least, according to the Montgomery jury. But I have questions. The twins have always enjoyed a snug relationship despite the obvious dissimilarities of their personalities. While throughout their lives they may have reacted differently to the same stimuli, a dialogue has apparently always existed between them. They may have disagreed, but each seemed to be aware of the other's thinking. Viewed in that light, does it make sense that

Betty would hire James White to murder her husband without Peggy at least having a hint of what was happening?

While Peggy and Betty were growing up, Betty was always the "naughty" twin while Peggy was the "nice" one. That description, in view of the circumstances, would now have to be changed to "evil" twin and "good" twin. But is Betty intrinsically evil and is Peggy intrinsically good? After her acquittal Peggy made a very curious comment. According to the Associated Press, after the verdict was announced, she thanked her legal team profusely and then told reporters: "I asked the Lord to send me a good lawyer, and He did." Was she acquitted because of good lawyering, a situation not entirely foreign to our judicial system?

In the long run, however, it makes no difference. Except for Betty's appeal, the case is now closed. While there is a possibility that Betty could get another trial, Peggy will never again have to legally respond to these murder accusations.

KE